M000030795

"YOU, MADAM, HAVE GOT NERVE."

"Have I?" Olivia gave a lighthearted laugh. "How divine. I have always wanted some."

"It is not in the least becoming," Brandon muttered fiercely. "It is damned unnatural. I should pack you off to your father and let him deal with you. It would serve him right."

Olivia pulled a face. "I scarcely think that is a sound solution, my lord. You see, he and I are not on the best terms at present."

She was gratified to see her husband was taken aback by the news.

"Pray, do not distress yourself on my account. Aunt and I shall be very content to remain in the quaint little house we've found on Hartford Street."

"Hartford Street!" he exploded, his body recoiling at the suggestion. "No wife of mine will reside on Hartford Street. You, mdam, shall reside at Park Lane or not at all. Is that perfectly clear?"

When he caught her around the waist and pulled her to him, her breath caught in her throat. She felt the danger of his lean, hard body against hers. Excitment coursed through her, reminding her of their one passionate night together.

"You shall come home with me tonight," he murmured.

BOOK YOUR PLACE ON OUR WEBSITE AND MAKE THE READING CONNECTION!

We've created a customized website just for our very special readers, where you can get the inside scoop on everything that's going on with Zebra, Pinnacle and Kensington books.

When you come online, you'll have the exciting opportunity to:

- View covers of upcoming books
- Read sample chapters
- Learn about our future publishing schedule (listed by publication month *and author*)
- Find out when your favorite authors will be visiting a city near you
- Search for and order backlist books from our online catalog
- Check out author bios and background information
- Send e-mail to your favorite authors
- Meet the Kensington staff online
- Join us in weekly chats with authors, readers and other guests
- Get writing guidelines
- AND MUCH MORE!

**Visit our website at
http://www.zebrabooks.com**

ONE WILDE NIGHT

Stacy Brown

ZEBRA BOOKS
KENSINGTON PUBLISHING CORP.
http://www.zebrabooks.com

ZEBRA BOOKS are published by

Kensington Publishing Corp.
850 Third Avenue
New York, NY 10022

Copyright © 2000 by Anastasia Vasko

All rights reserved. No part of this book may be reproduced
in any form or by any means without the prior written consent
of the Publisher, excepting brief quotes used in reviews.

All Kensington titles, imprints and distributed lines are available at special quantity discounts for bulk purchases for sales
promotion, premiums, fund raising, educational or institutional
use.

Special book excerpts or customized printings can also be created to fit specific needs. For details, write or phone the office of
the Kensington Special Sales Manager: Kensington Publishing
Corp., 850 Third Avenue, New York, NY, Attn. Special Sales
Department. Phone: 1-800-221-2647.

If you purchased this book without a cover you should be aware
that this book is stolen property. It was reported as "unsold
and destroyed" to the Publisher and neither the Author nor the
Publisher has received any payment for this "stripped book."

ZEBRA and the Z logo Reg. U.S. Pat. & TM Off.

First Printing: November, 2000
10 9 8 7 6 5 4 3 2 1

Printed in the United States of America

Prologue

England, 1857

"I do so love a carriage ride in the middle of the day!" Aunt Edwina exclaimed, clapping her pudgy hands together.

Olivia Parker smiled at the kind-faced woman sitting across from her.

"Madame LeBlanc promised to show me the finest silks and laces that have just arrived from France." She lifted her shoulders in glee. Curly gray hair framed her cheerful round face, and her bright blue eyes peered at the world with excitement from behind wire-rimmed spectacles. "I simply cannot wait to make our selection."

Olivia sighed and turned her gaze out the window to the bustling city streets. She despised these afternoons filled with fittings and endless discussions of fabrics. She would much rather be at home curled up with Anthony Trollope's latest offering, *Barchester Towers*, or galloping down Rotten Row at dawn on her feisty mare than engaged in the frivolous task of selecting fashionable gowns.

But her father had told her time and time again women were not to indulge in such ridiculous pastimes. She was far more intellectually inclined than was seemly. Among the fairer sex, submission was all that was required. Her sole obligation in life was to be obedient, reserved, and graceful. Everything else would be taken care of by the men in her life—first by her father, and in due course by her husband. Her every need would be seen to by someone else. In short, she was not required to think.

But she did think. She tried not to, but she couldn't help herself. She possessed a natural curiosity, which she managed to rein in most of the time for the benefit of her father.

"We are here!" Edwina cried, adjusting her straw-brimmed bonnet. *"Olivia!* Attend me, child!" she snapped. "Have you not heard a word I've said? Dear me, we will be late for your fittings. Come, child! Madame LeBlanc is the most expensive modiste in town. She simply does not wait."

Olivia rolled her eyes heavenward. "Yes," she sighed, alighting from the warm luxury of the carriage's inviting squab seats. "How could I forget?"

Disregarding her niece's lackluster attitude, Edwina waddled across the street and entered the stylish shop. She immediately greeted the exclusive proprietor and monopolized the conversation. Gabbing about the style and cut of gown she would like fashioned in only the finest brown taffeta, she took no notice of Olivia's apathy.

Gazing longingly out the shop window, Olivia

sighed. Bond Street offered enticing treats, and the small elite shop was terribly stuffy. A sly grin stole across her lips, and she darted a glance over her shoulder. Judging from her aunt's chatter, she and Madame LeBlanc would be occupied for hours.

"I shan't be a moment, Aunt," Olivia called out, opening the shop door. "I need a breath of air."

Before her aunt could stop her, Olivia slipped from the elegant dressmaker's shop. She started down the street, her gaze riveted to the luxuries displayed in the shop windows. In no time at all, the shopkeepers' tempting displays had her rapt. She took no notice of where her journey led her.

Drawing in a deep breath of crisp winter air, she smiled. It was wonderful to walk along without her aunt's constant cheerful banter to distract her. She felt free and, for the first time in her life, marvelously independent.

She had been walking for quite some time when she noticed a drastic change in the complexion of the neighborhood. The opulent shops close to Madame LeBlanc's had given way to shops that were somewhat dingy, and fashionable, well-dressed pedestrians were scarce—in fact, nonexistent. Before she could retrace her steps toward Bond Street, a grimy looking young man lurched out at her from a nearby doorway.

" 'Ere now, Miss, where d'ya think yer goin'?" he inquired, his dirt-smudged face unnervingly close to hers.

Alarm rippled down her spine. She took a shaky step backward. Instinctively, she clutched her ermine muff to her chest. "I was"—she glanced about her for an expedient avenue of escape—"walking," she offered lamely.

"Oh, aye. Were yer now?" he mumbled, his rapacious gaze jerking to her neck, where the ermine edging of her black velvet pelisse parted to reveal a pearl and diamond lavaliere.

Fear took root in her heart. Before she could cry for help, the ruffian snatched the gold chain, violently ripping the pendant from her person. She gasped in shock and tried unsuccessfully to defend herself and reclaim what was rightfully hers, but he cuffed her hard across the face.

A groan of pain escaped her, and she tumbled backward and fell. She knew a moment of terror as she hit the ground. Her eyes fluttered shut in horrified disbelief. This could not be happening to her.

And then, blessedly, she heard a deep, commanding male voice. "You there! What the devil are you about?"

The curt remark was followed by the muffled sounds of the startled thief scampering down the street.

Dazed, she tried to set herself to rights. A firm grip closed around her upper arm. She was pulled to her feet.

Still shaken by the vicious encounter, she uttered a frantic cry and tried to wrench free from yet another assailant. But a warm, velvety masculine voice gave her pause. "It's all right. I am not going to hurt you."

She glanced up and found herself staring into the bluest eyes she'd ever seen. Her throat went dry. All possibility of rational thought vanished. Standing before her was the most gorgeous specimen of masculinity she'd ever beheld. Eyes as blue as the sea, hair the color of rich sable, and broad cheekbones that flanked a long aquiline nose which suited his aristocratic good looks all gave him an air of male superiority.

Her knees went weak. She leaned against him, welcoming the refuge of his rock-hard chest.

"You've had quite a scare." His voice was low and wonderfully comforting. Her eyes fluttered shut, and she reveled in his strong, comforting embrace. "You're perfectly safe now. No one is going to hurt you," he assured her.

When she displayed not the slightest inclination toward pulling away, he took a gentle, albeit firm, hold of her slender shoulders and set her away from him.

Between the harrowing experience of assault and robbery and the astonishing gallantry of her gorgeous rescuer, she was numb. As if in a dream state, she could do no more than stare at him. In a smart swallow-tailed uniform of red and gold, a black bearskin hat tucked beneath one arm, her intrepid savior was obviously an officer in one of the Queen's regiments.

Most of the officers returning from the Crimea during the past year had donned fashionable beards, but somehow the muttonchops and full mustache were oddly out of place on her champion's face.

Knitting his brow, he examined her with a critical eye.

She was surprised by his stern, jaded countenance and the hard lines that edged his full mouth. His decidedly masculine, chiseled features were somewhat intimidating. Even so, she longed to reach out and touch the cleft in his proud chin and smooth the deep creases in his forehead.

In sharp contrast to his reassuring voice, his frown deepened.

"Are you quite all right?"

She seemed incapable of replying.

His compelling blue eyes searched her face, and

his gaze drifted lower, drinking her in with shocking thoroughness. She flushed several degrees hotter beneath his lazy, heated regard. She had never been brazenly admired by a man before. Her heart fluttered in her chest. It was rather exciting to be on the receiving end of a purely wicked scrutiny.

"Did that vagabond hurt you?" The sharpness of his tone wrenched her from her fanciful reverie.

She shook her head. Rubbing her sore neck with her dirt-smudged glove, she managed to find her voice. "No, he—my pendant! He stole my pendant!" she cried in dismay.

The officer's lips thinned. "Yes, well," he muttered, glancing in the direction the thug had fled, "he is well on his way now, much the richer for his trouble. It was foolish of you to be out alone. Defenseless young ladies should never be without an escort," he told her curtly. "You are fortunate not to have been badly hurt."

Her spine straightened. His choleric, condescending tone nettled her. *Defenseless young ladies*, indeed. As if she were a helpless child fresh from a nanny's care! *She* was not defenseless—nor was she all that young, really. He made it sound like an unforgivable flaw to be under the ripe old age of twenty-five. It was decidedly unflattering, particularly when she was mooning over him and imagining him as her dashing, romantic rescuer.

Regardless of how irritating she found his disdainful manner, however, she owed him a debt of gratitude.

"As it happens," she explained with surprising aplomb, given that her insides were wobbling rather badly, "I am not without escort. My aunt is shopping nearby. I," she admitted with some embarrassment, "stepped out for a moment and ended up"—she surveyed her questionable surroundings—"here."

The hard edges of his mouth turned down. "Yes, well, I suspect that will be the first—and the last—time you venture out alone."

A rueful smile touched her lips. "Yes," she admitted with a pang of sadness. Her gloved hand touched the spot on her green silk gown where her beloved pendant had once lain. "I warrant you are correct."

A smile softened his otherwise harsh features. "I am sorry you had to learn such a cruel lesson. Was the pendant of great value?"

She nodded her head, reflecting unhappily on her loss. "Yes," she said quietly, "it was very dear to me."

"In that case," he remarked, sincerity shining in his deep blue eyes, "I am doubly sorry."

She looked up at him, and, offering him a hesitant smile, said softly, "I . . . thank you for your concern, kind sir."

"You must allow me to see you safely back to your aunt." Taking her arm, he proceeded to escort her back to Bond Street.

Chagrined by her lack of judgment, she murmured, "Again, I am indebted to you, sir."

He frowned. "Nonsense," he said sharply. "Not at all. It is the least I can do."

As they walked, an awkward silence fell over them. Clearing her throat, she hastened to remark, "I very much suspect you saved my life."

He pulled a modest face. "I sincerely doubt your life was at stake," he drawled, "merely your riches."

Despite her raw nerves, she managed a smile. "Then it is fortunate indeed that I have none."

His hooded gaze swept over her. "My dear girl,

with beauty such as yours, a woman does not need a fortune.''

Flustered, she lowered her lashes and hoped the brim of her black velvet bonnet hid the deep flush in her cheeks. A secretive smile curled her lips. Her encounter with the thief had been blessedly eclipsed by her breathtakingly handsome companion's charm.

As if on air, she accompanied her dashing hero down the street. Unfortunately, their stroll came to an end far too quickly. When they reached Madame LeBlanc's, Olivia caught sight of her aunt. Edwina was bumbling about in a tizzy, demanding something be done to find her lost niece. Their driver was attempting to console her. From the looks of things, poor old Jim was achieving little success.

Her rescuer glanced in the direction of the distressed matron, who was flailing her arms in the air. One end of his mouth lifted slightly. ''Your aunt, I presume?''

Olivia heaved a sigh. ''I am afraid so.''

''I wager you are quite safe in her hands. Only the most stalwart criminal would dare approach such a formidable protector,'' he drawled with dry humor.

Olivia could contain neither her amusement nor the thrill of excitement that rippled through her at the feel of his breath warm and soft against her cheek. Pressing her gloved hand to her mouth, she tried to stifle her mirth.

After suffering the ranting of her overset aunt, Olivia climbed into the refuge of her father's black lacquered carriage and leaned out the window to address the handsome stranger. ''I cannot thank you enough for coming to my aid, gracious sir.''

''I only wish I had arrived in time to retrieve your jewels from the villain who stole them,'' he replied, pressing a kiss on her gloved hand. He gazed deeply into her eyes. "Assisting lovely damsels in distress," he murmured softly, "is an honor I find difficult to resist."

A rosy glow warmed her cheeks, and she smiled shyly.

With that, he hit the top of the conveyance and gave the order to drive on.

As the carriage rolled over the cobblestones toward home, Olivia sat back. Hugging her arms to her waist, she expelled a blissful sigh.

"Gracious me," her aunt cried, nearly hysterical, "when I think of the fate that might have befallen you were it not for that gallant officer"—she splayed her hand across her large bosom—"I could faint dead on the spot." She moaned and waved her lacy handkerchief to and fro to fan herself. "What will your father say?"

Olivia was only vaguely aware of her aunt's agitation. At present, she did not much care for her father's fine opinion. Her main preoccupation was with the officer with the arresting good looks who had come to her aid.

Beaming from ear to ear, she leaned against the soft velvet squabs and smiled. He'd called her lovely and he'd kissed her hand. She expelled a dreamy sigh. He was the most stunning man on whom she'd ever laid eyes.

Of course, she mentally chided herself, he was also the *only* eligible young man she'd ever had occasion to meet. Recalling his dazzling smile, she quickly disregarded that point. He was irresistibly charming— a courtly gentleman if ever there was one.

Not that she knew the first thing about men. Aside from those who frequently dined at Belgrave Square, the tall handsome man with eyes like a clear blue summer sky and hair as dark as coal was the first man with whom she'd exchanged more than three words. To date, she had led a completely sheltered life.

Her brow wrinkled. Perhaps too protected. If this afternoon's nightmarish experience was any indication, she was grievously ill-prepared for the challenges of the world. Until today, she had never come face to face with the seedy side of London.

However, she was not so naive as to believe that outside her cozy, safe environment life wasn't austere and cruel. Her assailant's dirt-smudged, angry face took hold in her mind. She shuddered. Without the protection of a man, a woman was a helpless victim.

A secretive smile curled her lips. Closing her eyes, she sat back and expelled an elated sigh. She would be pleased to accept the role of frail female—provided, of course, that her gallant protector cut as princely a figure as the chivalrous young officer.

Chapter 1

The death knell pealed out, signaling the final laying to rest of the late Earl Marlborough. The sound was harsh and appropriately forbidding, given the cold, gray morning. Clasping his hands behind his back, Brandon Wilde stared stoically into the dark pit, not really listening to the prayers the vicar recited in a monotone. The coffin containing his father's remains creaked as it was lowered into hallowed ground.

"Ashes to ashes, dust to dust," the vicar droned.

Mounds of earth landed with a thud on top of the coffin, until slowly the long narrow box was completely hidden. It was the last Brandon would ever see of his wastrel father.

Thank God.

Death. It was a harsh reality, one with which he was all too familiar. Unbidden memories assailed him of his first military engagement at the battle of Alma

River. His acts of bravery had won him respect among his peers, but his infatuation with soldiering hadn't lasted long. The horrible suffering of the men in Malta and the Crimea, the appalling conditions which he endured—lack of food, clothing, and sufficient fuel—altered his attitude toward pursuing a military career.

After the slaughter of thousands at the battle of Inkerman, he left the blood-soaked field wounded, disillusioned, and sick at heart. Were it not for his good friend Jeremy Pratt and the nursing efforts organized by Florence Nightingale, he might well be dead.

At times, he wished he had died there rather than returned to England. He delayed his return as long as he could, only to find his father dying and Cloverton Hall unchanged. All his childhood demons still lurked within, tattered souvenirs of his past. It conjured up deep-seated resentment and painful remembrances of things best forgotten.

The vicar snapped his leather-bound Bible closed, jolting Brandon from his grisly reverie. Turning to address the new Earl of Marlborough, the aged vicar remarked tersely, "God be with you."

He trudged off, leaving Brandon alone, a tall unwavering figure beside his father's grave. The wind howled and moaned about him, tugging at his raven hair and heavy black coat. The biting cold was good. The wind stung his face, reminding him he was still alive. He must have some semblance of feeling left deep down inside.

Apart from the physical discomfort of the damp chill, however, he felt nothing. It was the hour of his father's death. Brandon could not conjure up a single emotion.

His mind drifted back ten years to the death of his

mother. It burned in his memory like a torch. At that funeral, he'd been a boy of fifteen, not a man of five and twenty. His father, who was too drunk to attend the burial, had taken great pleasure in ridiculing his son's tears.

But Brandon had wept. He'd shed an ocean of tears over her stiff cold corpse, had sobbed until his tears ceased. With the loss of his mother, his heart had been torn from his chest. In its place was an empty, cavernous space he'd never been able to fill.

Since then, he'd lived on the periphery of life. He'd learned the hard way it was best not to feel anything. Sensitivity was an emotion he could ill afford. Drawing a deep breath of cold air, he turned his back on the plot where his father would lay for eternity and headed down the hill toward Cloverton Hall.

When he arrived, he learned a Gilbert Parker was waiting to speak to him.

Brandon's insides twisted into a sickening knot. Although the name was unfamiliar to him, he suspected the reason for the call. He had been home scarcely a week and already it had begun.

Only last night, Brandon had been apprised in general terms of the appalling financial situation he'd inherited. He'd read the steward's report and met with the family solicitor, who had been less than subtle in his depiction of the dire state of affairs. The visitor awaiting him in the blue salon was undoubtedly one of many tradesmen seeking payment.

Divesting himself of his black overcoat and beaver hat, Brandon braced himself for what promised to be a harrowing exchange. The prospect of having to beg for clemency did not sit well with him. As he reached for the doorknob, he noted with displeasure that his palms were sweaty.

Upon entering the room, a startling realization struck him. The caller was not a tradesman. The impeccably dressed, salt-and-pepper haired gentleman standing before Brandon flaunted biscuit-colored trousers, a brown velvet frock coat, and a beige brocade waistcoat. His tucked shirt was made of expensive linen. His spotted green cravat, Brandon noted, was undoubtedly fine French silk.

It reminded him that his own snug black trousers were frayed at the braid, his linen shirt yellowed, and his black waistcoat tattered. Moreover, his clothes were sadly out of fashion and reeked of camphor.

Turning from the fireplace, the stranger made a quick, albeit thorough, assessment of his host. An inexplicable gleam appeared in the man's piercing gray eyes.

"Lord Wilde, I presume. Gilbert Parker," he explained, grabbing hold of Brandon's hand and shaking it vigorously. "You are doubtless wondering why I have intruded on this most sorrowful day, my good man."

Brandon's forehead creased slightly. *My good man?* Obviously Mr. Parker did not know how to address his betters.

But it was of little consequence. The relief Brandon felt at not having to confront a bill collector made up for any social slight he might otherwise have felt. Besides, his military service had taught him there was more to a man than his birthright.

Brandon silently crossed the room to the drinks table. A cynical smile twisted his lips. Whether he'd been rich or poor, drinks were the one thing his father had always kept well stocked.

"If you are here for the burial," he remarked as

he sloshed a large dose of brandy into a glass, "you are a bit late."

"Funerals are such dreary occasions," Mr. Parker replied with an air of indifference. "I prefer to avoid them whenever possible."

Brandon nodded his head in agreement and drained his glass in one swallow. "Capital notion."

Helping himself to a comfortable seat on the threadbare blue velvet couch, Parker admitted, "I have come about a different matter entirely."

Brandon turned to examine the curious man. His crystalline blue eyes swept over the impertinent man with disapproval.

"Have you indeed? Well, then." A humorless smile touched Brandon's lips. "I see you have already made yourself at home. Why not dispense with formalities and state your case?"

Parker dismissed Brandon's sarcasm without comment. "I assure you, I do not intend to intrude upon your grief longer than is necessary."

Brandon refilled his brandy glass. He took a gulp of the amber liquid, and his insides began to thaw. Dropping into the unyielding wing chair, he inclined his raven head. "That is a relief."

"I wonder if you are familiar with the late earl's state of affairs," Parker's blunt manner set Brandon on edge.

Baffled by his tactless inquiry, Brandon sent him a queer look. "To what *affairs* do you refer, sir?"

Parker bared his teeth in what could only be described as a predatory smile. "Specifically, your father's—forgive me. I should say, *your* dire financial straits? I believe," he drawled, plucking an imaginary piece of lint from his impeccable sleeve, "the cumulative debt is somewhere in the range of twenty thousand pounds."

Brandon's jaw set like granite. "You seem rather well informed," he remarked, a decided chill in his voice. He despised the notion that his situation was public knowledge.

"Indeed," Parker murmured. "I know everything there is to know about the unfortunate circumstances in which you find yourself."

Brandon's glass paused *en route* to his lips. His azure eyes narrowed. "Precisely how is that possible?"

"I hold in my possession several large IOUs incurred by your late father, scads of promissory notes, and countless bills of exchange which he gladly accepted. You see, I was pleased to lend your father any amount I could, thereby ensuring I was his sole creditor."

The blood pounding in his ears deafened Brandon. He downed the remainder of his brandy and set the glass on the mahogany table. "And am I to assume from this very auspicious visit," he inquired briskly, "that you are looking for prompt payment?"

Parker inclined his head. "Indeed you may. But perhaps," he hastened to add, raising his index finger in the air, "not in the manner you might believe. There is a rather large mortgage on the property."

The muscle in Brandon's jaw pulsed. "I am aware of it."

A triumphant smile spread across Parker's face. "In that case, you would be well advised to sell the estate and to settle the account."

Fixing the odious man with a lethal glare, Brandon sprang to his feet. "Never," he growled, presenting the crafty man with his broad, proud back. He crossed the room to the fireplace. Resting his forearm on the mantel, he gazed pensively at the flickering flames.

Behind him, Parker tsk-tsked. "Never is a very long time," he reminded Brandon. "The estate is not entailed. Very irregular, I know, but nonetheless true. Nothing is stopping you."

Brandon swung around. "Nothing but honor. My father may have disgraced the family name, but I will never condescend to sell. You have mistaken the matter," he said hotly.

Parker stroked his chin thoughtfully. "So it would appear. And yet," he remarked, unruffled in the face of Brandon's resentment, "you may find you have little choice in the matter. You see, in addition to holding the bulk of your father's debt, the estate is mortgaged to me."

Brandon's lips curled in disdain. This grasping social climber turned his stomach. "You may think to garner an estate for yourself, but you will never claim the title."

A pregnant silence hung over the dank room. Rubbing his aching forehead with his thumb and forefinger, Brandon muttered after a tense moment, "Even if I do agree to sell—which I won't—you can never be a peer of the realm. That honor," he said contemptuously, "can only be given by right of birth."

Parker laughed out loud. "You are shrewd, my boy," he observed, amusement twinkling in his calculating gaze. "Far more clever than I gave you credit for. My association with the late earl may have colored my judgment where you are concerned. Like father like son, I had supposed. But in your case," he allowed, examining the proud set of Brandon's shoulders, "nothing could be further from the truth. Your father was a lecher, a gambler, and a drunkard. You,

I expect, are a man to be reckoned with. It is no secret you harbored no affection for your father. Mind you, no one would fault you for abandoning him to serve the Queen. And I've a feeling were you in my place," he mused, "you'd have done much the same to achieve your ends."

Brandon fixed Parker with an icy glare. "I am sorry to disappoint you."

Parker's brows furrowed. "I must admit, your reaction amazes me. I should think you'd be pleased to sell and be done with it. Do not be a fool, man." He sat forward. "Give in to temptation. Free yourself of the heavy burden your wastrel father placed upon your shoulders."

Brandon walked to the large casement window. Resting his hand on the sill, he gazed out at the overcast sky. "I shall," he stated with firm resolve, "in my own good time."

"Ah," Parker drawled sagely. "You think to marry a wealthy heiress with an allowance of twenty thousand pounds a year and a generous dowry, do you?"

Turning around, Brandon folded his arms over his chest and leaned back against the sill. He regarded Parker with blatant dislike. "Say what you've come to say and get out."

"No cause for hostility, surely? I've a sound solution to your dilemma that may serve us both well in the end." He rose to his feet. "If you will but hear me out?"

Brandon inclined his head in tacit agreement.

"You are quite right when you say I want an estate. I do. That is precisely why I became acquainted with your father. But, as you have alluded, I want more. Much more."

Brandon regarded Parker suspiciously. "What *more* could you possibly hope to gain?"

"Why," he chuckled softly, "a way into the peerage, of course. I thought you had surmised that already. I am prepared to forgive all debts, provided—"

Brandon eyes narrowed. "Provided what?" he prodded with keen interest.

"You marry my daughter."

A look of incredulity crossed Brandon's face. Grunting derisively, he straightened. "Forget it."

Parker raised his hands. "You agreed to hear me out. Olivia shall be Lady Wilde, and I shall have the satisfaction of knowing my grandson will be the next Earl Marlborough. It is a fair exchange."

Slinging his hands on his narrow hips, Brandon fixed Parker with a venomous glare. "I will never marry your daughter," he stated. "You must be mad to suggest such an arrangement. If you think to buy your daughter an eligible husband, you've come to the wrong man."

Parker cocked a dubious brow. "Have I?" Gathering his walking stick, hat, and gloves, he said with poorly feigned regret, "I should hate to demand payment in full and take possession by default. Quite a formidable sum. It could prove a trifle distressing for you." With that provocative remark, he took his leave.

Seething, Brandon raked his hands through his coal-black hair and cursed his iniquitous father to hell.

One month later, Brandon arrived at Parker's Belgrave Square address prepared to do business. He noted with satisfaction as he pounded his fist upon the red lacquered door that Parker's town house was modest. It paled in comparison to the grand Grecian-columned residence on Park Lane which had been occupied by Wildes for generations. Then again, Belgravia *was* less fashionable than Mayfair.

A middle-aged butler showed Brandon into a gauchely decorated back parlor, and Brandon crossed the threshold of the most hideous salon he'd ever seen. The lamps were a shade of red that defied nature, and they had gold tassels. The sofas were upholstered in garish gold and black velvet. In fact, everything in the room was vulgar.

From the cursory inquiries Brandon had made, Parker had the Midas touch. The man was as rich as Croesus.

Brandon's hands fisted around a piece of ivory parchment that contained a thinly veiled threat. According to his solicitor, Mr. Bosworth, it was merely a matter of time before Parker demanded payment in full and took measures to acquire Cloverton Hall for himself.

A snarl twisted Brandon's lips. The wily Parker had orchestrated the entire affair. If Brandon had not known better, he'd have sworn Parker had purposefully plied his father with liquor until he died of it.

Behind him, the door swung open. Brandon whirled around.

"Ah, Lord Wilde," Parker remarked, eyeing Brandon's gray sack coat that lacked a black armband. "Am I to assume you have decided against mourning your dearly departed father?"

"What business is that of yours?" Brandon asked.

Parker shrugged his shoulders. "It is none of my concern. To be candid, I never liked the man." He closed the door behind him and swiftly changed the subject. "To what do I owe this visit, may I ask?"

"You bloody well know why I'm here," Brandon said through gritted teeth.

"Excellent." Parker beamed, rubbing his hands together. "I take it you have decided to reconsider and accept my terms."

"Not on your life."

"Such a pity," he drawled, taking a seat behind the large mahogany desk, the legs of which were carved into savage dragons. "I shall simply have to pursue the matter to its completion."

Brandon planted his palms squarely on the desk. "You must give me more time," he insisted with a fierceness born of desperation.

"Time, it would seem, does not favor you. Your father's legacy has serious repercussions—unless you accept my offer."

Brandon hung his head. "In time," he vowed, "I will repay the debt in full. But you must give me more time."

Parker chuckled derisively. "Meet my daughter. You may find her appearance sways your decision."

Brandon stood tall. "Very well," he said stiffly. "I will endure an introduction. But that is all."

Parker eyed Brandon critically. "You are a hot-headed young buck. Best curb your passion before it rules your head and makes a fool out of you. You and I both know the only sensible thing is to agree to my terms. Why resist the inevitable?"

Brandon turned away to pace the confines of the room. "Nothing is inevitable," he muttered irritably.

Parker got to his feet and tugged on the bellpull. A moment later, the butler appeared and received instructions to summon Olivia.

"You wished to see me, Father?" a dulcet voice

queried from the doorway, breaking the tense silence that hung over the two adversaries.

Brandon swiveled around. His heart slammed against his ribs. Standing before him was a fair-haired vision of loveliness the likes of which he had set eyes on only once before. It was her, his lovely damsel in distress.

Struck dumb, he swallowed audibly and dragged his hand through his midnight hair. Good Lord. *She* was Parker's daughter? The pawn he hoped to use as a weapon against Brandon?

Garbed in a pale blue taffeta dress, tucked white blouse, and bow tie, she could pass for a schoolgirl fresh from a governess's care. But if the throbbing of his pulse was any indication, that did not diminish her appeal. Not one damned bit. His attraction to her was just as potent as it had been when he'd come upon her lying helpless in the street.

Her eyes were a startling shade of green. Or were they brown? He couldn't quite decide. Fringed with thick lashes, they were as large and startlingly beautiful as he recalled. Equally surprised by their renewed acquaintance, she gazed at him.

Despite his desire to refuse the interview, now that he knew the identity of the woman in question, he indulged the purely male impulse to admire her. He let his bold, assessing gaze pore over every inch of her with an impolite thoroughness that would have put most young innocents to the blush. She remained the picture of intoxicating femininity.

Her skin might have been that of a porcelain doll, he noted with a surge of fierce desire. Her moist pink mouth was full, slightly parted, and just as kissable as it had been that chilly afternoon not so very long ago. He'd been tempted then to pursue the rare beauty, but urgent matters at Cloverton had taken him from London sooner than he would have liked.

Her hair was the color of corn silk. Parted in the Madonna style, it curled about her fragile face with enviable closeness. He could envision how thick and luxurious it would be when not bound at the back of her head in that tight braid. He found himself imagining what it would be like to run his fingers through her hair and cover her full inviting mouth with his.

A jolt of incredulity coursed through him. What the devil had come over him? He would allow she was enticing to his senses and more than pleasing to the eye than any other woman of his acquaintance, but she was bait for her calculating father and his diabolical scheme.

Dragging his gaze from the heavenly vision of loveliness, Brandon glared at Parker.

Parker's gaze skittered from Brandon's expression. He addressed his daughter.

"Olivia, I would like you to meet Lord Wilde, Earl Marlborough. He has recently come into his title and is eager to make your acquaintance, my dear."

Her startled gaze flew to Brandon's rigid expression. A frown marred her otherwise perfect forehead. She looked disappointed by the discovery that he was titled, and he wondered if she was weighing the merits of divulging their previous meeting.

She obviously thought better of it and dipped him a polite curtsy. "A pleasure, my lord."

Brandon nodded his head curtly. "Miss Parker," he replied with stiff civility.

"That will be all, my dear. You may leave us. We have matters to discuss that do not concern young ladies."

"Yes, father." Olivia dutifully took her leave.

Brandon watched her slip from the room. Blood coursed hot through his veins. Infuriated by the tell-tale signs of his attraction, he growled at Parker, "What sort of gambit is this? She is hardly fodder for the London marriage mart."

Parker shrugged and reclined more comfortably in his chair. "The choice is yours. Marry my daughter, or face financial ruin. Which is it to be?"

"What you suggest is barbaric."

"On the contrary, it is entirely civilized. The harsh reality of social disgrace and financial ruin await you should you not agree. Marry Olivia. If you do not," Parker assured him, an ominous glint in his eye, "I shall see to it you are brought to your knees."

"You cannot expect me to marry a mere girl who is a complete stranger to me."

Parker shrugged carelessly. "I will allow that her appearance is somewhat youthful, but I assure you she is of a marriageable age. Since when did not knowing a woman present a hardship for a hot-blooded young man?"

Brandon fixed him with a heated glare.

"Come now. Age is hardly of significance where large sums of money are to be had, and I think you will agree she is not lacking in any way. She has led a sheltered life appropriate for her delicate female constitution. She is obedient, graceful, and although she may look fragile, she is healthy. All the ingredients for an excellent wife, would you not agree?"

Brandon's face contorted in disgust. "By God, you are despicable. She is your daughter, for God's sake. If you cannot find it in your heart to be lenient with me, at least be merciful where she is concerned. Do you care nothing for your child's happiness?"

Parker waved aside Brandon's objection. "She shall be happy with the knowledge that she has done her duty and made her father proud. A sound alliance with a peer of the realm is more than most women of common birth can hope to attain."

Brandon planted his hands on his waist and prowled the room, mentally weighing the merit of Parker's reprehensible offer.

He supposed he should be thankful his dissolute father had not disgraced the family name by selling the estate. Brandon could, in good conscience, do no worse. After all, it had been handed down some four hundred years from father to eldest son.

Damn and blast. What choice did he truly have save to marry the chit and be done with it? If the startling surge of physical attraction he'd experienced was any indication, he would not suffer excessively from the arrangement. Mercenary though the alliance might be, it was also damned expedient.

"Do not pretend you are not tempted," Parker goaded. "I saw the way you looked at her. She is like a perfect bud that will bloom into an exquisite rose. Many a man will envy you your young, fertile bride. Dress her in the finest silks and jewels and you will not notice her lack of experience. I guarantee it."

Brandon swung around to glare at Parker, burning contempt in his deep blue eyes. "If I wed your daughter," he clarified, "you agree to forgive all debts, including the mortgage on Cloverton Hall?"

Parker inclined his gray head in agreement. "A fair exchange, would you not agree?"

"And what if I am displeased with my bride?" Brandon asked. "What then?"

"You won't be," Parker grunted in reply, "for if you are, you shall soon find yourself without a sou to

your name. I am no fool. Olivia shall come with a
handsome dowry of thirty thousand pounds per
annum. It shall be yours . . . on condition."

Brandon's eyes narrowed. "What bloody condition?"

"Naturally, there will be serious limitations to your
control over her fortune."

"In other words," Brandon snapped, *"my wife* shall
keep me on a tight leash?"

Parker grimaced. "Nothing quite so drastic. You
have but to conduct yourself as a gentleman and live
within your means. All shall be well. Have a seat."
Parker motioned Brandon to the velvet-cushioned
chair in front of his desk. "It won't take more than
a moment to work out the pertinent details."

Feeling deeply resentful, Brandon stalked across
the room and slumped into the chair.

"There is one other matter that bears mentioning,"
Parker said cautiously.

Brandon's arctic blue eyes threatened to impale
his blackmailer. "And what might that be?" he asked
in a low, angry growl.

"Olivia must never learn the truth," her father
enjoined him. "The details of her betrothal will be
kept from her. Are we agreed?"

Brandon gave a curt nod. He saw no reason to
involve the girl in her father's sordid dealings.

"Excellent," Parker replied, gleeful as a schoolboy.
"Shall I tell you how I acquired my wealth? I amassed
most of my extensive fortune in the East. India and
China are lands of great opportunity for the shrewd
of mind and strong of heart. It is an interesting story,
to be sure. I am particularly proud of my recent coal
mining and shipping business ventures."

"Why am I not surprised?" Brandon said. "All of

Europe is in crisis over the speculation of railroad shares and *you* prosper." Leaning forward, he said, his voice laced with bitterness, "I do not give a damn how you accumulated your riches. Draw up the bloody agreement and let us be done with it."

"Indeed?" Parker murmured, completely unfazed by his future son-in-law's gruff remark. "I would think a man such as yourself would be curious to learn how to *earn* money rather than spend it."

Brandon's lips thinned. "You've struck a devil's bargain, Parker. It comes as little surprise that you managed to crawl out of the gutter. You have seen to it I have no choice but to agree to your odious terms. I must marry your daughter. The particulars of the matter are therefore of little consequence to me."

Parker frowned. "Come now, why so glum? You shall be acquiring a small fortune and a beautiful young bride in the bargain. You have retrieved your family's name from the jaws of scandal and shall retain a formidable estate. If you are wise, it will henceforth be entailed to my grandson. This day calls for celebration, surely," he remarked cheerfully, "not for dour faces."

"Oh, I shall celebrate," Brandon assured him, his tone deadly. "When our dealings are through and I never have to set eyes on the likes of you again, *then* I shall celebrate."

Olivia padded over the carpeted stairs and down the narrow hall toward her father's back parlor. She was slightly embarrassed to learn her handsome rescuer's true identity. Why should the Earl of Marlborough wish to renew *her* acquaintance? She could not credit that a peer of the realm had actually arranged to meet her, a commoner's daughter. Had he perchance been trying to discover who she was all these weeks?

No. She shook her head. That could not be. A man like that certainly would not have thought twice about her. More important, he was clearly as stunned by her arrival as she was to find her gallant protector standing in the middle of her father's study.

To her chagrin, he seemed irritated and downright rude, quite unlike the heroic officer she'd admired. When he'd turned to 'examine' her—for that could be the only word to describe the way his startling blue gaze had raked over her person—he wore an almost hungry expression. She flushed at the memory. No man had ever looked at her like that. With a surge of wicked excitement, she wondered if he found her as pleasing to look at as she did him.

Vowing not to think of the earl or his mysterious motives, she scratched lightly at the door to her father's private sanctuary. Upon hearing his greeting, she entered.

"Ah, my dear." He extended his hands to her.

She pressed a kiss to his cheek. "You wished to see me, Father?"

"Er, yes." He released her hands and presented her with his back. "I have some good news for you, my dear. You are to be married by month's end."

Her brows drew together. *"Married?"* she gasped, shocked by his announcement. "Whatever can you mean? I have no suitors, no callers."

He swiveled around to face her. "Does it surprise you?"

"Indeed, it does," she sputtered. "To whom, pray,

am I betrothed?'' An amused look dawned on her face. She was convinced he was playing a ruse on her.

He grinned at her. ''The Earl of Marlborough,'' he explained, overjoyed by the prospect.

Her face fell. *''Lord Wilde?''* she croaked. Good Lord, he wished to marry her?

''The very same.''

She gaped at her father. ''You cannot be serious.''

''Indeed, I am. At this very moment, his lordship is arranging for a license. You are to be married at Cloverton Hall. What say you to that?'' he asked, beaming with pride at his accomplishment.

Olivia clutched her forehead with her fingers. ''I scarcely know what to say,'' she mumbled, groping for a seat before she fell down. Her head reeled. Somewhere in the distant recesses of her mind, she was aware of her father espousing the excellent character of Lord Wilde and his expressed desire to make *her* his bride.

Agitated, she got to her feet and wandered over to the mantel. She turned the recent events over and over in her mind. She could surmise nothing from their two brief meetings that would elicit such a drastic move on his part. What had precipitated his lordship's proposal? What of the customary courtship? Surely that was necessary before he offered for her hand.

''Are you not pleased?'' her father wanted to know. ''Come, tell me you are happy.''

She shook her head as if to clear it. ''I . . . I do not understand.''

''His lordship has seen you and wishes you for his bride.'' Her father clasped her by the shoulders and turned her to face him. ''It is an honor, Olivia.''

She knitted her brow. ''Why should he wish to

marry me, a woman who is so clearly beneath his station in life?"

"It is what the earl desires," her father explained, tucking a stray lock of blond hair behind her ear. "And I believe it is a sound match, as well. You will be Lady Wilde. Do you not understand the honor he is bestowing upon you? Out of all the eligible young ladies in London, he has selected *you* to be his wife."

Nonplussed, she stared at her father. "Why me?"

He laughed. "Because you are beautiful, charming, and graceful, everything a woman of substance should be."

"How can he possibly be certain what I am like?"

"He finds your character and your appearance flawless and he wishes to marry you. That, my dear girl," her father said, tweaking her playfully on the nose, "is all you need know."

Mystified, she inquired, "Does he not wish to familiarize himself further with my character? Are we not to meet alone?" Astonishment mingled with panic. "Am I not permitted to at least speak to him before the wedding?"

Shaking his gray head, her father frowned. "Er, no," he muttered. "He has recently returned from the war and has many pressing issues to attend to."

She did not feel reassured in the least. "I am sorry, Father, but I cannot agree to his proposal."

Her father stiffened perceptibly. "I daresay he rather fancies you, my dear. And as I have already given your hand, *you* have little choice in the matter."

Her heart sank. "Father, please reconsider. If he is the sort of man who selects his bride on a moment's notice," she said, "you would be well advised to spurn him, Father, for my sake."

"It was not a moment's notice, that I can tell you. And you will have no reason to regret his attentions."

Her eyes sharpened. "How can you offer such an assurance?"

"You are a beautiful young lady, very rare and very precious. Believe me when I say the earl is quite taken with you. It is you and no other he will take as his bride. He has told me so himself."

Stunned by this turn of events, she stated quite firmly, "I think I should demand a lengthy courtship."

"Bah!" her father snapped. "What need is there for a courtship?"

"To marry a man who is almost foreign to me?" A stricken expression crossed her face, and she sank down on the velvet sofa. "I find the prospect somewhat . . . frightening," she admitted.

"Nonsense," her father assured her, dismissing her trepidation. "You've nothing to fear. You have only to be obedient to your husband in all things, as you have been to your loving father, and you shall make him a very happy man indeed."

She glanced up sharply. "Pray consider my feelings in the matter, Father. I—"

"Hush now." He pressed his finger to her lips. "The matter is settled."

"How can it be settled?" she demanded. "I have yet to agree—"

"*I* have accepted him." Her father's tone brooked no disagreement. "This childish fretting will not do, Olivia," he admonished her sharply. "It simply will not do. You must comport yourself as a lady, mature and refined. It is what the earl expects. It is what *I* expect."

She recognized his tone and knew not to press him

further. Expelling an unhappy sigh, she lowered her troubled gaze to the floor. Inside, her blood boiled.

He offered her an affectionate smile. "I have always done what is best for you, have I not?"

She wanted to scream at him, to make him stop this folly, but she could never address him in anger. He would not tolerate an emotional outburst from her. He had a hard, implacable nature and a fierce temper when crossed. Having been raised without the warm comfort and support of a mother's love, Olivia had learned at an early age not to gainsay her father and to accept him as he was. Despite his sometimes harsh manner, she had never questioned his love for her.

And yet there were times when Olivia doubted subservience was the exalted state for women that her father espoused.

Still, she had no choice but to accept his dictates. Who would support her should she rail at him and refuse his insane suggestion that she marry a complete stranger? Her poor bedraggled Aunt Edwina was no match for him. She had tried her best to be a surrogate mother to Olivia, but that did not help Olivia from feeling horribly trapped and, not for the first time, utterly alone.

Nearly bursting with resentment, she sat in silence, her back ramrod straight, her shoulders tense. But she offered him no reply.

"You will be the perfect Lady Wilde, my dear. I am more proud than I can say. Now go," he instructed, patting her on the cheek, "and tell your aunt I wish to see her. We've a wedding to plan and a lavish trousseau to select for you, my sweet."

The discussion was at a close. She was to be married, and that was all there was to it. She felt ill.

As she slipped from the room, a sense of dread enveloped her and a lump of fear clogged her throat. Lord, she was to marry a man who was at once a wildly attractive protector and a distant stranger. What could she expect from an arrangement with such a man?

Chapter 2

Three weeks later, thoroughly exhausted from the rigorous preparations for her new life as Lady Wilde, Olivia endured a seemingly endless train ride to East Anglia. Sandwiched between her chatterbox Aunt Edwina and her pensive father, she tried to keep her spirits high. After an even less agreeable carriage ride from the station, she caught her first glimpse of her new home, Cloverton Hall, from the carriage window.

Her father had boasted that the enormous edifice was considered one of England's finest homes. Gazing up at the gray stone overgrown with ivy, she felt a shiver creep up her spine. Although it was dusk, she could not imagine the sun ever shone on such a dreary place. It looked more like a cold prison than a warm, inviting home. But, several of the rooms had a pale yellowish hue, indicating life actually lurked within the gloomy hall.

Aunt Edwina danced attendance at Olivia's side,

merrily chattering about the grandeur and size of the place.

"Just imagine the balls you shall host, my dear," she cried. "In all your days, did you ever imagine such an honor being bestowed on this family? I still cannot credit our good fortune."

Olivia offered her aunt an indulgent smile. Short and pudgy, Aunt Edwina was exactly what an adoring widowed aunt should be. What she lacked in intelligence, she more than made up for in enthusiasm. Olivia loved her dearly, but she was hardly a source of guidance as to why an earl should marry a commoner—or, for that matter, the challenges that lay ahead for Olivia once she was married to a seemingly disinterested husband.

The earl was certainly aloof. He had not requested another meeting with her since their engagement, nor had he penned a single note to her professing his desire to make her his. Her father, not her betrothed, had presented her with her engagement ring. And although she could not be certain, she believed her father had paid five hundred pounds for a lavish trousseau designed to see her through the first two years of her married life.

Heaving a sigh, she stepped down from the carriage and took in the crumbling old estate with a critical eye. She very much doubted she and the earl would be hosting any gala balls at Cloverton Hall.

Taking her by the arm, her father escorted her across the pebbled drive. "You should not be nervous, my dear," he advised, patting her hand.

"I am not nervous, Father," she stated, her tone resolute.

They mounted the stone steps and entered a deserted front hall. After a brief delay, they were greeted by an appropriately dour-looking butler named Chalmers.

"His lordship has retired to his private rooms for the evening," the bald servant explained. "He has left instructions that a cold supper be served. Your rooms have been made ready. His lordship felt certain you would wish to refresh yourselves after your long journey."

Olivia saw a vexed look darken her father's features. Clearly, this was not the reception for which he had hoped. She placed her gloved hand on his tense forearm.

"I am very tired, Father, as you must be. His lordship was quite considerate to allow us time alone," she suggested, trying to cool her father's simmering temper.

"Oh, yes," Aunt Edwina chimed in. "I am exhausted. I should like nothing better than to retire for the night. I am sure I shall sleep like the dead. And so should you, child," she advised Olivia. "Tomorrow is a very exciting day for you." She giggled.

Olivia squelched the urge to groan out loud and managed a wan smile instead.

Her father gave a curt nod. But as Olivia accompanied her aunt up the stairs, she heard her father snap at the butler, "Tell his *lordship* I wish to see him. Immediately."

"But, sir, he gave express instructions not to be disturbed."

"I said *immediately.*" Her father stormed off toward what Olivia assumed must be the library. Odd that her father should know his way about Cloverton Hall. A frown marred her forehead. Had he been here before?

Gabbing about the luxurious estate, Aunt Edwina

clutched Olivia by the arm. "Can you believe your eyes? It is like a castle fit for a queen. Just think, by this time tomorrow, *you* shall be Lady Wilde," she exclaimed, splaying her palm against her large bosom.

Olivia's heart sank. Yes, indeed. Tomorrow she would marry a stranger who did not care enough for her feelings to greet her in person. Her wedding was clearly not to be a romantic occasion, and his lordship definitely would not be the image of a gallant groom.

Trailing wordlessly behind the sullen servant girl who led them down the long, dim hallway, she wondered why all who were connected with Cloverton Hall seemed downtrodden. Was it the plight of all who came in contact with the earl to be miserable?

When she caught sight of a flickering light beneath a heavy door, a wave of nervous energy swept over her. She felt certain those were his lordship's private rooms. An odd sense of foreboding invaded her chest. What manner of man was he that he chose to avoid her at all costs? More important, what were his intentions toward her? They'd met only once prior to his proposal and on that brief occasion he had displayed more kindness toward her than he had since their betrothal. Her father had explained that among the upper class, love was not a prerequisite for marriage. But Olivia could not shake off the nagging suspicion that something sinister had driven his lordship to ask for her hand.

Olivia and Aunt Edwina were installed in a spartan room at the end of the hall. It overlooked the weed-infested gardens far below. When the two were alone, her aunt clasped her beefy hands together and plopped down on the enormous feather bed. Swinging her legs to and fro, she remarked with a happy sigh, "This *is* nice. I am so very pleased we are to pass this evening together. You know, I regard you as my very own daughter. And tomorrow night, of course"—she blushed—"you shall join your husband." She laughed nervously. "I am certain your things will be placed in the adjoining master bedroom, as is proper. I shall see to it myself."

A sick feeling settled in the pit of Olivia's stomach. The thought of marrying a complete stranger was only eclipsed by the horror of having to endure all manner of shocking intimacies with the taciturn man. As much as she loathed to admit it, she was frightened.

What would life with the earl be like? She wasn't quite sure how to feel about her impending nuptials. Ever since that bizarre afternoon when she'd been summoned to meet him, she'd felt as though she'd been living in a dream world turned nightmare.

Despite Edwina's cheerful prattle, Olivia's mind wandered to the demands that would be placed on her as Lady Wilde. Her father made it all sound facile, but Olivia was not persuaded. Pleasing a cold, distant man promised to be the greatest challenge of her young life.

She felt a measure of concern for her father, as well. She'd sensed his agitation all the way from London. Perhaps she should seek him out and make certain that he was happy with the arrangements before she retired.

Not that she held out any hope of sleep. Aunt Edwina snored abominably, and Olivia's nerves were on edge. It might give her some consolation to speak to her father. Now, more than ever, she needed his calm assurance and steely strength of purpose.

Leaving her aunt happily reclining on a mountain of pillows in the middle of the enormous, lumpy feather bed, Olivia went in search of her father. Smelly oil lamp in hand, she descended the darkened staircase. As she neared the room she'd seen him enter earlier, she heard voices raised in anger. Her father's heated accusations were followed by the low, controlled tones of another man.

Curiosity mingled with concern. Her feet propelled her toward the door, and she rapped lightly. Then, without waiting for an invitation, she threw open the door.

A tall, broad-shouldered man whom she immediately recognized as her intended swung around to face her. His handsome countenance was a mask of blazing fury. She swallowed audibly and quelled the urge to turn tail and run.

Recognition crossed his face. Anger drained from his features, only to be replaced by that burning hunger she'd seen once before. His piercing blue eyes drifted over her with an agonizing, heated precision that made her toes curl. Totally unprepared for their meeting, she could do little more than stare at the man who had claimed her as his bride.

A stray lock of raven hair fell across his forehead, softening his otherwise harsh, forbidding features. He was clean shaven, she noted. His face seemed almost boyish without whiskers. She was secretly glad. His youthful appearance bolstered her confidence as his equal and not his infantile bride.

Standing before her in a pair of buff-colored trousers, his soft linen shirt partially undone to reveal a tantalizing wedge of bronze skin and rough black hair, he looked ruggedly handsome and unnervingly virile. Their eyes met for what felt like an eternity.

Her heart seemed to be permanently lodged in her throat.

Feeling awkward, she tried to smile, but found she could not. His heated gaze lingered on her face and boldly drifted lower to openly admire her bosom.

Lord, the *way* he looked at her—as if he vacillated between the urge to throttle her and the desire to devour her whole.

Apparently annoyed at being discovered in the throes of a heated argument with the father of his bride to be, Lord Wilde frowned.

Paralyzed with embarrassment, she stood on the threshold of his private library, feeling a fool. When she heard their raised voices and detected their argument, she should have returned upstairs.

Finding her voice at last, she said, "Good evening, my lord."

His searing blue eyes locked with hers and he inclined his head. "Miss Parker," he replied softly.

"Olivia?" her father queried from somewhere beyond the huge, broad-shouldered man looming before her. Outrage and surprise mingled in his tone. "What the blazes—"

Heat crept into her cheeks. "I—I did not mean to intrude," she blurted, mortified at the thought of being chastised by her father in front of the earl.

"You didn't," his lordship said, an easy smile playing around the edges of his sensual mouth. Turning away from her, he sauntered—that was the best word to describe it—to the drinks table and poured a large quantity of brandy into his glass, then drank some. "Your father was just leaving," he explained, keeping his back to her.

Her father shot his lordship a look of unmistakable dislike. "That is quite right, my dear," he said, getting to his feet. "The hour is late." Offering her a warm, reassuring smile, he extended his arm to her. "Come, you must be all in."

"Pray, Father, do not allow me to interrupt. If you would like to continue your"—she searched for the appropriate word—"discussion, I can wait."

"Not at all," he replied, patting her hand affectionately. "Our little chat is at an end for the time being." He cast a dark look at the earl. "Besides, you are never an interruption, my sweet."

Glancing from her father to his lordship, her heart grew heavy.

"Good night, my lord," she offered in a whisper-soft tone.

"Good night, Miss Parker," he said, without bothering to look at her. His deep, husky tone was all politeness. She could find no fault with it. But his manner was clearly resentful.

As her father slipped the oil lamp from her unresisting fingers and escorted her up the stairs to her bedchamber, he asked, "What is it you wished to see me about?"

"What?" she mumbled, her thoughts preoccupied with the acrimonious scene on which she'd intruded. "Oh. It was nothing," she murmured, wondering what on earth the two men had been fighting about. Tonight's heated exchange had left her with an uneasy feeling about her nuptials. Why on earth should his lordship dislike her father so? And more important, if he harbored no respect for her father, why would he wish to marry his daughter?

The wedding was not a grand affair. Brandon had refused to invite a solitary soul. Marrying a complete stranger under duress did not sit well with him, and he certainly did not wish to advertise his desperation. Anyone meeting the young innocent would guess in a trice he'd married her for her money—that and her looks.

The only people in attendance were Parker, whose presence Brandon chose to ignore, and Parker's perennially cheerful sister, who grated on Brandon's nerves. He glared at the gray haired, portly woman bobbing up and down with nauseating excitement. An irritated frown touched his lips. Did she never come up for a breath of air?

His bride, of course, was present. He glanced over his shoulder. As she walked slowly up the aisle toward him, he caught his first glimpse of her.

He gulped. Good Lord. She looked like a sacrificial lamb being lead to the slaughter. Frowning, he turned away. If his father were not already dead, he'd gladly have strangled the bastard.

Feeling her presence at his side, he glanced down at the diminutive blond who stood not quite shoulder height beside him. Following the style set by Queen Victoria, her satin gown was white and her veiled head adorned with orange blossoms. She was as silent as she was obedient, he noted.

His lips twisted. The entire affair was damned awkward. What the devil was he to say to her? What was she expecting from him? Whatever her expectations, they were undoubtedly more than he was willing to give.

Brandon tugged at his silk necktie. It was choking him. His dark blue frock coat, white waistcoat, and gray trousers were fresh from the tailor, but they felt uncomfortably restrictive.

The same morose vicar who had buried his father

mumbled the marriage rites. Brandon had to lean forward to hear what the devil he was saying. He wondered wryly if they were really being married.

The stone chapel was just as cold and damp as he recalled. The deuced place smelled musty. Not surprisingly, his debauched father had scarcely had an occasion to open the doors. The last time the chapel was used, prior to the late earl's burial, must have been when Brandon's mother was buried.

He quickly thrust that memory from his mind. He had enough problems to contend with this day. He did not wish to remember his painful childhood— not when he couldn't even remember his bride's Christian name. Until last evening, when her father had called her Olivia, Brandon had thought of her as Odelia, which meant "litte wealthy one," a misconception that probably stemmed from her generous dowry.

He darted her another glance. Her stony expression and softly intoned vows told him she was not happy. When the time came for him to take her small hand in his and slip the shiny gold symbol of possession on her third finger, she trembled. His gaze captured hers. Their eyes held for a scant moment before her lashes swooped down, shielding her from his probing gaze.

He should feel sorry for her. In the moments when he allowed himself to consider her as a person in any real way, he was sympathetic.

"You may now kiss the bride," the craggy old vicar announced, snapping his black, leather-bound Bible shut. Retrieving a large white handkerchief from his pocket, he proceeded to nosily blow his nose.

Feeling awkward with what most considered a tender moment, Brandon turned to face his bride.

He was thankful she met him halfway. At least he did not have to force her to accept his advances. Swallowing hard, he leaned down. He was about to give in to the temptation to kiss her rosy lips, but thought better of it and pressed a light, brotherly kiss on her cheek. Straightening up, he turned from her and strode from the chapel.

As he stormed back toward the house, he felt the heavy burden he'd been forced to carry somewhat lessened by his nuptials. He'd saved Cloverton Hall and restored the family fortune, but he would never accept Olivia as his wife. He refused to be controlled like a pawn on a chessboard. Parker would never see the day his daughter bore the Marlborough heir.

The meager wedding party arrived at the hall on his lordship's heels. When they were clustered in the drafty front hall, Parker congratulated his daughter.

"It is only appropriate that the bride and groom share a private toast to celebrate their nuptials," he announced, eliciting a glare from his son-in-law. Whatever relief Brandon might have experienced following the twenty-minute wedding ceremony dissolved instantly.

Glancing at the pale woman dwarfed by the white satin gown overflowing with pearls, lace flounces, and chiffon ruffles, Brandon frowned. No doubt her father had selected that ostentatious gown. He caught sight of the diamond teardrop earrings and necklace that lay against her soft porcelain skin. It reminded him of the Marlborough diamonds worn by his mother. The family heirlooms should have been worn by his bride, save for the fact that his father had gambled them away years ago.

Without further ado, Brandon marched into the blue salon, the only room in decent condition, to suffer through the awkward niceties. "Fetch some champagne," he barked over his shoulder.

Chalmers bowed in obedience.

Rubbing his temples, Brandon gazed out the window at the annoyingly bright sunshine flooding the overgrown gardens. How the devil was he going to endure the extravagant wedding breakfast Parker had planned? His father-in-law had insisted on a richly ornamented wedding cake. The cold game, lobster salad, chicken, tongues, ham, prawns, chutneys, fruits, and various sweets had taken the servants days to prepare. Behind him, he heard the door open. He surmised his bride had joined him for the dreaded celebratory toast.

Closing his eyes, he groaned aloud at the insistent hammering in his head. Last night, after his heated discourse with the wretched golddigger and the unexpected encounter with his comely bride, his mood had been foul. When he'd set eyes on her last night, the same rush of heat, the same mindless need to touch her had overtaken him. It irked him no small degree.

Wishing to purge himself of thoughts of his luscious bride and to forget the circumstances of his cursed marriage, he'd imbibed far too heavily. At present, he was paying for his overindulgence. Between the decanter of brandy he'd consumed and the three hours of sleep he'd gotten, he felt like hell.

"Are you unwell, my lord?"

At the sound of his wife's soft voice, he swiveled around. She was perched like a small bird on the worn blue velvet sofa.

"I have a headache," he explained, crossing the

room to help himself to a flute of champagne. He offered her a glass of the golden bubbly.

Raising her enormous doe eyes to his, she searched his expression with a guileless wonder that made him damned uneasy.

"I see," she replied softly, accepting the outstretched glass. Her fingers brushed against his. A surge of desire coursed through him. His jaw clenched. Taking a swallow of champagne, he turned his attention to the window once more. After several awkward moments, she cleared her throat.

"Father tells me upon your return from the war you were awarded the Victoria Cross," she remarked, striving for polite conversation.

But he was in no mood for small talk. "Your father," he muttered with contempt, "seems to be a veritable wellspring of information."

Ignoring his rejoinder, she remembered what a dashing figure he cut when they'd first met. With his tall black fur hat and gleaming red coat with gold epaulettes and shiny brass buttons, he had made quite an impression on her youthful heart. She had been utterly taken with him. Some semblance of the gentleman she'd admired must exist beneath his cold, gruff exterior. "How proud you must have been to serve as an officer in the Queen's Guards and be rewarded for your bravery," she ventured.

"Proud?" He laughed, but without humor. "If I hadn't minded living in cold, wet trenches on little to no sleep, consuming barely edible food when available, and watching my men bleed to death in the stinking mud because there were no medical supplies and even fewer doctors, it would have been a smashing time."

He heard her quick, indrawn breath and saw her

face grow whiter. Shock mingled with hurt, and she looked away.

Instantly contrite, he said awkwardly, "Forgive me. I should not have spoken so harshly. I have been under a tremendous strain of late."

Bowing her head, she studied her lap. "You are displeased with me. Upon closer inspection, am I not what you wanted in a wife?" she asked, raising her eyes to his.

Her soft speculation sent a bolt of shock through him. He shot her a confused sideways glance before refilling his glass with champagne. "Why do you say that?" he asked, his gaze deliberately veiled. He knew damned well why she'd said it, but he preferred to hide behind semantics rather than address her concerns.

She smiled a little wistfully. Expelling a sigh, she placed her untouched champagne flute on the marble table beside her. With surprising aplomb, she stood to her full height, which by his estimation could be no more than five-feet-four.

"Pray, my lord, let us have no falsehoods between us. I must confess I do not fully comprehend your desire to wed. Since you have made no effort to acquaint yourself with me, I can only assume you felt compelled to marry for reasons you do not wish to share."

His hooded gaze swept the length of her in a leisurely, sensual appraisal. *Very adroitly done,* he thought with a sardonic half smile. He took another swallow of champagne. Perhaps his bride was not as docile and meek as he imagined. His eyes lingered on her snug bodice. Indeed, she was quite a woman, one who offered lovely attributes—definitely worthy of further inspection.

"I am persuaded your head must be paining you greatly," she said, eyeing his empty glass with censure. "I shall leave you directly to your remedy. But first, allow me to make my intentions plain. Regardless of your attitude toward our union, you may rest assured that I intend to fulfill my duties as your wife. I am aware of your station in life. Although common born and bred, I shall give you no cause for complaint. You may have no fear on that account. I wish to make you happy, if I am able. I will run your household and be the mother of your children. More than that I cannot promise." After issuing that momentous statement, she gathered her billowing skirt and quietly left the room.

Heaving a deep sigh, Brandon slammed his glass down on the table. Confound it. He had no wish for a wife. What the devil did he have to offer the chit? By his estimation, he was the last man on earth who should ever marry.

His blood boiled at the thought of being trapped by his dead father's sins. Would the bastard's hold on him never end? He swore under his breath.

To marry for money was repugnant to him. His stomach turned at the thought of taking a wife merely to avert financial disaster—not that marriage to Olivia would be a hardship, exactly. Quite the contrary. She was a damned sight more fetching than he would have liked. Why could she not have been a poor, pathetic, homely creature? Then he might feel sorry for her, instead of feeling an overwhelming need to fight his growing attraction.

Devil take it. This wife of his would be damned difficult to ignore. Aside from being a regal beauty, she conducted herself with a quiet dignity that inspired tremendous respect.

Still, he had no desire for a wife. Whatever emotion he might once have been capable of had died a long time ago. The simple fact was, regardless of the inexplicable pull he felt toward the woman, he had nothing to give her.

Besides, his household ran itself. The servants went about their business as they had done since time immemorial. For that matter, he had not the slightest inclination toward children, let alone a mother for them.

He drove his fingers through his jet black hair. Bloody hell. What was he going to do about her?

When next Brandon saw his wife, he'd removed his frock coat and necktie and was reclining at the head of the table opposite her father, waiting for the wedding banquet to be served. To his surprise, his bride had shed her wedding finery and was wearing a dark green velvet dress and ivory lace bertha. The plunging neckline of the gown drew his attention. The bodice fit her lovely shoulders and ample breasts with revealing snugness.

A slow smiled touched his lips. He sampled some of his late father's excellent claret, leisurely savoring the taste. Perhaps this marriage would not be as much of an ordeal as he had originally envisioned.

Taking her seat at her husband's right, across from her aunt, she murmured her apologies for being tardy.

"No matter," the odious Parker remarked. "You look lovely, my dear, and are well worth the wait." Parker lifted his gaze to his taciturn son-in-law. "Would you not agree, my lord?"

"Mmmm," Brandon murmured, taking another

sip of claret. His hooded gaze caressed her bare shoulders and round bosom. "Well worth it."

Shifting on her seat, Olivia tried to ignore the heat of his stare. It was rather difficult. Did the man have no manners? Lounging in his chair like a rogue, he was staring at her with a wolfish gleam in his eye. She wondered if there were a gentlemanly bone in his body.

Pinning a bright smile to her otherwise pale face, she wisely drew her aunt, never one to be reticent, into conversation. Anything was better than to suffer the discomfort of his lordship's hungry gaze in awkward silence.

"We are fortunate to have such lovely weather," she remarked.

"Indeed, we are," Edwina agreed, munching on a slice of cold chicken. "You were such a beautiful bride. I must confess, my lord," she told Brandon, "I wept for joy at the sight of how charming she looked."

Waving away the platter of ham, Brandon murmured in a husky tone over the rim of his claret glass, "Lovely."

Clearing her throat, Olivia looked down at her plate. It was overflowing with lobster salad, cold meats, and jellies. With him watching her like a rabid dog, she wondered if she could eat. She darted a glance at his plate and noticed his food was untouched, but the footman had filled his lordship's glass with claret for the third time.

"Edwina and I plan to leave for London in the morning," her father announced.

Olivia's head snapped up. "Must you, Father?" Her voice sounded frantic even to her own ears.

Her father frowned. "Your husband will want time alone with his new bride. Is that not so, my lord?"

"Indeed," came his lordship's deep velvet voice in reply.

Swallowing audibly, Olivia toyed with the food on her plate. Dread coiled around her heart. The last thing she desired was to be cloistered in this dank mausoleum with her brooding husband. If he was this rude and showed not an ounce of deference toward her family, what would he be like when they were alone?

Chapter 3

It was well past midnight when Brandon finally went in search of his bed for the night. Silvery moonbeams shone through the large casement windows of his bedchamber, casting shadows across the hardwood floor. Groping in the dark, he struck the flint and lit the oil lamp beside his bed.

He was bone tired, he realized with a lusty yawn, and more than a little tipsy. The hour was fast approaching one, far too late to summon his valet. Faithful old Saunders would be asleep by now. Having been passed on to Brandon from his late father, the elderly man-servant would undoubtedly be accustomed to the ungodly hour, but Brandon did not have the heart to bother him.

Expelling a sleepy sigh, Brandon sank down on the side of the bed and tugged off his black boots, then shrugged his unbuttoned white waistcoat off his shoulders. Ripping his white pleated linen shirt over

his head, he tossed it aside and reached for the waist-
band of his trousers.

The bed linen rustled behind him.

He practically vaulted off the bed. To his astonishment, lying sound asleep in his large tester bed was
his golden-haired bride. He'd expected her to spend
the night in her own rooms. Obviously, his bold bride
intended to assume her place as his wife. Raising the
oil lamp, he gazed down at her. Reams of shimmering
blond hair fanned over his pillow, framing her fragile
face. She looked positively angelic in sleep's repose.
During her wakeful hours, her exotic hazel eyes encircled by long thick lashes peered at him, giving him
the uncanny sensation she was trying to unlock the
secrets he held deep in his soul. He preferred to keep
his privacy.

His eyes traveled the delicate column of her neck
to the soft lacy neckline of her whisper-thin nightgown. Her small hands, bearing the gold symbol of
his possession, rested on top of the sheets.

His stomach clenched. The covers were at her
waist, baring her full, round, pert breasts to his roving
gaze. The shadow of her dark areola shone through
the filmy gauze. He gulped. His tongue seemed suddenly too large for his mouth, and his throat had
gotten too small.

"Good Lord," he said aloud, setting the lamp on the
bedside table. Rubbing the tension from the back of
his neck, he swore under his breath. White hot desire
pulsed through him. What the devil was he going to
do about *this?* An insidious voice whispered in his
head, *She is yours, your wife to do with as you please.* And
he'd like nothing better than to possess her body and
soul—except for the fact that Parker wanted an heir.

Brandon would be damned before he'd give him a grandson.

Turning the lamp down, he stripped naked and crawled into bed beside her. Despite the throbbing ache of attraction, the second his head hit the pillow, he was asleep.

Brandon awoke from the cold. He realized in a sleepy daze that he lacked covers. Shivering, he tugged on the counterpane, but it would not budge. Cursing, he rolled over and came into contact with a warm, soft figure.

Groggy from sleep, he snuggled closer to her warmth. Whoever she was, he thought, wrapping his shivering body around her, she was warmer than a hot brick. Burying his face in her silky hair, he sighed. She smelled wonderful, like fresh lilacs. His arms tightened around her. She was incredibly soft, and her delicious heat permeated his chilled bones. What a delightful bed warmer, he thought, smiling, and drifted off to sweet oblivion.

Olivia was burning up. The heat emanating from the heavy weight pressed against her was stifling. She tried wriggling loose, but two muscular arms of steel locked about her, drawing her closer to the burning heat. She lurched against the great bulk, but that only seemed to spur him on. Clutching her tightly to his bare chest, he shifted his weight. Rather than being free of the naked colossus, she was now partially beneath him.

A husky voice, thick with sleep, murmured against her lips, "Lilly, my darling. I've missed you, love."

Before she could explain that she was not Lilly, nor did she know anyone named Lilly, his open mouth, hot, wet, and demanding, came down on hers. Squirming beneath him, she twisted her head and pressed her palms against his enormous shoulders in a vain effort to stave off his advances.

It was no use. The more she writhed beneath him, the more ardent his kisses became. His hands were inside her nightgown. She gasped against his mouth in surprise. He was palming her breasts. His scandalous caress made her breasts peak and ache in a oddly pleasant way.

Her shock grew to dismay when his tongue slipped between her lips and stroked the soft recesses of her mouth. Moaning her surprise, she clutched at his shoulders and endured the invasive kiss. She should have found the experience repulsive. But quite the contrary, the slow slip of his tongue deeply stirred her senses.

When at last he lifted his mouth from hers and ceased to toy with her breasts, she was panting for air and felt flushed all over. Worse yet, his bold touch evoked a tingling rush of pleasure deep inside her. He nuzzled her neck and pressed a kiss behind her ear. She quivered. His hands slid beneath her gossamer gown to skim her bare hips and thighs.

He lifted her nightgown to reveal her naked body. The next thing she knew, he was kissing her throat and showering wet kisses over her breasts. Then his tongue was caressing her abdomen. All the while, his hands roamed over her soft round hips and smoothed her bare buttocks.

When he lifted his head to her breasts, his mouth closed over one hardened nipple and sucked with hunger. She could no more control the whimper that escaped her throat than she could resist clutching his raven head to her breasts, eager for more.

What he did next left her bereft of speech. His hand slipped between her legs to touch the sensitive apex of her thighs. She trembled. He trailed kisses along her cheek and kissed her neck. His breath was warm and moist against her skin. She sighed.

And then his fingers parted her slick feminine folds and caressed her most private place. She gasped against his mouth.

Fear mingled with nerves. "My lord," she panted breathlessly in the darkness.

"Brandon," he murmured softly, his finger intimately stroking her until she thought she'd go mad from the spiraling pleasure.

"B-Brandon," she whimpered, swallowing hard.

Moaning, she bit her lower lip against the rising tide swelling deep inside her. He fondled her, kindling her need until it exploded in a maelstrom. Crying out in ecstasy, she clutched at his shoulders, her fingers biting into his hard muscles.

He rose over her. The handsome contours of his face were etched in the moonlight, and her heart kicked against her ribs. His weight pressed heavily against her, and she realized with a measure of panic that he would join his body to hers.

She was his wife. He had every right to touch her, to take pleasure in her body. She must submit to him, must endure whatever he had planned for her. Still, she found herself braced for what was to come.

Finding it paramount that he acknowledge the woman with whom he was about to physically join, she uttered breathlessly, "Brandon, my name is Olivia, *not* Lilly."

A deep rumble that was almost a groan sounded in his chest. "I know who you are," he murmured softly against her lips. *"Olivia."* He whispered her name on a breathless sigh of desire. Nudging her thighs wide, his deep throaty voice whispered against her ear, "*Sweet* Olivia, my beautiful bride. How I long to make you mine."

The feel of his huge body bearing down on her was not unpleasant, exactly. She never wanted this sweet pleasure to end, but if what her aunt had told was true, it soon would. She could endure their coupling if she had to, however painful it promised to be. His large swollen member pressed against her soft feminine core, slowly easing inside, stretching her wide. Swallowing, she closed her eyes and waited for the agony to which Aunt Edwina had alluded. Feeling her small, tight passage resist his entry, he hesitated and stared down at her in the shadows.

"What is it?" she whispered, mildly disappointed that he had shied away from completion. "Don't you want me?"

"Oh, I want you." He groaned deep in his throat. "You can have no idea how much."

"Then . . . have me," she urged, breathless with her own need.

Grunting his accord, he withdrew from her slightly. His hands clutched her narrow hips and lifted her to receive him. Gazing deeply into her eyes, he drove inside her until he was fully sheathed deep within her. Despite her wet, welcoming, warmth, she gasped at the feel of his thrust. It filled her more completely than she had ever imagined possible.

Her breathing was coming in heavy pants, as was his. Wrapping her thighs around his hips, he pushed against her, easing even deeper inside her silken passage. Arching her back, she moaned softly at the indescribable feeling of his full, deep invasion. His arms went around her, cradling her beneath his weight.

He kissed her mouth, slowly, deeply, passionately, then moved within her, withdrawing only to drive deep until tiny shivers of pleasure rippled through her. All thoughts of discomfort vanished. His tongue drove deep, caressing the soft recesses of her mouth, mimicking the tempo of their lovemaking, and she found herself swept away, caught up in the raging tempest.

Whimpering, she gave herself up to the intense inexplicable feelings burgeoning deep inside her. She felt a strong connection to him that was more than merely physical. It was as if they had found a level of communion in the quiet, intimate darkness that was just beyond their reach in the light of day.

Their hungry, eager mouths twisted, tasted, kissed while they climbed to new heights of ecstasy in each other's arms. She clutched him to her, straining against him, desperate to reach the pleasure she sensed was building. She moved her hips, writhing, straining, undulating beneath him.

The tiny waves swelled into spasms. A spiraling crescendo washed over her. Her fervent cries matched his deep guttural groans as he drove into her, hard and fast.

And when she was splintering into a million pieces of blissful fulfillment, he surged deep inside her one last time, meeting her in paradise.

For a long moment, he lay heavily against her, their bodies still intimately joined. His face was buried in the hair at the nape of her neck. As he held her close and breathed deeply, she knew he was struggling to regain some semblance of sanity. Astounded by the earthshaking experience, she was at a loss for words.

Then he brushed his lips against her temple, her cheek, and once against her mouth. Expelling a deep sigh of satisfaction, he rolled off of her and sprawled out on the bed beside her. She lay in the darkness listening to his labored breathing.

What, if anything, she should say? Her brow knitted. What did one say at a time like this? She wasn't sure what to conclude from his passionate lovemaking, or, for that matter, from his resentful attitude hours before.

Although she was not blind and sensed he found her attractive, she had been totally unprepared for the rapture they'd just shared. Taken completely unawares by her own passion, she wasn't sure what to do next.

Despite their physical closeness, of which there now could be no doubt, they were, in fact, virtually strangers. Their wedding ceremony this morning had been horribly cold and distant. Afterward, he had made little effort to assuage her fears that she was not the bride of his choice.

How, then, could they ignite in flames of passion? And why had he bothered to initiate her into the physical realm with unparalleled finesse?

She did not know what to think. She wanted him to talk to her, to comfort her, to reassure her the man in her arms was the man she'd married, rather than the strained, remote stranger she'd known thus far. She was not expecting declarations of love, but by all rights he should say something. Anything.

Sighing, she turned her head on the pillow to look at him. His features were masked in darkness. Pushing up on her elbow, she leaned over him. "Brandon," she whispered.

No reply.

She heard his slow breathing and knew he'd found sleep. Disappointed, she lay back down and stared at the ceiling in the darkness, trying to fathom what had just transpired.

She'd had no inkling kissing would be *that* intimate, nor had she been prepared for her body's natural response to his roving touch. She was still tingling from his possession. Aunt Edwina had made no mention of tingles.

In fact, Olivia was profoundly startled by the intense pleasure she'd found in his arms. Was it always like that? Powerful, explosive, all consuming? Aunt Edwina had alluded to a great deal of discomfort and warned her she would simply have to suffer through the act dutifully.

Suffering was a far cry from what she'd felt in the heat of his embrace. The memory of their bodies joined as one, his deep penetrating thrusts that awakened a spiraling ache of ecstasy, made her flush hot all over again. It was common knowledge that wives were not expected to find satisfaction in the marriage bed. Most men performed the act for the sole purpose of begetting an heir. Having secured a son, they sought mistresses for their physical enjoyment.

Strange, she thought, rolling onto her side to hug her pillow, he did not seem to mind her inexperience. Nor did it seem to have diminished his enjoyment. Quite the contrary. He had made his pleasure in her body patently clear. She had enjoyed that as well. Pressing her palms to her red-hot cheeks, she was glad they were lying in the dark together.

A pang of uneasiness assailed her. Was it because he believed her to be someone else? Is that why he'd found her desirable? No. She had made certain he knew who she was before she gave herself to him.

And he had said her name in that husky, passionate way that told her he wanted *her* and no one else.

Still, her treacherous mind was curious. Who on earth was this Lilly person? she wondered with irritation. And why should her husband be dreaming of *her* on his wedding night? It was indecent to whisper another woman's name in his wife's ear whilst in the process of making love. Had the man not an ounce of shame?

Rolling onto her back, she hauled the covers up to her chin. Why was she giving in to such foolish insecurities? He was her husband. What he did and who he knew prior to their marriage was of no consequence. She was his wife now. They were bound together by God. Coming closer to her sleeping husband, she placed her cheek on his shoulder. He murmured something in his sleep and wrapped his arm around her waist, drawing her close against his hard, naked body.

For a time tonight, she'd felt close to him physically, had experienced an emotional connection that startled her. The indescribable bond they'd forged was heartwarming beyond all her expectations. That her seemingly cold husband was capable of such tenderness surprised her and gave her hope for a contented future as his wife.

And yet the fleeting closeness had ended far too quickly. Snuggling against him, she vowed to remember the deeply touching intimacy they had shared and build on it. It was the only foundation they had from which they might forge a happy marriage.

The following morning, Olivia awoke in a muddle. Disoriented, she stared blankly at the heavy crimson velvet drapes shrouding the bright sunshine that poured through the casement windows. Dark paneling and furniture dotted the distinctly masculine decor surrounding her. Her brow furrowed. This room was not familiar to her.

Lord! Her hand flew to her mouth. She was married and sleeping in her husband's bed. Her head jerked around. She fully expected to find his lordship lying naked beside her, but the bed was empty. The only vestiges of his existence were the soft indent in the pillow and the rumpled bed linen. She was not particularly eager to see him this morning. She felt certain she would not be able to look him in the eye without remembering what they'd done last night.

A small clump of gold chain glittering against the snowy pillow caught her eye. Tugging the sheet up over her bare bosom, she leaned up on her elbow. To her amazement, her diamond and pearl lavaliere lay there. A cry of joyful surprise escaped her lips. Retrieving the cherished piece, she fingered the pendant in astonishment.

How in the world had he gotten it back? She quickly donned her most prized possession. She could not have wished for a finer wedding present. A quizzical frown touched her forehead. What a strange and contradictory man she had married.

Sighing, she stretched her arms over her head and yawned. Leaning back against the pillows, she felt tired and listless. A secretive smile touched her lips. Her fingers toyed with the pendant around her neck. She was overjoyed by its recovery, but it was more than that, much more. Last night had been the single most extraordinary night of her life.

When he'd awakened her, looming over her, a virile

naked man, she'd been quite terrified and, she allowed in the light of day, fascinated.

As much as his conduct had surprised her, his physical appearance was equally startling. Her father had explained that Brandon had fought valiantly during the last battle of the Crimean War and had almost lost his life, which explained the nasty scar on his left side. She'd noticed the hard bumpy skin beneath her fingertips when he was kissing her last night and again when he was inside her and her hands had greedily caressed his naked torso.

It was somewhat romantic to imagine her husband as a war hero wounded in the fray. He must be a noble and honorable man. His physique certainly was formidable. His hard, well-muscled chest and shoulders were larger than she'd reckoned they would be. The night before their wedding, when she'd met him in the library, she'd caught a glimpse of his bare chest covered with coarse hair, but she had no idea how attractive he would appear completely divested of his shirt.

She could not deny it. She was strongly attracted to her husband. His lovemaking was no hardship, either. Quite to the contrary, she realized, coloring to her roots.

Thus far, while a trifle distant and moody, her husband had been a considerate, patient lover, not to mention kind and thoughtful. She was deeply touched by the return of her lost necklace. If last night's episode was any indication, enduring the rigors of his bed might not be as awful as she originally envisioned. No, she was not entirely unhappy with her marriage.

* * *

Filled with hope and a firm determination to make her marriage work, Olivia entered the breakfast room. To her surprise, Brandon was nowhere to be found.

Instead, Chalmers awaited her. He handed her a stiff white parchment that bore the Marlborough seal.

Frowning slightly, Olivia accepted the note. Sensing the situation was somewhat irregular, she nervously darted a glance about her. "Has his lordship already eaten, then?" she asked the manservant quietly, hoping her father would not hear.

Chalmers clasped his hands behind his back and gave a slight shake of his head. To her dismay, in front of her father and Aunt Edwina, he said, "I believe his lordship departed very early this morning." And with that appalling statement, he promptly quit the breakfast room.

Olivia's heart sank. She quickly tore open the wax seal and read the missive. As her eyes swept across the page, hot color scalded her cheeks. Had she really imagined they would have any kind of a life together? How utterly foolish she had been. She read the note.

My dear Olivia,

I am most heartily sorry not to address you in person, but you were sleeping so soundly when I awoke that I was loath to disturb you. I must away to London. I have many pressing engagements that require my immediate attention. In light of my father's recent death, I have plans to take my seat in the House of Lords.

It is my sincere hope that you will be at ease at

*Cloverton Hall. You may rely on the servants should
you have want of anything in my absence.*

*Your most obedient servant and devoted husband,
Brandon*

Folding the letter, she placed it beside her plate.
"He has gone to London and does not say when he
shall return to the country."

Aunt Edwina stopped eating, her fork paused mid
air. She blinked at Olivia in astonishment.

"Gone to London!" her father exploded. His chair
scraped against the floor as he jumped to his feet.
Before she had the opportunity to gainsay him, he
snatched the parchment and read the contents for
himself.

"Father, *please*," she beseeched, extending her
hand to him for the return of her private note, "I
beg of you. Consider my feelings in this matter."

But he would hear none of her pleading. He crum-
pled the note in his fist and tossed it to the floor.
"I shall bring him back and force him to issue an
apology," he snarled.

"No, Father," Olivia stated calmly. "You will do
nothing of the kind."

"I can and I shall," her father countered. Storming
around the room like a savage beast, he muttered
under his breath about the earl's outrageous, insulting conduct. "I will not allow him to squander
my daughter's dowry on gaming tables and painted
ladies!"

Olivia felt as if she'd been punched in the stomach.
Painted ladies? She had not considered her husband
might seek his pleasure with other women in London.
God, oh God. Last night . . . everything they'd shared.

It meant nothing. Absolutely nothing. Was she no more to him than a warm body from which he sought momentary pleasure?

She felt sick. She was his wife, and he had treated her like nothing more than a common trollop. He was no gentleman. He had proven that on more than one occasion. Swallowing hard, she managed to compose herself.

"As you told me, many marriages," she reminded her irate father, "particularly among the peerage, are arranged between virtual strangers. I will . . . adjust."

"By God, I will make him crawl for this," he bellowed, his fisted hand raised.

"If you do"—she struggled to maintain her tenuous control—"I shall never speak to you again."

He stopped in his tracks and stared at her. *"What* did you say?" he breathed.

Bewildered, Edwina glanced from her furious brother to her obdurate niece. "What has come over you, child?" she asked, clearly amazed that Olivia should dare contradict Gilbert. "You must follow your father's dictates in all things."

Olivia turned to her aunt. "And what of my husband's dictates? Am I not to follow his as well?" she demanded, tears pricking her eyes.

Edwina paled considerably. Bowing her gray head, she studied her hands.

"I am sure his lordship has legitimate reasons for returning to London," Olivia continued in a low, controlled tone. "After all, Father, it is not unusual for the nobility to vacate their country houses in February, is it? I shall respect his privacy and hope he sends for me in time."

"The devil you will!"

"Father," she said, "do not intervene. What has

transpired between his lordship and myself is none of your affair." She drew a deep, steadying breath. "You had no right to read his letter to me."

"No right?" her father echoed in stunned disbelief. "I have *every* right. You are *my* daughter."

She got swiftly to her feet. "And I am *his lordship's* wife," she reminded him bitterly. Placing her linen napkin beside her uneaten breakfast, she told him calmly, "I have done as you asked because I am your daughter. You, of all people, know my heart was not gladdened by this union. It would appear that his lordship harbors similar reservations about our marriage. Let that be an end to it."

"An end to it?" he echoed, incredulous. "By George, it is not!"

The painful lump in her throat nearly gagged her. "Do not interfere where you are not wanted, Father," she warned, her tone ominous.

He gasped in shock. *"Not wanted?"*

She kept her gaze lowered to the floor as her shaky legs carried her across the room to the door. "You are free to take your leave of the country, if you are so inclined. Now that Bran—the earl has gone, I am persuaded there is precious little at Cloverton Hall to occupy your interest. I shall be content to while away the hours with Aunt Edwina for company."

"Am I to be dismissed by my own daughter?" he ranted. "Everything I have ever done has been out of love for you! How can you speak to me in this heartless manner?"

She paused for a moment at the threshold. Keeping her back to him, she said, nearly choking on the words, "I collect you believed the alliance would be judicious and fruitful. All that is left for me is to hope your initial judgment was not entirely incorrect."

"How dare you send me away in disgrace?" he demanded, with an air of command that had never failed to bring her to heel in the past.

Tears stung her eyes. Her face contorted with pain. She desperately wanted to make Brandon come back to her. But her husband was free to do as he pleased. Despite the fact they were man and wife, despite the blissful moments she'd spent locked in his arms, despite his passionate lovemaking, despite his heart-warming kindness in giving her such a thoughtful wedding gift, she had absolutely no hold on him. She would not force him to play the part of a smitten husband when his inclination clearly ran in a different direction.

"It is I who am in disgrace, Father," she said, her voice raw with emotion. "You are free to do as you like." With that, she quit the breakfast room.

Chapter 4

The room was dark, and yet Brandon knew every soft contour of the woman lying in his arms. He'd kissed her full, inviting mouth time and time again, palmed her round breasts with his hands, driven deep inside her sweet welcoming warmth, felt her beautiful body tighten around him until he thought he'd go mad from the exquisite pleasure her satin sheath afforded.

The woman he held in his arms always gave freely and fully of herself, holding nothing back. He loved that about her. And tonight would be no exception.

Rolling onto his back, he brought her over him. She straddled his hips, her pale blond hair enticing him with its irresistible luster. Draped across his chest, it shrouded the two sultry lovers in soft yellow silk. He drove his hands into her silken hair, framing her face with his palms.

His heart squeezed in his chest. God, but she was

beautiful. So incredible to touch and even better to have.

Slowly, she bent her mouth to his and kissed him, driving him wild with the tantalizing strokes of her tongue and soft caress of her supple lips. Desire unfurled hot and thick in his blood. He clutched her to him impatiently, eager for the inevitable passionate consummation that took them both to heaven.

But she pulled back, trailing hot wet kisses across his chest and down his stomach. He closed his eyes, reveling in her exquisite, seductive beauty. His blood pulsed like a tempest in his veins, and he groaned with a need so potent, so intense, he thought he would explode if he did not possess her soon.

His arm went around her soft, slender waist, drawing her down on top of his chest. He cupped the back of her head, bringing her sweet intoxicating lips to his. His open mouth hungrily slanted over hers. Sliding his hand down the smooth ivory column of her back, he rocked her hips against his. Feeling the dewy warmth of her need, he surged upward and thrust deep inside her satin heat.

She welcomed him, as she always did, with a sigh of sweet pleasure. Arching her hips against his, she met his deep, hard strokes, kindling his burning need. She coaxed him lovingly toward completion and soared to new heights of ecstasy in his arms. The tension coiled tighter and tighter inside him. He could never have his fill of this woman.

Unable to sustain his tenuous control, he groaned and reached for her, desperate to kiss her lips, hold her to him, and possess her with the all-consuming passion that threatened his sanity. They would reach an excruciatingly sweet climax, the same deep, wondrous exchange they'd shared from the very first time they'd touched. It was pure rapture.

The agony of his pleasure was acute. God, oh God. It was so good with her, so incredibly sweet, so deeply moving. He'd never experienced this intense emotional bond with any other woman. And he never wanted their lovemaking to end. He felt as though his heart would burst from his chest.

Gasping for breath, he woke with a start to find himself alone in his large canopied bed. A fine dew of perspiration covered his skin.

Dragging his hand through his sweat-soaked hair, he swallowed. The forest green counterpane and bed hangings over the dark mahogany tester bed were those of his London town house bedroom. Judging from the sun peeking through the heavy velvet drapes, it was late morning. He threw himself onto his back.

Bloody hell. It was a dream. Just a blasted dream.

His eyes drifted shut and he scrubbed his hands over his face. His chest rose and fell rapidly from unspent desire. He slammed his fist into the pillow beside him.

The same confounded dream. Always the same blasted fantasy. And the fair-haired angel with the figure of Grecian goddess and the amorous skills that astounded him? His lips twisted. *She* was his wife, and he knew it. All during the smoldering encounter, he always knew it.

She was the woman with whom he made love night after night. That was what made it so powerful.

No. That was not it entirely. The deep, abiding *feelings* the dream evoked shook him. It was not purely sexual, although there was that. It was more, much more. She made him feel alive and strong and content.

He'd spent the balance of his life working at feeling numb. Most of the time, it was not a particularly hard endeavor. At least, it had not been until he'd married his fair-haired angel. He had gone around half dead inside.

Somehow she had changed all that. Night after night, she came to him in his dreams and tugged at his heartstrings. It reminded him in graphic terms that he still had emotions. It was startling and confusing and bloody damned awful.

Crushing his aching skull between his palms, he swore under his breath. He must be the only man in England who lusted after his own wife. He was glad she was at Cloverton Hall and not close at hand. With the memory of their wedding night burning ever brightly in his mind and haunting his sleep nightly, he might well embarrass himself and take her at first sight.

"Damn and blast," he muttered under his breath. He wished he'd never touched her. She'd poisoned his blood or some such nonsense, he thought, rubbing his eyes with his palms. Whatever the reason, he could not get her out of his mind. Or his bed.

What he needed to rid his mind of her was a mistress. Why not offer Maria Chesney carte blanche? After all, he'd been forced into marriage. He did not owe his wife love and fidelity.

The buxom war widow had made it clear, on more than one occasion, that she was available and eager. She was a consummate flirt—not that he minded, though her suggestive banter was less than subtle.

Given his preference for drinking and gambling of late, however, he'd had little time or energy left for sexual pursuits. Particularly not when every woman he saw paled in comparison to his ravishing wife, who visited him nightly in his dreams.

Devil take it. He had to get the beguiling woman out of his head. Perhaps he should accept Maria's overt offer, if for no other reason than to prove to himself his preoccupation with Olivia stemmed from nothing more than sexual frustration.

Yes. A mistress was indeed a capital notion. With the alluring brunette to occupy his time and satisfy his carnal needs, he would not give his comely bride a second thought.

Olivia meant nothing to him. With a warm, willing Maria in his bed, he would soon forget his wife and the utterly ridiculous, albeit terrifying notion that he might actually be developing feelings for her.

Expelling a lusty yawn, he threw back the sheets and walked nude across the thick Aubusson carpet to the washstand. Sloshing some water from the white porcelain pitcher into the large bowl, he bent over the basin. He splashed some much needed cold water on his face and on the back of his neck.

Glancing up, he caught his reflection in the mirror. Bloody hell. He stared at the image of the man reflected in the glass. Lord, he looked like hell. Haggard. Old. Jaded.

As he scrubbed his hand across his chin, a twinge creased his forehead. He'd aged ten years since the war due to excess drinking and hard living. His face twisted. Confound it. He wasn't following in his debauched father's footsteps, was he? No. Never that. He could alter his habits anytime he wanted—not that he wanted to.

Squeezing his bloodshot eyes shut, he rested his

head against his forearm. "What the hell am I about with my life?" he wondered aloud.

Turning from the unholy image of a man on the brink of moral disaster, he grabbed his black velvet robe and dragged it around his naked body. Throwing open his bedroom door, he bellowed irritably into the hall, "Saunders! Where the devil is my bath?"

Reclining in the large copper tub, Brandon leaned his head back and let the steaming water seep into his weary bones. He was not feeling at all the thing— thoroughly exhausted from that devilishly inviting dream and churlish. And if the clamor in his head was any indication, he was suffering, as usual, from last night's carousing and needed another drink.

"Saunders," he mumbled, shutting his eyes against the familiar throbbing pain, "fetch me a tisane. My deuced head is killing me."

"Yes, milord," the ancient-looking valet replied and slowly shuffled from the room.

Brandon massaged his pounding temples. Between his gambling, heavy drinking, and flirtations with the ladies, it was little wonder ranking male members of the *ton* had christened him "Lord Wild." He deserved the nickname, for it suited his excesses of late quite well.

Since his father's demise, Brandon had lived on the edge, seeking his pleasure where he could. He frowned at that admission. *But why the blazes shouldn't I enjoy life for a change?* he thought irritably. He'd done his blasted duty to Queen, country, and the damned family name. And, by God, he wanted to live. He set out to indulge his every whim and fancy. He had only one regret.

What would his wife think of his wicked excesses? Did she know? Had her father informed his dutiful daughter of her husband's escapades? His lips twisted. Hell, he hoped not. He did not want her to know.

The little baggage invaded his thoughts at the oddest moments: A pale yellow lock of hair curled against the ivory column of a woman's neck; a flash of dark, alluring, inquisitive eyes darting a glance his way; the softly intoned murmur of a delicate female voice, melodious laughter drifting through the air, and he found himself remembering her. Olivia, his child bride with a courtesan's figure and a passion that blazed well beyond his reckoning.

He kept remembering the way her breathless sigh had felt against his burning lips, the way her dainty hands felt clinging to his broad naked shoulders as he gloried in his sensual exploration of her soft, welcoming body.

His hand massaged the tension coiling in the back of his neck. Dash it all, he wished he had never touched her.

It was not as though he owed the damned chit a thing. Even so, he had to admit she *was* deuced intriguing. A bemused smile touched his lips. Truth be told, he was not entirely disappointed with the bargain he'd struck with her grasping father. He was thoroughly enjoying the spoils of marriage without the burdens of a clinging wife—not that Olivia could ever be described that way.

In retrospect, he wished he'd handled his departure with a bit more finesse. When he'd awakened and seen her soft alabaster skin and shimmering golden hair, he'd panicked. In the light of day, the realization of what they'd shared left him terrifyingly vulnerable.

The last thing he wanted was a *real* marriage, so he'd left as quickly as he could. At the time, he thought it was a sound solution for them both. He could never be any kind of a husband to her, and she would be happier without him. It was best that he leave and never look back.

He laughed aloud at that misapprehension. Her blazing passion held him prisoner as no bands of matrimony could.

Upon his hasty return to London, her irate father had come to see his son-in-law. Brandon had summarily turned him out and left strict instructions with his butler, Carrington, to refuse his overbearing father-in-law admittance in the future.

Subsequently, Brandon had received countless threatening notes from Parker, all of which he promptly tossed in the fire.

It was ironic. Parker's avaricious nature had finally worked to his wayward son-in-law's advantage. Having reveled in securing a marriage to a ranking member of the peerage for his daughter, Parker could hardly decry the match without causing an unwanted scandal.

Saunders's return interrupted Brandon's contemplation. The valet's shaky blue-veined hand held a tulip-shaped glass filled to the brim with his lordship's cure.

Brandon swallowed a sip of the miracle elixir that, on days such as this, helped ease his throbbing head.

"Lord Pratt is here to see you."

Brandon's brows snapped together. "What? At this hour?"

Saunders discreetly cleared his throat. "It is nearly three o'clock, my lord."

The look of surprise on Brandon's face was swiftly followed by sheepish embarrassment. "Very well," he said agreeably, swallowing the remainder of the tisane in one gulp. He got out of the tub and wrapped his robe around his wet, glistening body. Toweling his hair dry, he instructed, "Show him in. We can talk while I dress."

"Very good, my lord," Saunders replied.

Brandon donned a pair of gray trousers with braid. He was searching through his mahogany armoire for a white linen shirt when Jeremy Pratt entered the room.

"To what do I owe this untimely visit?" Brandon asked.

Jeremy closed the door behind him. "Yes, you might well ask me that," he replied, his tone clipped.

Retrieving a crisp shirt from the armoire, Brandon shut the doors and turned to face his friend. Before Brandon could don his shirt, Jeremy thrust a pile of pound notes in his face. Frowning, Brandon gazed uncomprehendingly, at the formidable sum.

"You don't remember, do you?" Jeremy snapped.

"Should I?" Brandon shrugged on his shirt and tucked it into his trousers.

Jeremy slammed the pile of money on the table next to the wing chair. "You might at least recall that you lost such a sum last evening to Lord Dawson."

"If I lost it, how is it you are returning it to me?" Brandon asked, unperturbed.

"I won it back for you," Jeremy explained sharply.

Brandon lifted the decanter of brandy beside the large pile of money and poured himself a glass. Taking a sip, he reclined comfortably in the chair. "You need not have."

Incensed, Jeremy glared at him. "No, I need not have. Had you been sober and in control of all your faculties, I would not have."

"I don't need a nursemaid," Brandon muttered, downing the remaining brandy in one gulp.

Dubious, Jeremy cocked an eyebrow. "Don't you? Look at yourself, man," he charged in disgust. "You're drinking far too heavily and carousing like a vagabond. What the devil has come over you? In all the years we have known one another, I've never seen you in such a deplorable state."

Brandon's lips tightened in a grim line. "I don't need you to tell me what I am." He gazed down at the empty glass. "I've never despised myself more."

"For God's sake, at least tell me why. Why are you doing this?"

Brandon slammed the snifter down on the table and vaulted to his feet. "I don't know why . . . exactly."

"That is absurd," Jeremy countered angrily. "A man ought to know why he is driving himself into an early grave."

Digging his hands into his pockets, Brandon bowed his head. "I wish I were dead. Why the hell didn't you let me die?" he asked bitterly. "If you hadn't been so bloody noble, I would have bled to death."

Jeremy stared at him for a long, hard moment. "Is there nothing for which you will take responsibility? Now it is *my* fault you have decided to become as decadent as your father before you. You are not even man enough to admit why you drink."

"It banishes the demons in my head," Brandon muttered.

"We all have demons. Do you truly believe after the war any one of us doesn't?"

"Not like mine." Brandon spoke with contempt. "When I drink, I can live with myself. I can forget." He rested his forehead against the mantel and closed his eyes. "The past haunts me. And the present sickens me."

"And what of the future? Have you no thought of that? If you stopped feeling sorry for yourself long enough, you might recognize you have a wife and a title to look after."

Brandon glanced over his shoulder. One corner of his lips lifted in disgust. "My *wife*," he intoned bitterly, "owns me. Or her father does. And as for my exalted title, I despise it and everything that goes with it."

"My heart bleeds for you," Jeremy snapped. "Circumstances forced you to marry an heiress. What cruel fate life holds."

Anger sparked in Brandon's eyes. "Do you think I look at my life, at what I've had to do, and do you truly believe I am proud?"

Jeremy shook his head sagely. "You've been wallowing in self-pity so long you've lost all sense of reality. What you need is to get your bearings. Return to Cloverton Hall," Jeremy urged, clapping his friend on the back. "Reunite with your bride. Start afresh. Leave the past where it belongs—dead and buried."

Brandon shook his head. "Not everyone finds love like you and Christine. Olivia"—he hesitated for a moment, contemplating his beautiful bride— "she ... I—no." He shook his head. "It would never work."

"You will never know until you try." Jeremy's tone was harsh.

"It is out of the question," Brandon snapped. "I despise Cloverton Hall, and I have no use for a wife."

"Nor a friend, either, it would seem," Jeremy remarked, his tone caustic. Sweeping his hat and gloves from the green velvet sofa, he advised curtly, "Banish the memories that haunt you so before you find yourself lost beyond redemption."

Brandon turned on his friend. "You banish them," he said angrily. "I cannot."

Jeremy heaved a defeated sigh. "Very well. I've done my best. If you are determined to destroy yourself, there is nothing I can do to stop you."

"I never asked for your help," Brandon replied.

Jeremy wrenched open the bedchamber door. "I sometimes regret saving your wretched life, old man." He slammed the door in his wake.

Alone with his thoughts, Brandon paced the room like a caged tiger. His mind drifted back to Olivia. What *had* she found to occupy her time at Cloverton? She must be bored to tears. For him, Cloverton Hall held only depressing, unhappy memories, better off forgotten. He should not have left her there.

He scowled at his thoughts. Hell. He wasn't feeling the pangs of anything suspiciously like guilt, was he? She was so young, so innocent, so sheltered. He winced at the thought of how she must have felt when she learned he had abandoned her. Deserted. Alone. Unhappy.

He rubbed the tension from the back of his neck. He hadn't deserted her . . . exactly. She had her aunt for company. And besides, girls that age seldom had use for husbands.

Jeremy's point, however unpalatable, was well taken. At some point, Brandon must return to the country. He cringed at the thought of facing his wife.

* * *

Garbed in a moss green silk gown with a white muslin short coat and a green velvet net to protect her hair from the dust, Olivia stood in the middle of the rose morning room, gazing about her in disgust. The once opulent salon was in a state of complete disrepair, as were most of the salons.

Nearly two months had passed since Olivia's father had stormed from Cloverton Hall. Nursing her wounded pride, Olivia tried to accept her countrified existence.

It was undeniably insulting, not to mention hurtful, to be discarded by her husband like a used hankie. But there was no help for it. It appeared she was to rusticate in the country with her dowdy aunt while he enjoyed a lavish lifestyle in London.

She might have no choice but to reside in the damp, dreary old mausoleum, but she did not have to remain idle. Nor did she have any intention of doing so. She set out to restore Cloverton Hall to its former glory.

Thus far, the blue salon had been completely revamped and the gold sitting room had been reclaimed from the jaws of moldy destruction. But the estate was enormous, and it needed an appalling amount of work.

Chalmers appeared bearing a week old copy of the *Morning Post*. Accepting the paper, she noted with a frown it had come from her father.

Tucking it beneath her arm, she heaved a sigh. "The first thing that must be seen to is the roof," she announced, slapping the dirt from her hands.

Chalmers raised his eyes to the ceiling. Birds were perched on the jagged edges of a gaping hole. "I shall have some of the lads take a look at it straightaway. They should be able to render a repair by week's end.''

"Yes," Olivia concurred, marching to the windows and pulling at the heavy velvet drapes, fairly crusted with mold and dirt. "That would be best. And then,'' she gasped, choking on the billowing cloud of dust that had erupted from her tugging, "we shall have to see about papering the walls. They'll need a good scrubbing to remove the mildew first.''

"Yes, my lady," Chalmers dutifully agreed. He hastened to assist her with her undignified task.

The entire window treatment, rotten wood and corrupt fabric, came crashing down on the pair of them. Chalmers lifted Olivia out of harm's way. Sputtering from the dirt, Olivia coughed and waved the air clear. Sunlight streamed in, casting light on an enormous portrait above the fireplace. She stepped closer to gaze at the exquisite woman depicted in the life-size painting. "Who is she?''

Chalmers looked up at the portrait. "She was mistress of Cloverton Hall before you, my lady.''

Olivia turned to look at him in surprise. "You mean she was Lord Wilde's—my husband's mother?''

Chalmers nodded his head. "Lady Annabelle Huxley.''

Olivia glanced up at the raven-haired beauty. "She is lovely,'' she murmured.

"Mmm, that she was, my lady.''

The family resemblance was unmistakable. She could almost feel the expression in Annabelle's eyes. She was so like Brandon—the same dark hair, the same compelling blue eyes, and the same playful smile. Unbidden images arose of Brandon leaning over Olivia, his eyes gazing into hers as the two became one and he drove deep toward her soul, taking her to heaven in his arms. And then he was gone, like a highly erotic aberration of some kind.

Heat pervaded her cheeks at the vivid recollection of his body intimately joined with hers and the feel of his hard and pulsing length deep inside her. Clearing her throat, she thrust the memory from her mind. "What happened to her?"

Chalmers averted his gaze. "I shouldn't like to say, my lady."

Olivia glanced at him sharply. "Why ever not?" she asked, taken aback by his reply.

The butler wore a grim, shuttered expression. "It is not my place. His lordship would not wish it."

"As his lordship is not here and I have asked you a question, I see no reason why you should refuse to answer," she said, her tone brisk.

Chalmers lowered his gaze to the floor. "She bled to death."

Horrified, Olivia gasped. "Was she ill?"

The elderly butler shook his head. "No, my lady. She was with child."

"What became of the baby?"

"She was not . . . very far along," he explained, awkwardly.

Olivia lowered her gaze to the floor. "Oh, I see."

"No, my lady, I do not think you do."

Her head came up. She stared at him, sensing there was more he wished to impart. "Perhaps you would be good enough to explain it to me."

"The master's father, the late earl, was a hard man. Her ladyship was as gentle as he was coarse."

"They were not well matched, then?"

Chalmers shook his head. "No, my lady, indeed they were not. It is generally believed he caused her death."

Olivia's brows drew together. "How?"

"He was a drinking man and never one to pass up a bit of . . . skirt."

Like father, like son, Olivia thought. She felt ill at the idea she was nothing more than a "bit of skirt" to Brandon.

"Go on," she managed.

"From time to time, a violent rage would come on him. She and the young master paid the price."

Olivia grew pale. "Do you mean to say he beat her to death?" she breathed in horror.

"No. The fall caused her to lose the child," Chalmers explained.

"But . . . she did not fall on her own?" Olivia ventured to suggest.

"It would be difficult to believe she had, my lady."

"Could it have been an accident?" Olivia asked, disturbed by the notion of cold-blooded murder.

"The master was always quite deliberate in his actions," Chalmers stated, with sad resignation in his voice.

Olivia swallowed audibly. A shudder swept over her. She looked up at the gilded picture. "Are there other portraits like this one in the house?"

Chalmers shook his head. "Upon his return, the present Lord Wilde asked that they be taken to the attic. All but this one," he remarked, motioning toward the enormous painting. "That boy loved his mother, my lady."

"How old was my husband when she died?" Olivia asked, gazing up at the woman depicted in graceful charm and beauty.

"Fifteen."

She shot Chalmers a sidelong glance. "And . . . he knew?" she asked quietly, sensing the wise old servant gleaned the point of her inquiry.

"I believe so, yes."

She released a miserable sigh. Bowing her head, she felt sick at heart. "How tragic for him." She had no cause to feel compassion for her cold, heartless husband, but she sensed he'd suffered greatly—first as a boy from his abusive, drunken father and now as a man from the ravages of war. He was a complex, difficult person.

"It was a terrible loss for the young master. You see, they were devoted to one another."

Olivia covered Chalmers's hand with her own. "Thank you for being honest with me."

Bowing his snowy white head, he murmured, "As my lady pleases. Shall I have tea prepared in the sitting room?"

A smile softened Olivia's features. "Yes, please do."

"Do not remain overlong, my lady. There is a chill in the room that is not altogether pleasing," he advised with some concern.

Olivia nodded her head. She knew he meant the details of the past, which hung in the air like a frigid demon. "I won't be more than a moment."

Inclining his head, Chalmers quit the dank, smelly room.

Walking over to stand by the window, Olivia unfolded the newspaper and scanned the first page. Her lips thinned. It was soon evident why her father had chosen to forward the society paper to her. Her husband figured largely as the leading aristocratic socialite. "Recently returned to London, Lord Wilde is thoroughly enjoying his new position as Earl Marlborough.''

She scowled at the paper. "I wager he is," she fumed. Obviously, her lord husband had no need for a common wife, not when he could entertain himself with the sophisticated Lady Chesney, described as a beautiful and radiant young war widow.

Olivia tossed the vexing rag to the floor. No doubt the horrid Lady Chesney was his precious Lilly.

Hugging her arms around her waist, she let her teeth worry her lower lip. It was more humiliation than she could bear. How dare he shame her? Flaunting a mistress, indeed. It was not to be borne.

Her shoulders slumped. Her marriage was a shambles. Worse yet, she was helpless to repair the damage. Of course, something could be done—if she had the gumption for it. It might prove rather difficult, but it was high time and long overdue.

She must stand up for herself. She'd lived her entire life under someone else's dictates. Now she wanted to live according to the dictates of her heart. And, by God, she had a right to do so.

Resolved to take matters into her own hands, she intended to fight for equal footing in her marriage. Or at least, she amended, her stomach fluttering at the mere thought, as much as his lordship would allow.

If the earl prized mature, sophisticated women who brought a wealth of experience to the relationship, then she would give him what he wanted. She was intelligent; her tutors had told her countless times she was an adept pupil.

Olivia had suffered her country interment for too many lonely days and nights. She had endured sufficient degradation at her husband's hands to last a lifetime. If she held out any hope of winning her husband's attention, she decided she must transform her girlish appeal into womanly charm.

Sophistication was what she lacked, but she could secure the necessary experience. Indeed, she was given to understand it took precious little when the spirit was willing—and she was more than slightly determined. Those dreadful, boring etiquette lessons she'd been forced to endure most certainly applied to sophistication. With the proper sort of preparation and the will to succeed, she would manage.

The trouble was, she thought, tapping her chin thoughtfully, where would she find a proper home in which to stay whilst she played out her little gambit? She could scarcely show up on her husband's stoop looking woebegone and desperate and plead with him to take her in. It simply would not do.

She could ask her father. Now that his temper had cooled, he would be only too happy to undertake to rent a house on her behalf. Eager for a reconciliation, he would gladly assist her in any way she asked.

She paused for a moment to reflect on the idea. Shaking her head, she decided against the notion. On this occasion, she would accomplish the task entirely on her own. It would be the first of many autonomous decisions she would be required to make as Lady Wilde. The sooner she began to rely on her own judgment, the better. Given that she had no man of affairs, she would simply have to take matters into her own hands.

Although slightly irregular, she could place an advertisement for a situation herself, one which would suit her requirements perfectly.

She glanced at the portrait above the fireplace and

expelled a woeful sigh. "I sincerely hope your son proves more worthy than your husband."

She marched from the decrepit salon into the cheerful sitting room. A baffled Aunt Edwina watched in confusion as Olivia penned an advertisement expressing the need for lodgings. Summoning Chalmers, she made her bold announcement. "I should like you to send this letter to London, if you please. Posthaste."

"Yes, my lady." He departed, carrying on a silver tray the missive that would change her life forever.

Aunt Edwina blinked at her niece from behind her round spectacles. "But, my dear, why should you wish to arrange for lodgings—and in London, of all places?"

Olivia flung herself down on the sofa like a lady of the night. She cocked one brow devilishly. "How else shall we enjoy London society?"

Edwina nearly spilled her tea. "You don't mean to say that you . . . that I—"

A wicked gleam appeared in Olivia's eyes. "Indeed, I do, aunt."

"But," her aunt stammered, "what will your father say?"

"I care not a farthing for his fine opinion," Olivia declared, folding her arms over her bosom.

Edwina gazed at her niece as though she had gone stark raving mad. "W-what of your husband?" she cried in dismay.

Olivia's lips thinned. She got to her feet and drilled her fingers against her upper arm. "Leave him to me, aunt," she intoned with a determined gleam in her eye. "I know how to handle him."

Approaching the large casement window, she looked at the gray sky and soggy grounds patiently waiting for spring to burst forth. A small smile tugged at the corner of her mouth.

"You have not heard the last of me, Lord Wilde," she said softly to herself. Her smile turned positively devilish. "Two can play at this game."

Chapter 5

Scarcely a month later, Olivia found herself in London with Aunt Edwina by her side. Lord Bloomsberry's ballroom was nearly overflowing with guests. The glittering assemblage was quite impressive. Gazing about her at the powdered faces and myriad bejeweled ladies, Olivia wished she had selected a less impressive event to commence her splash into London society.

"Oh, my dear," Edwina declared, clutching Olivia's arm, "I must confess when you confided your plan to enjoy London society without the benefit of your husband's escort, I was scandalized. But now"—she clasped her white-gloved hands together—"I am ever so pleased you decided to take me with you. The pageantry quite takes my breath away." She gazed about the resplendent ballroom. "I declare, I'm too excited for words!"

Olivia could lay claim to no such excitement. Her

nerves were more than a little overset. She had pinned much on this evening. Tonight marked the start of a new life for her. Gone were her naive, schoolgirl manners. Now, thanks to her most excellent tenacity, which she prayed would not fail her, she was about to launch into an uncharted world. As the sophisticated Lady Wilde, she was ready to take on the stylish *ton*— and, for that matter, whatever the wicked Lord Wilde could hand out.

"I must say, it is a trifle warm in here," Aunt Edwina complained, waving her ivory fan to and fro. "And I am most horribly parched. I think I shall find some libation." She waddled off.

Left to her own devices, Olivia surveyed the crowded room. She smoothed her white gloves over her arms and nervously patted the back of her hair. It was curled and elaborately fastened with satin ribbons, lace, and roses, the height of fashion. She only hoped all the pieces stayed in place.

Upon their arrival in London the previous week, she'd visited a dozen of so of the most prestigious households in Mayfair and left her calling card. She was overwhelmed by the number of invitations she had received in return. This evening was the first of many social events on her busy schedule. Indeed, this evening's soiree had the dubious distinction of being the first ball of her entire life.

Outside of small, intimate gatherings or the dinner guests at her father's town house in Belgrave Square, she'd seen no society at all. Armed with a strong will, however, she felt confident this evening would be a smashing success. By tomorrow, everyone would know of the charming Lady Wilde. *Her* name would doubtless appear in the *Morning Post*.

She had no idea how his lordship would react

when he discovered his dowdy bride had taken it upon herself to enjoy London society without so much as a by-your-leave. Languidly waving her fan, she told herself she cared not a wit for his consent. Despite her outward appearance of calm and firm resolve, however, her insides were churning fiercely.

"Ah, Lady Wilde," Lady Bloomsberry exclaimed, wading through the crowd to greet Olivia. "What a treat it is for us to welcome you on your first evening out in London."

Olivia forced a bright smile to her face. Her middle-aged hostess was bedecked with so many jewels that her scrawny neck was entirely eclipsed.

"I would not miss it for the world," Olivia crooned with false enthusiasm.

"I should like you to meet my daughter," Lady Bloomsberry remarked, waving her arm in the direction of a plain, mousy-haired brunette. "This is Clara. She has just come out. I thought you might enjoy each other's company. You are, after all, so very close in age, and you have only just come from the country yourself."

Olivia stiffened at the subtle jibe, but offered the woman's hopelessly unattractive daughter a kind smile.

"I am persuaded you two shall enjoy the evening tolerably well. After all, Lady Wilde, you have scarcely seen much society since your marriage." Lady Bloomsberry took in Olivia's elegant white taffeta dress with a critical eye. "How quaint you are, my dear." She gave Olivia's cheek a condescending pat with her gloved hand. "It is a wonder your husband abandoned you to the country at all—and so soon after your nuptials, poor dear." Her catty smile threatened to crack her white face powder.

"He has not abandoned me, madam," Olivia countered coolly.

Convinced otherwise, Lady Bloomsberry offered her an indulgent smile. "Of course not. At least, not for long. I daresay, men must consider the necessity of an heir. Rest assured my dear, only *you* may provide him with that." She expelled a careless sigh. "Do not concern yourself. I feel certain Lady Chesney's charms will fade."

Olivia's face flamed.

"After all, what is beauty compared to youth?" Lady Bloomsberry asked, her red mouth curled with cruel amusement.

Olivia glared at the hateful woman. "What indeed, Lady Bloomsberry?"

The smile slid from Lady Bloomsberry's face and her lips pinched. With an annoyed huff, she gathered her skirts and disappeared into the throng of glamorous lords and ladies.

"Have you been long in London?" the timid Clara asked, apparently trying to eclipse her mother's rudeness.

"No," Olivia replied, wishing her aunt would return and rescue her.

Clara fell silent and let her gaze drift over the enormous ballroom swarming with eligible suitors.

"I say," Clara remarked, catching sight of someone. She expelled a sigh of pure feminine appreciation. "Who in the world is *that*, do you suppose?"

"Who?" Olivia surveyed the crowd for the man in question.

Giggling, Clara pointed across the room. "Why, he's the tallest gentleman in the room. And so well dressed. Have you ever seen eyes that blue?" she asked dreamily. "Is he taken, do you suppose?"

Olivia's gaze followed the direction of Clara's. "I daresay he is, yes."

Clara glanced at her companion in surprise. "How can you be so sure?"

"Because I very much fear," Olivia said, "he is married to me."

Clara's brown eyes widened in shock. "Then . . . that makes him," she said, clearly scintillated by the discovery, "Lord *Wilde.*"

"Mmm-hmmm."

"My," Clara crooned, eyeing him with girlish delight. "No wonder his reputation precedes him."

"Indeed." Olivia frowned.

Impeccably dressed in an ebony double breasted frock coat, silver brocade waistcoat, gleaming white linen shirt and cravat, and snug black trousers, he had the audacity to look absolutely stunning. Damn the man. If the erratic throbbing of her pulse was any indication, the effect was not lost on her.

A wave of nervous excitement washed over her. His chiseled profile was more harshly forbidding than she remembered, and his jet black hair was cropped shorter than she recalled. His eyes, however, were just as breathtakingly blue. Languidly chatting with a striking brunette, he was completely in his element. If appearances could be trusted, he was charming his gorgeous consort with unparalleled finesse, something he'd never bothered to do with his own bride.

Olivia felt as if she'd been punched in the stomach, but she could not bring herself to tear her eyes away. Hearing rumors of her husband's infidelities was one thing. It was a different matter entirely to come face to face with him in thrall to another woman's charms.

Brandon laughed at the unkind joke Maria Chesney had just made. The sight of unattractive Clara Blooms-berry scuttling through the crowd, desperate to make an alliance worthy of her station, was a source of great amusement to his catty companion. Her cruel streak was decidedly unbecoming—not that he cared. Having been surrounded by heartless people most of his life, he was accustomed to them. She was as cold and unfeeling as he imagined himself to be. But she was also very beautiful and openly available, precisely the right sort of woman for his purposes. It would not be a hardship for him to pleasure himself with her body night after night, nor would he feel an ounce of remorse for harboring not the slightest affection for her.

"Honestly," Maria remarked, indolently plying her fan, "the girl is positively hopeless. One can only wonder why her mother bothered to have her come out at all."

Brandon shrugged. "Perhaps she has high hopes for her," he offered, not particularly interested in idle gossip.

In fact, he was bored to tears. But, he acknowledged, conversation was not the reason he sought Maria's company. He was far too sober, however, to endure the remainder of this dull evening. He had lifted a crystal flute to his lips to remedy his current sober condition when his hand paused *en route*. He stared across the room.

Lady Chesney took note of his sudden paralysis. Her pale blue eyes followed the direction of his riveted gaze, and she caught sight of a gorgeous blond creature. It was little wonder he was captivated by the fair-haired beauty. Standing across the crowded ballroom, bedecked in a white satin gown with a guilelessly feminine lace bodice, she looked almost angelic, even to Maria's prejudiced eyes.

"Never say," she derided, "the wicked Lord Wilde is tempted by untried debutantes?"

Ignoring her, he continued to stare at the golden-haired enchantress. His jaw set like granite, and he swore under his breath.

Mildly distracted by his reaction, Maria glanced across the room once more. "She is rather captivating, I must say. Who on earth is she?"

"My wife," he growled. Without so much as offering the gaping lady at his side a polite bow, he strode across the crowded dance floor as Maria watched in utter disbelief.

"So," she groused aloud, her lips thinning, "*that* is Lady Wilde." Her long, lean fingers stroked the pearl choker around her neck. "The little twit might prove a trifle annoying," she muttered.

Olivia's frantic gaze darted about her for an expedient escape. None came to mind. This was not supposed to happen. Not here. Not tonight. What the devil was *he* doing at Lady Bloomsberry's ball? Infamous gentlemen were certainly not in attendance at fancy dress balls. Or were they? In her planning, had she failed to take into consideration the small circle of London's haute society?

Assessing Brandon's hardened features, she took a craven step backward. Her tongue darted nervously between her suddenly parched lips. Of all the balls in London, why did he have to attend this one? What could she say? More important, what on earth was she going to do? She must think of something. How could she possibly hope to shock him with news of her midnight escapades, if he ruined them before they began?

In long, angry, purposeful strides, he advanced on the spot where she stood, barely pausing to slam his glass on the marble pedestal by her side.

Oh dear. She swallowed. He looked every inch a handsome, angry giant. For one harrowing moment, she thought she might embarrass herself by losing the meager contents of her stomach. But she squared her shoulders as she attempted, to no avail, to stare him down.

Towering over her, Brandon glared at her. Olivia realized she'd stopped breathing, and she forced herself to draw a breath before she fainted dead on the spot.

"My lord," she intoned in a bare whisper before she dropped into a elegant curtsy before him. Given how much her knees were shaking, it was a miracle she managed it.

He caught her up short and brought her to her full height. "What the hell are *you* doing here?" he growled, his azure eyes blazing with anger.

"I was about to ask *you* the same thing."

His lips curled. "Forgive me. I seem to be at a loss. Did I, or did I not, leave you in the country?"

"Indeed. For weeks and weeks."

His eyes narrowed at her tone. "Then what, pray, are you doing here?"

"I am enjoying Lady Bloomsberry's hospitality," she replied with the same remarkable poise she'd exuded during their dreadful wedding.

He glanced about them, making certain their intimate tête-à-tête went unnoticed. Bloody hell. That damned dress clung to every gorgeous curve of her bodice. She looked, he acknowledged with a potent swell of white hot desire, ravishing. Damn and blast. She was lusciously soft and wonderfully feminine, even more alluring in the flesh than in his dreams. And she'd been damned enticing in those dreams last night, naked and willing in his arms.

"I can see that," he ground out, unsated desire making him cross. "What the devil possessed you to come to London?"

She shrugged her shoulder carelessly. "I was inclined to enjoy the society. Is that not why most people take leave of the country and come to town?" she asked, her tone pointed. "Unless, of course, one intends to take a seat in Lords."

Her words hit their mark. So she was annoyed with him for abandoning her in the country. Blast it all, she had nerve. "How dare you come to London without my permission? You've no right to inconvenience me in such a manner."

She arched a brow. "Haven't I?"

His gaze threatened to scorch her. "I do not recall issuing any invitation."

By this time, their lively exchange was attracting interested spectators.

"Confound it," Brandon growled under his breath, "the entire ballroom is staring at us."

Glancing about her, Olivia could see he was entirely correct. The gawking lords and ladies were practically salivating.

To make matters worse, Aunt Edwina was crossing the room. Spilling several drops of tepid lemonade as she pushed her way through the throng of guests, she lumbered toward her niece. Stunned by the sight of the wild ruffian who had married and promptly abandoned poor Olivia in the country, Edwina came to an abrupt halt.

"Oh," she cried in dismay, blinking at him from behind her spectacles. "My lord. I did not expect to see *you* here."

Scowling, Brandon dragged his hand through his hair. "Damnation," he muttered under his breath, "was it strictly necessary to bring *her* along on your jaunt to town?"

Before Olivia could reply, his steely fingers closed over her upper arm. He propelled her, none too gently, toward the balcony doors. She was forced to break into a brisk trot to keep up with his long swift strides.

"But, my dears," Edwina called after them, "will you not take some refreshment?"

The night air felt pleasantly cool against Olivia's burning cheeks. On one hand, she was glad of the timely reprieve. On the other, she was not at all eager for a renewal of their heated discussion.

The secluded surroundings left her at a distinct disadvantage. Even at the best of times, her husband cut an imposing figure. Right about now, he looked ready to commit murder, and she very much feared he intended her to be his next victim.

Darting a quick glance about the darkened balcony, he came to stand over her, his hands slung low on his hips.

"What the blazes do you think you're playing at, showing up here?" he demanded.

She opened her mouth to speak, but he wasn't finished.

"By God, you've no right to inconvenience me in

such a manner. Have you taken complete leave of your senses? Without so much as a by-your-leave," he railed, "you traipse to London and appear unannounced—at Lady Bloomsberry's ball, no less."

"I was announced," she told him, at her prim and proper best. "The footman enunciated my name quite clearly. I lament the fact you did not hear it, my lord."

Taking a menacing step closer, he glared at her.

Wetting her lips, she cleared her throat and prayed her voice did not quiver. "I am equally distressed to find *you* here this evening, my lord. Imagine my surprise. I certainly had no desire to make *your* acquaintance. Perish the thought," she said, with a feigned look of horror. "Verily, it was *my* express wish to enjoy myself this evening. I came to London to familiarize myself with the many charming gentlemen such good society has to offer. Your presence here does rather curtail my introductions, does it not?"

His eyes narrowed into artic blue slits. "What blasted *introductions?* You," he reminded her, stabbing his finger through the air, "are my wife. I expect you to observe the proprieties, not traipse here and there whenever the mood hits you."

"I am ever mindful of my exalted status as your beloved bride, my lord. But I wonder," she asked him coolly, "if you have perhaps forgotten the vows you took?"

"No, by George," he muttered, his gaze skewering her. "I have not forgotten. Nor am I likely to. If your outrageous conduct is intended to make me mindful of my husbandly duties, you are wasting your time."

"I am flattered, my lord, that you would imagine such an elaborate scheme on my part. In truth, I have

no wish to intrude on your, er . . . existence. I think
it best we lead separate but equal lives.''

He frowned at her. He wasn't quite sure what the
deuce separate but equal lives meant. He still could
not believe she had taken it upon herself to come to
London. Almost before the thought crossed his mind,
his face paled. His gaze jerked to her abdomen. "You
are not . . . with child?''

He looked ill at the prospect, and she despised
herself for the telltale signs of embarrassment that
streaked across her cheeks. It was heartless of him to
speak cavalierly of her condition when she'd fretted
over just such a possibility for weeks after he'd left.
Mercifully, her menses finally came and set her mind
at ease.

"I daresay the stylish gowns of the season conceal
a multitude of sins, but pregnancy is not one of
them." She reached for his hand and splayed his
palm intimately across her abdomen. The heat of his
palm seemed to penetrate the weight of her crinoline
gown. "You see, your child does not grow in my womb.
You need not concern yourself that our last encounter
left me indisposed, my lord. Indeed, it would appear
we are both totally unaffected.''

His gaze locked with hers. The hell he was! He
wanted her more now than ever. His hand spread
wide, grazing the soft feminine apex at her thighs.
She quivered. His nostrils flared with desire.

Her enormous, exotic green-brown eyes searched
his smoldering blue ones. Slowly, haltingly, he leaned
down and bent his head to hers. She leaned into him.
Her neck arched toward his kiss, and his breath was
hot and moist. Her lashes fluttered shut in anticipa-
tion. The evening breeze rustled the trees, and he
jerked back.

Dragging both his hands through his hair, he turned his back on her. "I am glad you're not with child," he said, his tone clipped. "But if you wished to come to London, you should have written and asked my permission."

"Oh, dear me, no. *That* would never do," she replied, pulling a mock frown. "Had I written, I very much doubt you would have sanctioned my visit. Then where would I be?" She was all calm and conversational. Inside, she was shaking like a leaf and still reeling from his near kiss.

He swiveled around. "In the country," he said roughly, "where you belong."

"I see your dilemma." Her dainty brow furrowed in consternation. "I daresay this presents a problem for us both, does it not?"

"Quite," he bit out. Digging his hands into his pockets, he prowled the deserted balcony. "You will return to Cloverton Hall posthaste," he told her, his voice harsh with command. "The entire disagreeable episode will be forgotten." He sliced his hand through the air in a gesture of finality.

She folded her arms over her bosom. A grimace touched her lips. "In other words, I shall rusticate in the country until such time as you deem appropriate, while you occupy your time with frivolous females— not unlike the one hanging on your every word this evening."

Her tone was spiteful, but she could not help it. She was experiencing her first taste of jealousy, and it was bitter. "And I should imagine you will visit gaming tables, where you shall undoubtedly lose hoards of blunt, and endure long nights at your club with your many gentleman friends, sharing embellished war stories whilst imbibing expensive French brandy. Oh, no. I think not, my lord.''

His penetrating gaze threatened to impale her where she stood. ''By God, madam,'' he breathed, ''you have got nerve.''

''Have I?'' She uttered a lighthearted laugh. ''How divine. I always wanted some. It is rewarding to know I've at last found it.''

''It is not in the least becoming,'' he muttered fiercely. ''It is damned unnatural. I should pack you off to your father and let him deal with you,'' he threatened, a menacing glint in his eye. ''It would serve him right.''

She grimaced again. ''I scarcely think that is a sound solution, my lord. You see, he and I are not on the best of terms at present.''

She was gratified to see that Brandon was taken aback by the news.

''Pray, do not distress yourself on my account. Aunt and I shall be very content to remain in the quaint little house we've found on Hartford Street.''

''Hartford Street!'' he exploded. His entire body recoiled at the mere suggestion. ''No wife of mine will reside on Hartford Street.'' The muscle in his cheek pulsed with energy. ''You, madam, shall reside at Park Lane, or not at all. Is that perfectly clear?''

She expelled a weary sigh, appearing for the moment to be defeated. ''If you are certain that is the best arrangement,'' she demurred, her manner guileless, ''I am sure we shall be happy to oblige you.''

Placing his hands on the stone balustrade on either side of her hips, he leaned over her. She tried to ease back from his encroaching heat, but her spine ground against the hard stone.

"Oh, you shall oblige me," he assured her, his tone ominous.

He caught her around the waist and pulled her to him. Her breath caught in her throat. She felt the danger of his hard lean body against hers. Excitement coursed through her veins, reminding her of their one passionate night together. "You shall come home with me this night," he murmured. His muscular thighs pressed against hers. Her pulse throbbed erratically, and a rush of warmth flowed through her.

On a purely physical level, she was drawn to him. She could hardly resist the tug of attraction, and she longed for him to touch her, to kiss her and make her his.

"Very well, my lord," came her breathless reply, "if you insist."

He chuckled deep in his throat as his hooded gaze drifted over her face and settled on her soft, full lips. "I do."

A smoldering flame lit his gaze. She found his purely sexual appraisal strangely exhilarating. His hand slid over her neck to gently graze her ivory skin. For a moment, she thought she saw a flicker of tenderness in his eyes. She wondered if he found her as stirringly appealing as she did with his chiseled features etched in the silvery moonlight.

She gazed into his smoldering blue eyes. Drawing a shallow breath, she wet her lips. "What of my aunt?"

All evidence of emotion vanished from his face as quickly as it had come. He pulled away from her abruptly.

"Rest assured I shall see you both settled this night. One can only hope," he drawled, "that the news of your inopportune arrival has not spread through London like wildfire."

"What?" she derided pertly, hurt by his blatant disregard for her feelings. He acted as though she were an annoying gnat he could brush away with the flick of his finger. "With Lady Chesney's charms abounding? I scarcely think anyone would take note of my presence here tonight."

A dark frown crossed his features. He glared at her, but ignored her jibe. "I shall have your things brought around to Park Lane in the morning," he uttered with stiff civility.

"That is very gracious of you, my lord."

"Not at all. It is customary for the earls of Marlborough to reside in Mayfair whenever they come to London," came his brisk rejoinder. "It is the least I can do for *my wife*." The caustic bite of his voice cut her to the quick. She averted her face from his heated stare.

Placing his palm at the base of her spine, he escorted her into the ballroom. She trembled at the intimacy of his touch. Upon returning to the swarming dance floor, he said brusquely against her ear, "Collect your aunt. My footman will attend you outside."

She watched her elegant husband channel through the crowd and reunite with his lovely brunette. Her stomach tightened in a sickening knot. As he bowed before the object of his affection and pressed a kiss to the lady's outstretched hand, Olivia turned away. Suddenly, she regretted her decision to come to London.

Chapter 6

Olivia waited outside in the confines of his darkened carriage for her husband. After nearly an hour, she was fit to be tied. Her fingers drilled a repetitive beat against her knees. It would seem his lordship could scarcely tear himself away from the stunning brunette's clutches.

The only thing preventing Olivia from marching inside and demanding his escort was her staunch sense of decorum—that and fear. A good deal of fear. She lacked the mettle to confront him again in public. He was no gentleman. He might refuse her outright. Then where would she be?

She had, of course, anticipated encountering her wild, unscrupulous spouse at some point. But when she envisioned that event, it had taken place on her terms in the morning room in her quaint town house, where she was able to prepare herself before receiving him. She certainly had never imagined undergoing a nerve-racking interview on a secluded balcony whilst his lover waited in the wings. It was an acutely humiliating experience.

To make matters worse, Edwina was slumped across the black leather carriage seat, fast asleep and snoring. Loudly.

Heaving a sigh of frustration, Olivia balled her hands into fists. "This is intolerable!"

As if hearing her cry, the carriage door swung open. Swinging an elegant black cape around his broad shoulders, her husband materialized before her eyes. Giving her no notice at all, he shouted orders at the driver and jumped inside the cramped conveyance.

His gaze swept over his wife's rotund companion propped against the side of the carriage, snoring heavily.

"I see we are all here," he said with barely concealed displeasure as he reclined on the leather seat beside Edwina.

"Indeed, my lord," came Olivia's crisp retort. "For quite some time. Tell me—I am but curious—was Lady Chesney the reason I was forced to wait in the chilly night air for nearly an hour?" Her voice reeked of jealousy and anger, but she did not care. She could not maintain her cool facade a moment longer.

He gave her a hard look. "As a matter of fact," he said gruffly, "she was."

"I expected as much. How is your darling Lilly?" she asked curtly.

His brows snapped together. "*Lilly?* Where the devil did you hear that name?"

She turned her gaze out the window. "You murmured it to me on our wedding night," she remarked, unable to bring herself to look at him. "I believe you mistook me for her." Her cheeks colored at the

memory of his lean body driving into her again and
again until she nearly cried out from the sheer pleasure of his hard, penetrating thrusts.

"Did I?" he inquired dryly. "Forgive me. My recollection of that night must differ somewhat from
yours."

Pushing the vividly erotic memories from her mind,
Olivia quit her inspection of the pitch-black streets.
"Indeed?" she pressed. "How so?"

His full sensual mouth quirked slightly and his eyes
locked with hers. He folded his arms lazily over his
chest, reclining more comfortably on the seat. "I
distinctly recall the identity of the woman in my arms.
My sincere apologies, madam," he said in a sultry
murmur, "if I led you to believe otherwise."

Heat scalded her cheeks and her lashes fluttered
downward.

"In any case," he went on to say, enjoying her
disconcerted expression, "you need throw no jealous
fits. Lilly is dead."

Olivia's eyes jerked up. *Dead?*" she breathed in
shock.

He nodded. "It would be more than a year now.
So you see"—he flashed a smile that did not reach
his arctic blue eyes—"no cause for theatricals."

She swallowed. "Who . . . was she?"

He shrugged. "Someone I knew once. It was a long
time ago and better off forgotten."

She could not stop herself from asking, "Were
you . . . in love with her?"

"In love?" he repeated, with obvious disdain for
such a romantic fancy. He turned his attention out
the window. "I shouldn't think so, no."

Olivia glanced down at her lap. "You must have
cared for her to mistake your bride for her on your

wedding night," she murmured, twisting her white gloves between her fingers.

Expelling an annoyed breath, he propped his long booted legs onto the seat beside his inquisitive wife. "She was a Russian peasant girl. I saved her from a group of British soldiers who thought to occupy their time with her for a while and then cast her aside when they'd had their fill. She was grateful to me." He shrugged. "After that"—he fell silent for a moment—"when you believe you may die at any moment," he explained, his tone solemn, "you come to depend on other people, perhaps more than you would under normal circumstances."

"I see," Olivia murmured, embarrassed by his frank depiction of his wartime lover. She was not accustomed to such blunt speech. In fact, there was not a single thing about her husband that was familiar to her gentle upbringing. Keeping her gaze on her lap, she tried unsuccessfully to force away the image of him wrapped in a lover's embrace with his darling Lilly.

Sitting forward, he slipped his forefinger beneath her chin and forced her to look at him. "You seem hell-bent on thrusting yourself into my life," he said, his tone ruthless. "You are wasting your time. I give you fair warning: I am entirely devoid of emotion."

"I wonder, my lord," she said, her eyes searching his harsh countenance, "if you are as heartless as you claim?"

He offered her a cruel smirk. "You may rely on it."

"Then"—she allowed her voice to become soft as silk—"you and I must have a very different recollection of our wedding night, to be sure. For the man

I held in my arms was neither cold nor heartless. Quite the contrary.''

"Come now, what can one midnight tryst with a lover mean to me," he remarked with callous indifference, "when I've so many to chose from?''

Olivia flinched and bowed her head to conceal her hurt. She would have to develop a tough skin if she hoped to break through her husband's callous exterior.

Olivia's slippered feet padded softly up the stone steps that led to her husband's white-pillared London mansion. A wave of anxiety washed over her. Her visit to town was not proceeding according to plan. While she did wish to pique her husband's interest, she had no express desire to live with him—at least not at this point.

"Oh," yawned Aunt Edwina, as she lumbered across the vibrant red carpet at the elegant threshold, "I am done in.''

Brandon's gaze swept over the rumpled woman. "I expect we all are," he replied with chilling politeness. "Never fear. Carrington shall show you to your bed for the night.''

"Oh, it is good of you to trouble yourself on my account, my lord," Edwina replied, beaming at him.

Olivia frowned at her aloof husband as her aunt's pudgy fingers tugged on her sleeve. "I can scarcely conceive of it, my dear," Edwina whispered. "Here we are in a fashionable London town house.''

Sighing, Olivia forced a paper-thin smile to her lips and darted a glance at her taciturn husband. He was conversing in a low tone with a rather officious man who was obviously the esteemed butler.

Her lips pursed. She wondered if his lordship admired a single thing about her. He certainly did not prize good manners, for it was his habit to be less than civil when the mood took him. Nor would it seem that he felt inclined to be generous with his affections. He was rude to the point of neglect.

Her brow wrinkled in confusion. She could not reconcile the snippets of kindness he'd revealed with his churlish character. Although fleeting, they were nonetheless a part of him, albeit a very small part. Why had he come to her aid that day so very long ago? And why had he gone to the trouble of retrieving her cherished lavaliere and giving it to her as a wedding present? She could no more comprehend his moods than his desire to wed her in the first place. Certainly a man should harbor some affection for his bride, or some respect despite the fact that among the upper crust love was not a prerequisite for marriage. Apparently, Olivia thought, dragging her disgruntled gaze away from her husband's handsome face, neither was common courtesy.

The butler Carrington inclined his slightly balding head toward Edwina. "If you will follow me, madam?"

"Yes, of course," Aunt Edwina happily acquiesced. Pressing a kiss to Olivia's cheek, she feigned a ferocious need for sleep and followed the butler from the lavish foyer up the wide red carpeted staircase.

Finding herself alone with the huge aristocrat who was her lord and master, Olivia was suddenly acutely uncomfortable. Darting a nervous gaze about the enormous front hall at the white marble Grecian statues and gilded framed landscapes, she prayed Brandon would cease his staring and speak to her.

When he made no move to address her or to break

the uncomfortable silence, she drew a deep breath and forged ahead.

"I must confess, my lord, I am feeling rather fragile. I am certain a good night's rest is what I require. Which are my rooms?"

His lips twitched slightly. "As to that," he remarked, slipping his hand around her upper arm, "I should like a word."

Olivia felt the color drain from her face. Smiling with lips that were dry as sand, she gathered all her courage and accompanied his tall, lean figure into the drawing room.

He clicked the door shut behind her. A sinking feeling invaded her chest. He couldn't possibly expect her to share his bed. She slanted a glance at his profile. Or could he?

No. It was out of the question. She would refuse him. She must—provided, of course, he took no for an answer. She found herself inexplicably drawn to this saturnine man. She could not hope to maintain her equilibrium if he took her to his bed.

He sauntered across the stately room to the drinks table, lifted a large crystal decanter of brandy, and poured a fair amount of amber liquid into a snifter. Turning about to face her, he took a large sip. "I find myself in a rather awkward position," he said, those gorgeous bedroom eyes of his making her stomach flutter.

Dropping onto the brown velvet settee, she drew a deep calming breath and asked, "What might that be, my lord?"

His heated gaze swept over her. "Being a primarily male domicile for the last fifteen years or more, I fear this house affords little comfort for gently bred young ladies. It has been shut up for quite some time.

My father was inclined to reside in the country these past ten years or so." He bared his teeth in a cool smile. "I never shared his partiality for Cloverton Hall. When I returned from the war, I found few alterations were necessary to suit my bachelor life in town. In short"—a roguish grin tugged at his full, sensual mouth—"I've no place to put you."

Faith, the way he was looking at her gave her the impression she had broken out in spots. "I see." Her tongue darted between her parched lips. "Could I not sleep with my aunt?" she inquired, secretly hoping he would agree.

Shaking his head, he polished off the remainder of his drink in one gulp and set the glass down on the silver tray. "I think not," he replied, his voice low and husky. "Servants have a tendency to talk."

As if he gave a tinker's damn about gossip. "Pray then, what do you suggest, my lord?"

A slow, provocative smile crept across his ruggedly handsome features. "Why," he answered in a low, sexy purr, "you shall pass the night in my bed. Where else?"

She quit breathing. For a scant moment, she entertained the insane notion of accepting the arrangement. She could win him with her body. Other women kept a man's attention in just such a manner. But she knew in her heart she was not up to such a formidable challenge. He'd demonstrated he could be cold, callous, and unkind when the mood struck him. She would lose her heart to him in a trice, and he would hold himself from her with alarming ease.

No. She must refuse him her body. It was the only way she could safeguard her heart. If she held out any hope at all of equal footing in this marriage, she must make him value her for her own merits, which far exceeded being a passing fancy in his bed.

Clearing her throat, she got to her feet. "It grieves me more than I can say to refuse your very generous offer," she said, her tone laced with subtle sarcasm, "but I am afraid I must decline."

He stiffened perceptibly and his features went stony with anger. "I see." His blue eyes turned frosty. "In that case, I shall seek my comfort elsewhere this evening. I daresay a green girl such as yourself," he went on, his tone brutal, "would be offended by my wicked intentions this night. I shall spare you the lurid details."

Her lashes swooped down. If he sought to humiliate her, he had succeeded. Raising her eyes to his, she met his deliberate stare with a steely resolve of her own.

"It is not my intent to invade your private life. You may go about your business as you wish. I shall not intrude."

"I am vastly relieved to hear it. Out of deference to your delicate sensibilities," he drawled sarcastically, "I shall seek other lodgings until such time as I decide what is to be done with you."

Olivia knew where he would go. Straight into his beautiful Lady Chesney's open arms. She clasped her hands together at her waist in what she hoped appeared a demure fashion. In truth, they were shaking horribly.

Salvaging her last remaining vestiges of pride, she said, "I wish you a pleasant evening, my lord."

He inclined his raven head. "I am persuaded I shall pass a satisfactory night, madam."

Retrieving the lamp from the gleaming mahogany table, she walked toward the door.

"Pleasant dreams, my sweet," he mocked softly as she brushed past him.

Slipping from the opulent drawing room into the dark chilly hall, she shivered. "All my dreams are pleasant, my lord," she tossed over her shoulder.

He gave a deep, throaty laugh. Standing in the drawing room doorway, he leaned his broad shoulder against the doorjamb and watched her mount the shadowy horseshoe staircase. "I wager they are, my sweet," he called to her. "But not as fanciful as mine."

As she slowly mounted the stairs, the soft yellowish glow of the lamp was eclipsed by darkness. His mouth thinned into a grim line. He refused to admit to himself her rejection had cut him to the quick. He was a master at squelching his emotions and denying any suggestion of pain. Anger, his old and trusted ally, rose to his defense and mingled with burning resentment. Damn her eyes. She was too confoundedly attractive by half.

The cursed thing of it was, he wanted her. Now. Tonight. And the provocative little tart had boldly refused him. Her brash conduct was not to borne.

What the devil was she doing in London? For a fleeting moment, he allowed his ego to be flattered by the idea that she was pursuing him, not that the idea of a real marriage appealed to him. But he would not deny he wanted to enjoy his husbandly rights— which she had brazenly refused to grant him.

Despite her outrageous impertinence, he was not proud of his cruelty toward her. When she had pressed him during the carriage ride home, all his defenses had risen. Her remarks about love and the like edged toward dangerous ground of which he wanted no part. He'd deliberately issued a setback in an attempt to wound her.

Later, when he'd offered her his bed, her blunt rejection stung his pride. She deserved the verbal lashing she'd received.

He drove his fingers through his hair. Hell and damnation. What the deuce was he going to do? With his bride an ever present temptation just beyond his fingertips, his life promised to be hell on earth.

"You were splendid, my dear!" Dressed in her cotton chemise, Aunt Edwina sat perched on the edge of the vanity bench in the rose-colored bedroom. Olivia closed the bedroom door behind her and sighed. She was not feeling splendid at all. At the moment, she was seriously doubting the wisdom of her decision to come to London.

"Absolutely brilliant!" Edwina clasped her hands together in praise. "I must confess, I had my doubts. When I saw his lordship at the ball this evening, I all but suffered an attack of the vapors. But you managed marvelously well. I declare, not a solitary soul would have believed you were not as you pretended—a woman of the world. You comported yourself with unparalleled elegance. His lordship must have been surprised."

"Did I?" Olivia queried, her tone doubtful as she dropped down on the large feather bed, her shoulders slumped in defeat. "Was he?"

"Oh, my dear, can you have any doubts?" Gathering a blanket about her bare shoulders, Edwina came to sit beside her woebegone niece.

A smile softened Olivia's otherwise taut features. She gazed at her sweet, guileless aunt. Poor dear, other people's motivations were beyond Edwina's reckoning. As far as she was concerned, the whole world was full of sugar and spice and everything nice. Faced with the conundrum of what to do with a cold, distant husband who clearly did not want her as wife, Olivia felt painfully alone.

Aunt Edwina patted her hand with affection. "You look unwell, child." Frowning, she brushed a stray lock of hair from Olivia's forehead. "What distresses you?"

"I cannot say for certain," Olivia replied, getting to her feet. Sighing, she clasped the tall maple bed-post and rested her forehead against it. "I fear I have made a grave error in coming here. I hope you will forgive my rash judgment, but I think it would be best if we returned to the country with all possible haste."

"Never say so," Edwina replied, taken aback by Olivia's change of heart.

Olivia's lips thinned. "I very much fear *his lordship* is less than pleased."

"Fustian. I saw the way he looked at you. Such admiration in his eyes! He is smitten," the older woman insisted, wagging her finger in the air. "I am sure of it."

Olivia rolled her eyes and sighed. "I think not, Aunt. Lady Chesney is the sort of woman he prefers. I cannot possibly compete with that," she admitted, depressed.

"What utter rubbish. Heed me well, my dear," Aunt Edwina advised sagely, *"you* are his *wife*. Lady Cheeky is a passing fancy, nothing more."

"It's Chesney, Aunt," Olivia was quick to correct. "And precious little good that does me when he is seeking his pleasure this very night in her arms."

"Men take mistresses from time to time," Edwina

allowed. "It is of little concern. He shall come to you, in his own time. Mark my words."

Olivia slanted her aunt a dubious look. "Thank you. I cannot tell you what a measure of relief that is to me. When, pray, do you suppose that might be? Before or after he has graced the threshold of every bedroom in London?"

"If it is your desire to keep him," Edwina advised, "you must make him want *you* above all else."

"But how?" Olivia cried, raising her arms. "I am not of his class. I am a gently bred commoner who ought to have stayed where she belonged." She plopped down on the enormous feather bed beside her aunt. "What on earth was I thinking?" She hung her head. "London is the worst place for me."

"I reckon you came to London," Edwina remarked, "because you thought to make him fall in love with you. You cannot turn back at the slightest resistance."

Olivia's head came up. She gave her aunt a startled look. Edwina was more intuitive than Olivia had given her credit for being. Olivia opened her mouth to utter a forceful denial, but found she could not. She did want his love and his respect. She had neither.

"I suppose you are correct," she admitted. In her naivete, she had believed a happy life with her husband was possible. What a fool she was. Happiness and fulfillment were not in Lord Wilde's vocabulary. All he wanted was a convenient bed warmer. When she had refused him his conjugal rights, he had not so much as batted an eyelash.

"What a disaster this has all turned out to be. Everything is horribly muddled. He wasn't supposed to know of my existence until *after* I'd made a splash. We were not supposed to be *here,*" Olivia lamented, looking around her at the elegant heavy maple furnishings. "He was to come to *me* on *my* terms."

"Yes, well, here we are," her aunt murmured, frowning.

"To his way of thinking, I am a gauche child," Olivia groaned. "A passing inconvenience, nothing more. How can I make him want me for myself when I have nothing with which to lure him? No sophistication, no mystery, nothing. He had the nerve to call me a green girl."

"In some ways you are," Edwina remarked, eliciting a heated glare from her niece. "Oh, do come along. What is wrong with being young and inexperienced, may I ask? It is what most men desire in a wife."

"If I hold any hope at all of winning Brandon's affections," Olivia reasoned aloud, "I must approach him on his own terms. A man like that would never want a gently bred girl. That much is patently obvious. You must agree?"

"Mmm, possibly," Edwina replied.

Olivia folded her arms at her waist, her expression determined. "I must create a sensation. That is all there is to it."

"Oh." Edwina giggled. "How utterly wicked. Never say you plan to become notorious?"

Olivia slanted her aunt a frown. "Celebrated would be nice."

Edwina's eyes grew wide. "Consider, dearest," she remarked with some excitement, *"your name* might very well grace the society pages!"

"What a delicious prospect," Olivia replied, grinning from ear to ear. "I must transform myself into a brazen hussy."

Edwina mulled over the notion. "It sounds delightful. What a rousing diversion! But have you considered the recompense you may face? You could end up rather badly hurt. After all, you are a complete innocent. And as all of London knows"—she sighed—Lord Wilde is a veritable wolf."

Olivia frowned, but in truth, she could find no fault with Aunt Edwina's logic. "Why should a man like that wish to marry at all, do you suppose?" she wondered, her frustration mounting.

Aunt Edwina cocked her curly head to one side. "I'm sure he had his reasons. Duty. Honor. Leave off for tonight, dearest." She yawned. "Get some rest. It will all look brighter in the morning. You'll see."

Olivia doubted the light of day would shed anything positive on this unbearable circumstance, but she left her aunt in peace and walked down the carpeted hall toward her makeshift quarters. She felt certain she would pass a miserable night.

Entering the distinctly masculine room, she eased the door shut and sighed aloud. She glanced at the enormous tester bed against the far wall and her heart sank. The knowledge that she was to sleep on the same sheets which had graced his naked body only the night before, while he was bestowing his physical affections and Lord knew what else on another woman, made Olivia want to cry.

Bolstering her strength, however, she shoved away from the door and vowed her feelings would not be so easily trod upon. Shivering, she peeled off her white taffeta gown and laid it on top of the dark green velvet sofa.

Standing in her sheer linen chemise, she caught sight of her reflection in the large cheval mirror. She tugged at her long blond hair, loosening it from the tight curls, and shook her head. Was she so horrible to look at? Totally lacking in his eyes? She smoothed her hands over her breasts, down her narrow waist, over her slender hips and across the flat of her abdomen. *What does Lady Chesney have that I do not?* she wondered, gazing at the provocative sight of her hair flowing around her like a siren's. Her lips turned down, and she sighed in misery. *Everything.*

Dejected, she turned away from her reflection and scurried across the cold floor to his lordship's gargantuan bed. First chance she got, she decided, crawling between the frigid linen sheets and tugging the covers up to her chin, she would set his lordship straight on a matter of great import. She could be every inch as sophisticated as Lady Chesney ever thought of being. Oh yes, she vowed, snuffing out the lamp on the rich mahogany bedside table and shivering against the icy sheets, his lordship was in for a big surprise.

Chapter 7

Early the next morning, it came as little surprise to learn from Carrington that his lordship would not be joining his wife for breakfast. Olivia pursed her lips. No doubt he was otherwise engaged with Lady Chesney. Life with Lord Wilde was going to be much more difficult than Olivia had originally envisioned. She was not particularly interested in waiting with bated breath for him to grace her with his presence.

Thankfully, her maid Jenny had arrived from Hartford Street with Olivia's trunks. At least Olivia would have her things about her and not pass another night in her shift. A brisk gallop in the park was just the thing to lift her spirits, followed by a nice warm breakfast. Perhaps later, she'd do a bit of shopping with her aunt, and then she would pay a few social calls to become better acquainted with London society.

Garbed in a snug-fitting black velvet riding habit with white lace collar and undersleeves, she donned her straw-brimmed velvet hat and white lace veil. Satisfied that she looked presentable, she departed Park Lane for a stimulating trot through Hyde Park. It was her usual habit to have a groomsman accompany her, but given the multitude of concerns weighing on her mind, she prized what little privacy she could find and refused Ned's assistance.

" 'Is lordship won't like it," he warned.

"I am sure his lordship will adapt," she countered briskly, and kicked the gray into a brisk trot.

"But, my lady," Ned objected, calling after her, " 'tis me job!"

She glanced over her shoulder at him. Offering him a sunny smile, she called out, "I shall answer to his lordship."

Scratching his balding head, Ned muttered aloud, " 'Is lordship 'as got his hands full with 'er, I wager."

Stylish Rotten Row was crowded with riders exercising their mounts. Though boasting of their newest purchases from Tattersalls, the gentlemen were also complaining of heavy gaming losses at Goodwood. Abandoning the sandy track, Olivia steered her mare through the warm, blossoming park toward the Ladies' Mile. She nodded her head in polite greeting to the stylish passersby and paid particular attention to the gentleman riders. To her delight, they seemed more than eager to return the favor. Becoming notorious would be far easier than she had imagined.

"Cor!" a raggedly dressed man cried out, catching sight of Olivia on horseback.

His rotund wife came up short by his side. " 'Er now, what the devil's gotten into you, then?" she asked, irritably adjusting a threadbare shawl around her corpulent shoulders.

"Look ye 'ere, ol' Bess," he said, pointing across the Park.

His wife released a deep sigh. "Aye, I'm lookin' at all them people gots more than us," she groused, folding her arms over her drooping bosom.

"Not fer long, my lovely."

Bess shot her husband a queer look. "What are y'on 'bout, Clive?"

"I seen somebody who might change our luck."

She heaved an impatient breath. "Oh, aye. Who might that be, then?"

"Lady Wilde."

"And who might she be when she's at 'ome?"

"Cast yer mind back a few years, love. I'm sure you can remember old Parker. Gave me my first job."

"Which you lost right quick."

"So I did. But I got away with more than the shirt on me back."

"What's that to do with her?" Bess demanded, waving her hand in Olivia's direction.

"You never know, Bess old girl," Clive said. "Now that she's come into a bit o' money o' her own, she might be interested in helping an old friend of the family. I'll just pay her a visit and see, shall I?"

Her spirits high, Olivia was about to take a refreshing trot around the course when a shabbily dressed man approached her on foot.

Blocking her path, he flashed a crooked smile up at her. "Remember me, Miss?" he asked, removing his tattered hat.

Reining in her feisty mount, she replied coolly, "I am afraid you have mistaken me, sir." She was about to escape the grimy-looking man when he caught hold of the mare's harness.

"Now," he purred in a cunning tone, "is that any way to treat an old friend?"

"Old friend?" she queried, a shiver of trepidation creeping up her spine. She darted a glance about her. The park was blessedly crowded. She breathed a little easier. "I scarcely think you are an associate of mine, past or present."

"No need to get uppity, now is there, Miss, Just coz you've had a bit of good fortune and old Clive here has fallen on hard times. I thought you might find it in your Christian heart to be charitable with them that gots less than you."

Recognition dawned in her eyes. *"Mr. Winterbottom?"* she breathed in surprise. He had indeed fallen on hard times. He looked nearer to a beggar boy than a man of affairs.

He chuckled deep in his throat. "I thought you might recall. How could you forget a trusted employee and friend of the family?"

"You were neither a trusted friend nor a valued employee. As I recollect, you were dismissed with just cause and given a generous severance under the circumstances."

"Ah," he remarked, a scheming glint in his eye, "so you do remember old Clive after all."

"Vaguely. What I do recall disinclines me to offer the likes of you charity or anything else."

"Don't judge me so hard. Can I help it if I got sticky fingers?"

"Your tenure with my father was relatively short-lived. My father never liked you and I never liked you. Now, if you would be so kind as to unhand my horse, I shall be on my way and forget this unfortunate meeting ever took place."

Resentment lit his beady brown eyes. Refusing to do as she asked, he leaned closer and glowered up at her. "You've got no right talkin' to me like that," he spat, his tone menacing. "Who do you think y'are? Queen Victoria?"

Olivia's hand tightened around her crop.

"I know all about you. You think you're so high and mighty now that you've married the Earl of Marlborough. But old Clive here knows the truth. You're nothing but a whore's bastard child," he hissed at her. "Do you hear? A whore's daughter is what you are!"

Frantic to be free, Olivia drove the heel of her boot into her mare's side and slashed at the hateful man with her whip. Wrenching free, her horse took off in a gallop, tearing across the park.

"I can prove it, too!" he shouted after her, rubbing his sore cheek. "Don't think I won't! You'll be hearing from me, little Miss. Then we'll see who's the haughty one! I've got proof. Do you hear? Proof!"

By the time she managed to rein in her mount, she had reached the park entrance. Tears were streaming down her face. Desperate to escape the onlookers and forget the disturbing episode, she urged her horse into a brisk trot and made for Park Lane.

Ned rushed to her side and helped her dismount. "What 'appened, my lady?" he asked, seeing her tear-stained cheeks beneath her sheer veil.

"Nothing," she explained, shaking her head and sniffling. "It was nothing at all." Laying her gloved hand on Ned's forearm, she implored him, "Say nothing to your master. His lordship will never grant me a single freedom if I burst into tears with childish caprice."

"Very well, my lady. But I'd feel better if y'allowed me or one o' the boys to act as chaperon next time."

She smiled her thanks and nodded her agreement. With shaky hands, she gathered her skirts. As she climbed the front stairs to the Marlborough mansion, feeling frightened and confused, she realized she was trembling all over. "Horrid man," she said aloud.

Joyful memories of a childhood filled with happy stories about her late mother rushed to the forefront of her mind—how graceful and kind she was. According to her father, her face could light up a room and her melodious laughter brightened his mood. Everything she knew about her mother indicated she was a devoted wife and a loving companion. She had died due to complications during childbirth.

Her father had always maintained that although he had lost his wife, he had gained a daughter. In so doing, Olivia had become his salvation after his devastating loss. How dare that repugnant Winterbottom cast aspersions on her mother's character?

Anger welled inside Olivia at the thought of his vicious suggestion. She shook her head in disgust. It simply cannot be true.

It was well past noon when his lordship finally put in an appearance at the Park Lane mansion. After the untimely appearance of his tempting wife at Lady Bloomsberry's ball and her curt setback last night, he'd been frustrated and thoroughly piqued and went directly to his club, where he proceeded to get royally foxed. He complained, for as long as anyone was inclined to listen, about the deficiencies of the fairer sex and remained all night at his club.

Knowing he planned to get completely bosky, Brandon had left express instructions to have a bath drawn and a large tisane waiting upon his return. Hence he was rather surprised to encounter his vexingly alluring wife in the front hall. He took in her diminutive form. Clad in a yellow silk gown that accentuated her narrow shoulders, full round breasts, and slender arms, she looked enticingly beautiful. An unwanted flare of desire spread through his loins.

Her gaze traveled over his tousled hair, bloodshot eyes, unshaven face, and disheveled clothing, making him acutely aware of her dim view of his scruffy appearance.

"I am not feeling at all the thing this morning," he uttered stiffly. "Pray, excuse me." He made to walk past her, but she would not allow it.

"Put you mind at ease, my lord. I have no wish to condemn you."

Heaving an irritated sigh, he swung around to face her. "I am relieved beyond measure," he drawled. In truth, his mouth was as dry as dirt, his head was hammering, and every bone in his body cried out for sleep.

"I must confess"—she gurgled with amusement—"you look quite a sight."

His lips thinned. "If you wish a word, madam, pray say so and I shall oblige you, but if it is your desire to critique my appearance, you'll find I'm in no mood," he warned.

She hesitated for a moment, her eyes sparkling with an intriguing flame. "Perhaps," she allowed, "a private discussion is in order."

They crossed the expansive front hall, and he thrust

open the library doors and motioned impatiently for her to precede him. She swept across the threshold with the grace of a swan. He shut the doors and leaned back against them. Folding his arms across his chest, he pinned her with a hard stare. "Out with it," he said roughly. "You'll find I haven't the patience for cat-and-mouse games."

With a whoosh of silk, she whirled about to face him and clasped her hands together at her waist. "Excellent." She looked him straight in the eye. "Neither have I."

He flashed a mirthless smile and shoved away from the double doors. "I am so very pleased to hear," he drawled, his tone sardonic, "that we are, at last, in agreement."

She let her disparaging gaze sweep over him. "I would scarcely lay claim to that, my lord."

Her cool words set his temper on edge. His gaze fell to the gold and pearl pendant draped around her neck. Before he could quell the urge, he picked up the delicate piece and cradled it in his hand.

Unbidden memories of the night they spent together rushed to the forefront of his mind—the unforgettable taste of her sweet, supple lips, her breathless sighs, the feel of silky thighs cradling his hips as he drove deep inside her and made her his. A rush of white hot desire coursed through his veins.

Despite his vow to resist what sweet temptation she offered, he found her more than slightly alluring this morning. A frown touched his lips. Devil take it. Under the circumstances, he had no reason to be drawn to her. But he was, with a vengeance.

Only last night, the woman had scorned his advances. Her blatant rejection should have put him off, but it hadn't. Quite the contrary. He wanted her with a fierce craving that startled him.

"It was good of you to take the trouble to retrieve it for me," she said softly.

He shrugged away her gratitude and dropped the pendant. "It was no trouble at all. After our meeting, I retraced my steps and happened upon the street urchin who stole it from you. It took little effort to persuade him to return it to my safekeeping."

"Nonetheless, I was deeply touched by your thoughtfulness."

"You need not be. Do not imagine any gallantry on my part," he remarked sharply, eager to dispel any romantic notion she might hold. "I assure you it was merely a twist of fate, nothing more."

She lowered her lashes. "I see," she murmured. "In that case, why did you not return it to me sooner? You might have given it to me that day in father's study. Why didn't you?"

His eyes swerved away from hers. "I . . . did not anticipate meeting you."

"But you came to ask for my hand. Surely you imagined we might meet."

He shrugged off her inquiry. "I did not give it much thought."

As she caressed the cherished pendant, a whimsical smile touched her lips. "And I had imagined you intended its return to be a wedding gift." She let the jeweled necklace slip through her fingers. "How foolish of me."

Wandering to the window, she kept her back to him for a long moment. Gathering her wits about her, she swiveled around to face him. Her chin was set with an air of confidence. "I am glad that small misunderstanding has been ironed out. I think it wise to settle our relationship from the outset so as to avoid any possible confusion in the future."

Her tone grated on his ears, in stark contrast to the affect her womanly shape was having on his pulse.

"I think it best to agree here and now," she said, "that you are free to seek your pleasures where you will, provided I am at liberty to do the same."

A look of blank astonishment crossed his face.

"Do not look so undone, my lord. No one need hear of our private arrangement."

His temper fueled by the need to purge himself of the tempting sight of his shapely wife garbed in a tightly revealing gown, he demanded gruffly, "What bloody *arrangement*?"

"Why, independent lives, of course. We shall both live fully and freely. Is that not agreeable to you?"

Frowning at her, he fell into a leather chair and propped his legs on top of the desk with a indelicate thud. With impatient fingers, he tugged at his neckcloth. "What twaddle is this?"

"It is no twaddle, my lord," she hastened to assure him. "After all"—she eyed him with disdain—"you plan to enjoy yourself in town, that much is patently obvious. It is no secret fashionable ladies admire you."

Despite her outrageous speech, she was having a highly desirable affect on him. Hell, he was seriously questioning his motives for leaving the country all those months ago.

He had to admit, as he let his eyes feast on her lovely figure charmingly revealed to its best light, there were a great many things about his new wife he had yet to discover. Take, for instance, the soft feminine rise and fall of her ample breasts enviably caressed by the tight frock. The neckline barely concealed the dusky nipples he'd lavished with his tongue on their wedding night. A tempting lock of soft blond hair draped across her neck.

He liked to watch her mouth. It was soft and full and supple—if memory served, the perfect size for him. He suddenly recalled the honeyed taste of her, the feel of her bare satin skin beneath his calloused hands. Why he had not plunged deep inside her tight, wet sheath and pleasured himself to the hilt instead of leaving for Boodles last night was an enigma, to be sure. After all, this marriage offered few amenities. Why not enjoy what attributes his luscious little wife had to offer? He was capable of seduction. If their wedding night was any indication, she would be easy to lure into his bed.

Oh, yes, he thought with a slow smile, he wished he'd taken her last night and again countless times before the dawn. He sighed at the heady thought. What he would not give to make his nightly fantasies a reality.

"And it goes without saying that any child I bear will, of course, be of your issue," she continued.

He sat bolt upright. "I beg your pardon? *What* did you say?"

"I would certainly never fob another man's child off as the Marlborough heir." Frowning, she shook her head at the very idea. "Heaven forbid."

The full impact of her outlandish speech took hold in his pounding brain. He looked at the infernal woman as though she were a candidate for bedlam. His piercing blue eyes narrowed to slits of ice. "You expect . . . you honestly believe," he blustered, his fury mounting with each word, "that I would . . . that I would allow you to," he shouted, clearly affronted by her proposition, "you actually imagine I will stand idly by whilst you—"

She arched a golden brow. "Engage in the very same liberties you yourself enjoy?" she supplied quite calmly. "Indeed, I do. It is only fair. Come now, admit it. You have no use for a wife. Why be stingy?"

His mouth tightened into a grim line of fury and he vaulted to his feet. In a blink of an eye, he crossed the distance between them. "Have you lost your wits entirely?" he demanded.

"On the contrary," came her blithe rejoinder. "I believe I have just found them. My recommendation is a sound solution to both our problems."

"I am disinclined to agree."

She offered him a dubious look. "Do come along, my lord. A clinging bride is rarely of any use to a man such as yourself. You must agree."

His only reply was a white-hot glare. The muscle in his jaw pulsed in painful cadence with the blood pounding in his head. He'd like nothing better than to throttle her. No, he wouldn't. He had something far more gratifying in mind.

"Conceive, if you will, of our married life together," she stated. "You having to avoid me, concealing your tête-à-têtes, while I contrive to meet gentlemen on the sly." She frowned and tsk-tsked. "Very dull indeed. Why not enjoy ourselves while we still can? Duty shall call us to the drab country existence before long, and you are not getting any younger. I certainly have no desire to rob you of your best years."

"Rob me of my best years?"

"For my part," she went on in a conversational tone, "I shall, of course, be the picture of propriety at all times. You need have no fear. I simply wish to take a lover." She shrugged her shoulders as lackadaisically as if they were chatting about the weather. "Is that such a crime? Surely"—she ran her fingertip along the books housed on the shelves—"you can have no objection to my having one measly man in my bed when you've had so many women. Only consider the alternative—acting the part of the dutiful, adoring husband, cleaving to your wife, and, in due course, producing the dreaded family heir." She heaved a weary sigh. "How utterly mundane. You cannot wish for such a dull life."

He gnashed his teeth. By God, the little tart was baiting him. "Most assuredly not," he said stiffly. "Considering the unpalatable alternative"—his tone was harsh—"I concede your point. There is no harm in what you suggest. It is only fair. Take a lover if you wish. I'll not stand in your way."

She paled slightly but quickly recovered her cheerful facade. "You see? Only last evening you were fretting over what should be done with me. And now think how agreeable my stay here shall be."

"Not entirely agreeable to my way of thinking," he ground out, his irritation showing. "But if it's a paramour you seek, you may have one. Now," he muttered, his manner brusque, "if our amicable little chat is at an end, I am in serious need of a hot bath and a shave." He strode across the carpet toward the double doors.

"There is one other rather inconsequential detail," she called out. "I hesitate to mention it, of course."

She did not sound a bit regretful. Heaving an annoyed sigh, he clenched his jaw and swung around to face her. "And what, pray," he said, his tone razor sharp, "might that be?"

Toying with her bell sleeve, she cocked her head to one side. "I fear I lack ... experience. I am ashamed to admit it to *you*." She smiled coyly. "But I am completely unschooled in the ways of attracting . . . well, men. And you, my lord, are accounted to be adept at amorous engagements. I thought perhaps you might condescend to assist me with my plight." she glanced at him from beneath dusky lashes.

"By George," he breathed, thoroughly enraged, "you go too far, madam."

She looked crestfallen. "Very well." She sighed. "I shall just have to muddle through somehow, seeking my lessons where I may."

Shutting his aching eyes, he swore under his breath and rubbed his hand across his tired eyes.

"You are not feeling at all the thing this morning, and here I am flinging demands at your poor aching head." She offered him a sympathetic moue. "I am a beastly wife, am I not?" she asked, running the palm of her hand across his hard, broad chest. "Still, I must confess, you are a puzzlement. Do you have no wish at all for a wife?"

He gave her a menacing look. "I should think it patently obvious, madam, that my inclination runs in a different direction entirely."

Her gaze locked with his. "Then pray," she countered, emotion lighting her sultry brown-green eyes, "why did you take one?"

"Surely," came his sarcastic reply, "even you must be aware. Every man comes to an age when he needs a wife, if for no other reason than to ensure the dreaded family heir."

Slipping from him, she turned away, but not before tears welled in her eyes.

"Then I warrant," she said quietly, "you must have been grieved indeed when your seed did not take root."

He stiffened at her barb. Lord, she was being difficult. He had a mind to pack her off to the country forthwith—except for those blasted tears and that delectably soft, enticing body. Devil take it. She was far too tantalizing than was seemly in a wife.

He shouldn't care a jot about her feelings. All the same, he realized with an irritated frown, he hated himself for making her distraught.

Once before he'd seen a woman despondent—his mother. She had seemed to cry all the time, always due to some hateful thing his father had said or done to her. As a boy, it had made him feel wretched inside. Helpless. All twisted up in painful knots. He did not like being reminded of those occasions. Nor did he warm to the notion of having to contend with his wife's hurt feelings.

"Forgive me," he apologized hoarsely. "I did not mean to overset you."

Dabbing at the corner of her eyes, she whirled about to face him and pinned a bright smile on her face. "Oh, my lord, I could never hold *you* responsible for *my* feelings. After all, I am merely your lowly bride. You can owe me nothing at all. What I do find most vexing, however," she remarked, resuming her chipper tone, "is your hesitation to assist me in my quest for a diverting companion. I should think a man who has little use for a bride save for the proliferation of his family name would be only too glad to be rid of my unwanted presence."

Any sympathy he might have felt for the little hellion vanished instantly. How he could have imagined she was like his mother was beyond him. *His wife* was anything but frail. His jaw clenched hard. "If you desire a lover, take one," he flung at her. "I've said I'll not stand in your way."

She smiled mirthlessly. "That is very magnanimous of you, my lord. But your permission is not the only license I require. Alas"—she gave a cheerless sigh—"I shall simply have to look elsewhere for a more willing tutor."

"You little witch," he breathed, furious. His burning gaze bore into her, and he toyed with the highly gratifying notion of smothering her pert lips with his own, peeling that enticing gown from her luscious little body, and having his way with her on the library floor.

"On second thought," he told her, his tone sharp, "I shall be only too pleased to instruct you. You seem to have adopted the conniving ways of your sex. Indeed"—his searing gaze swept over her—"courtesan blood must flow through your veins. You play the part of temptress to perfection, my sweet."

Taken aback by his response, she demurred softly, "Why . . . thank you, my lord. You are kindness itself."

He fixed her with a look of blazing. "Think nothing of it." Turning on his heel, he crossed the room in long angry strides. Yanking open the paneled doors, he glanced over his shoulder. "I gather, from your eager countenance," he said nastily, "you are a quick learner. We shall commence your instruction forthwith."

Too stunned to move, Olivia could do no more than stare at her husband's proud back as he stormed from the room. The slam of the door jolted her from her perplexed state. She sank into the large burgundy leather chair that faced her husband's desk, quaking from head to toe, and with good reason. Fighting fire with fire had gotten her into a spot of trouble.

Good Lord. She clutched her forehead between her thumb and forefinger. What was she to do now?

She had no intention of *taking* a lover. She never dreamed he'd allow her such shocking freedom, nor did she wish it. It was a ruse to provoke him—and he was more than a trifle provoked, she admitted, blowing the air out of her cheeks.

Her brow furrowed. What sort of an uncaring cad had she married? He was supposed to refuse her such shocking liberties, not volunteer instructions. Any decent man would have read her the riot act for suggesting anything as outrageous as taking another man to her bed. What in heaven's name was she going to do now?

His parting words rang in her ears. *We shall commence your instruction forthwith.* Chewing nervously on her lower lip, she wondered what he meant by that remark.

Brandon stormed up the winding front staircase, uttering every colorful expletive he knew. If he could ring her slender lily white neck, he would. Gladly. Heedless of his aching head and parched mouth, he barreled down the hall to his bedroom. *Their* bedroom. Ripping off his cravat and frock coat, he tossed them on the floor and bellowed for Saunders. Slumping down on the side of the bed—*his* bed, where that temptress had slept—he tugged off his leather boots and threw them aside.

"Bloody hell," he growled under his breath. He'd never felt this much pent-up energy in his life. "Damned woman," he muttered irritably, "could drive a man insane without half trying." And he had a sneaking suspicion she was trying. Hard.

Angrily, he tore off his white linen shirt and rolled

it into a ball, then threw it across the room. She was far too tantalizing to have at his fingertips.

He got to his feet and tugged off his trousers. Blast it all. He dragged his thick velvet robe around his body. Scratching the thick white scar that traversed his chest, he sank down on the bed and scowled. He simply had to come to terms with the fact that his wife was a confoundedly attractive woman who, at the moment, resided in his home.

Take a lover indeed. The impudent wench astounded him.

But he knew her gambit. He had no choice but to accede to her outrageous request. If he didn't, he would be forced to express his burning desire to have her and no other.

He would not be backed into a corner so easily. Oh, no. He would never allow her that sort of power over him. It was bad enough to have suffered her wily father's manipulations. Brandon would not be controlled by his wife, regardless of how damnably attractive she was.

Saunders emerged from the connecting room and shuffled across the floor.

"Your bath is drawn and hot, my lord. Shall I bring your tisane now?" the old curmudgeon inquired with customary dryness.

Brandon gave him a dark, reproachful glare. "No," he bit out, getting swiftly to his feet, "You need not."

Nodding his agreement, the aged valet proceeded to collect his master's belongings from the floor.

"Just as you say, my lord," he replied. "It is so delightful to have a lady about the house, is it not? I cannot tell you how long it's been since we've seen the likes of her 'round the place. Forgive me for saying so my lord, but you are indeed a very fortunate man."

Brandon gave him a murderous glare. If he did not know better, he'd suspect his designing little spouse had bribed his once loyal household staff. One day in *his* house with her soft, feminine wiles and she had finagled her way into everyone's good graces. Except his, of course. He was vacillating between the unbecoming urge to spank her very nicely rounded bottom and a purely male instinct to take her to bed for the next month.

The following afternoon, Olivia took tea with her aunt in the sitting room. The decor served to improve her mood, with its richly appointed draperies, cheerful wallpaper, and coordinating striped upholsteries. She tried to avert her gaze from the gold-framed portrait of an endearing youth who bore a strong resemblance to her husband. The rakehell seemed determined to live up to his wild reputation. At present, Olivia could do no more than accept his ways.

"Shall I serve, or would you like to?" Aunt Edwina inquired, dropping heavily into the chair that flanked the delicate sofa.

Sighing, Olivia said, "I think it best if I undertake the service. Your hands shake a trifle."

"Last time," Edwina admitted, giggling, "I nearly scorched poor Gilbert."

Olivia shot her aunt a quelling look. "I do not wish to be reminded of father," she said, handing her a porcelain cup brimming with milky tea.

"Oh. Of course not, dear," she agreed, falling silent.

Sitting back on the couch, Olivia took a leisurely

sip of tea. Her thoughts drifted to the tall, handsome stranger who was her husband. She did not expect to see her recalcitrant spouse for the remainder of the day. No doubt he was vexed because she'd out-witted him. That would be ironic, considering it was she who was outwitted in the end. Her fretful ponder-ing was interrupted by the appearance of Prudence, the downstairs maid.

"A note arrived for you early this morning, my lady," she said, nervously bobbing a curtsy. "It was from a messenger boy. I was given strict instructions to deliver it to you and none other."

Retrieving the note from the tray, Olivia shot Edwina an exaggerated frown. Examining the note, she saw that the single sheet of paper bore no seal.

"Is it from Gilbert?" Edwina wanted to know, clearly hopeful that the breech between father and daughter would soon be mended.

Olivia shook her head. "No, it is not from Father."

"Then who?" her aunt pressed.

Olivia shrugged and tore open the mysterious mis-sive. "Perhaps," she teased, "I have acquired a secret admirer." As her eyes traveled the page, the smile slid from her face. The words scrawled boldly in black ink shook her.

You might have been reasonable, treated me with the decency I deserve, but no, you had to act the part of a lady. Ain't that a laugh? I wager you'll be surprised to learn your mother was nothing but a whore.

Old Clive here is willing to overlook your initial hastiness, provided you come good with the blunt. Your father, the wily old fox, took great pains to protect your dirty little secret. While I was in his employ, I happened to come across a love letter. It was hidden in a secret compartment of your late mother's desk.

Needless to say, your father was none too happy to learn of it. Can't say as I blame him, seeing as how the letter states quite plainly that you are the bastard child of the Duke of Kent.

I've a feeling you'll pay handsomely for my silence. After all, we wouldn't want his lordship to get wind of this unhappy truth, now would we? Might prove a trifle embarrassing for all concerned.

Meet me at Madame Tussaud's tomorrow afternoon, four o'clock sharp. If you are thinking of refusing my very generous offer, do not. I want what is coming to me. One way or the other, I intend to get it.

Staring at the note, her hand shaking, Olivia tried to digest the shocking contents.

"What is it, dear?" Edwina inquired. "I declare, you have gone ghostly white."

"What?" Olivia murmured.

"You look a fright. What is it?"

"Nothing of consequence." Olivia quickly folded the note to conceal its contents. "It was a surprise, that is all."

Satisfied with her niece's explanation, Aunt Edwina sat back to enjoy a slice of lemon cake. "I must say, his lordship's cook is delightful," she chattered happily. "We shall not suffer from want of delicious cakes, that is for certain."

As her aunt expounded upon the many delights of town living, Olivia grappled with her dilemma. What was she to do? Winterbottom was lying. He had to be. It couldn't be true. She did not even know the Duke of Kent. She was tempted to toss the contemptible letter in the fire and forget about the disgusting little man's threat entirely.

But what if he makes good on his threat? a nagging voice asked. He could have no evidence, but it would not do to have such accusations circulating around the Earl of Marlborough's new bride. She had enough problems on her hands without fueling Brandon's desire to be rid of his wifely nuisance.

Her odious blackmailer was right. Her tenuous marriage, if one could call it that, would never survive should the ghastly rumor come to light. Such a sensation would disgrace her husband's good name, not to mention what it would do to her own reputation.

She could not shake a nagging uneasiness. It could not be true. Could it?

Lifting her precious lavaliere, she turned the piece over.

To my beloved A.P. from F.K.

Amelia was her mother's name.

"Who is F.K.?" Olivia asked, interrupting her aunt's idle prattle.

Taken aback by the question, Edwina blinked at her niece in some surprise. "I am sure I do not know, dear. You must remember, your father purchased that piece for your mother at an estate auction. It might have belonged to anyone."

A pensive frown crossed Olivia's face. She'd heard her aunt regale her with that same story countless times, but now, she was not sure what to believe. Could F.K. be the Duke of Kent?

No. It was too fantastic. It simply was not possible. She knew who her father was. Winterbottom was merely fishing for money with his vile insinuations. Horrid man. He would doubtless say anything to draw her in.

Dismissing the vicious accusation as pure rubbish, Olivia put the entire matter from her mind.

"As the hour is fast approaching five," Edwina remarked with a mischievous gleam in her eyes, "I thought we might take a turn about Green Park or perhaps take a ride in his lordship's stylish phaeton."

A smile softened Olivia's pensive features. If Brandon was presently annoyed with her outrageous request for equal footing in their marriage, an unorthodox romp through the park in his coveted phaeton would doubtless send him over the edge.

"I daresay that would be ill-advised, but I am certain a carriage ride could be arranged, if you fancy one."

"Well, we might consider the phaeton," Aunt Edwina pressed, put out by Olivia's refusal. "After all, if it is good enough for his lordship's mistress, I daresay it is suitable for his wife and her aunt."

Olivia slammed her cup and saucer down on the silver tray. He'd taken that harlot out in his phaeton? Loathsome, egotistical beast.

"Well, I mean to say," Edwina sputtered, "if he can take that tart out, why shouldn't we have a go?"

Despite her distress over Winterbottom's attempt at extortion, Olivia had to quell the urge to laugh. "Quite right," she concurred, dismissing Winterbottom's letter. "Shall we take a stroll with our parasols, then, despite the absence of my lady's maid?" She arched her brow mischievously. "Or will we cause scandal, do you suppose?"

Her aunt clasped her hands together. "Oh, I do hope so, my dear!" she exclaimed, giddy as a schoolgirl.

Chapter 8

Poor Ned was scandalized by the prospect of the lady of the house handling the phaeton on her own.

"I dunno if 'is lordship would be pleased," he stalled, rubbing his scruffy chin with his fingers.

Olivia waved her hand in the air, dismissing his concern. "I can assure you, Ned, I am entirely capable of handling it on my own."

Ned did not look persuaded. "Beggin' yer pardon, my lady, but his lordship is mighty particular 'bout his phaeton."

"His lordship is indisposed at present. Far be it from me to disturb him with such a frivolous request." So saying, she stepped into the sleek black phaeton and grabbed the reins. Aunt Edwina required a bit more assistance. Approaching her from behind, Ned gave her a ungentlemanly shove.

"Ooof!" she exclaimed, toppling into the black leather seat. Struggling to set her roly-poly figure to rights, she dislodged her straw hat. Olivia caught it and placed it squarely on her aunt's mound of gray curls.

Clicking her tongue at the horses, Olivia snapped the reins.

"There," Edwina remarked after catching her breath, "this is nice."

"Mmmm." Olivia slanted her aunt a conspiratorial smile. "I am ever so glad you thought of it."

As the black horse meandered from Park Lane to Green Park, Olivia felt a sense of independence.

"Shall we ride about the park for a time?" she asked cheerfully.

"Delighted," her aunt concurred.

They had not gone more than a few yards when Olivia caught sight of a shabby cap, tattered plaid coat, and worn trousers that could belong to only one person. A quake of fear swept over her. Leaning one shoulder against an enormous tree, he removed a piece of grass from between his teeth and offered her a broad, knowing grin.

Sickened by the sight of him, she turned away.

Coils of dread closed around her heart. Had he followed her here? Good Lord, he must have. A shiver of dread ran down her spine. Was he watching her? Trailing her?

Apprehension bore down on her like a suffocating weight. Were his threats as dangerous as that? She had put the vicious letter from her mind, thinking it no more than a desperate ruse to garner money, but clearly her encounter with the foul man was not a coincidence. He would not be as easily put off as she initially thought.

She darted another glance in his direction. He was propped up against the tree, a hateful smirk on his face. Reaching out, he rubbed his grimy fingers together in a not so subtle suggestion for money.

"Aunt," Olivia blurted, "I grow weary of the park. Might we try it another day when I am feeling more energetic?"

Edwina looked surprised. "Certainly, my dear." Her eyes narrowed behind her spectacles. "Are you quite sure you are well?"

Olivia pasted a smile on her pale, drawn face. "Perfectly well." Turning off, she brought the conveyance to a standstill. "Wait for me in the phaeton. I won't be a moment."

"Here? In the middle of the park? But why?" Edwina sputtered.

"Please, Aunt, do as I ask," Olivia snapped.

Edwina paled slightly. "Very well," she murmured, disturbed by Olivia's gruff manner. "But do hurry, I shouldn't like to be on my own overlong."

Olivia gave her aunt a spontaneous hug and hopped down from the phaeton. When her aunt was no longer in sight, Olivia hurried down the path toward her odious blackmailer. Glancing over her shoulder to be certain Edwina couldn't see her, she gathered her skirts and quickened her gate to join Winterbottom. He slipped behind the large elm, where he could be certain their sordid meeting would be concealed.

"Well now, isn't this a right nice surprise? Got me note?" he asked, leaning his back against the broad tree trunk.

Her lips compressed. "Indeed," she uttered coolly.

He leaned toward her. His proximity set her on edge. "How 'bout some blunt then, eh?" he asked, his eyes dancing greedily. "A little taste of things to come."

Her heart galloped in her chest, but she refused to let her uneasiness show. "What makes you think I'll pay you a farthing?" she asked him sharply. "It is all lies, every word of it."

He cocked his brow. "Y'think so, eh?"

"I know so. My father will confirm the truth."

"Oh, aye. He knows the truth, all right. But he won't tell you none of it. Mark my words, you'll never get the truth from the likes o' 'im. He's a good one at keepin' secrets."

"Thus far, you have done nothing but issue idle threats. You have no proof. I've yet to see any evidence this damning letter actually exists. How do I know you truly have it in your possession?"

"Oh, I've got it, all right." He gave her a calculating look. "Don't believe me, huh?"

"No, nor do I intend to pay you anything until I see it for myself and am satisfied it is authentic."

"Well," he drawled, rubbing his stubbled chin, "that's too bad now, ain't it? Coz I haven't got it on me person just now."

"Then I advise you to stop pestering me, or I shall be forced to go to the authorities. Blackmail is a crime, Mr. Winterbottom."

"Is that a fact?" he chuckled nastily. "I don't know much 'bout the law, but I can imagine what his lordship will say when your mother's damning letter arrives tomorrow with the morning paper at Park Lane. Is that a risk you're prepared to take?"

Her lips thinned. "I see your point," she said tightly, her cheeks burning with indignation.

"Thought you might. Now how's about it?"

"I don't carry money on my person."

His beady eyes danced with avaricious pleasure. "A rich *lady* like you?" He cocked his brow dubiously.

"I wager you can get whatever you like from that husband o' yours. Why," he leered, eyeing her with lascivious pleasure, "I'd pay a king's ransom for the likes of you in my bed."

Revolted, she lifted her skirts and hurried across the green as his hateful laughter rang in her ears. Cursed man.

A terrible thought occurred to her, and she stopped short. What if, despite her efforts to thwart him, he sent the letter to Brandon anyway? Her heart thudded in her chest.

He wouldn't. Money was what he was after. Even the rapacious Winterbottom knew better than to show his hand at this juncture. She had time to discern what, if anything, was to be done.

The vile man was right on one point: She could not possibly approach her father. He was devoted to her mother's memory. Even the hint of such a suggestion would overset him. He would be heartbroken to imagine his daughter would ever entertain such vicious slander. And yet what choice did she have but to consider Winterbottom's calumny as potentially damning? The ramifications were too distressing to contemplate.

Olivia would simply have to handle the situation on her own. How, she was not at all sure, but she must rid herself of the unwanted pest and soon.

The tension of the moment brought tears to her eyes, but she brushed them away and swallowed the rest back. She paused for a moment against an elm tree to regain her composure. Drawing a deep, calming breath, she managed to collect herself and walked slowly to meet her aunt.

Edwina was fretting. "What kept you?" she asked

in a fit of nerves. "I was concerned when you did not follow directly."

"You need not have been. I thought I saw someone I knew, that's all." She climbed into the phaeton hastily.

Gathering the reins, she snapped the leather against the horse's rump. A handsome gentleman tipped his beaver hat as the phaeton exited the park.

Edwina giggled and nudged her niece in the ribs. "What a sly one you are," she teased, winking. "Thought you saw someone you knew, indeed. Sneaking off to meet your paramour. Cheeky vixen. But don't worry," she whispered, "I won't breathe a word to his lordship."

Olivia glanced at her aunt in momentary confusion. "Oh . . . yes," she stuttered, a bit awkwardly. "How clever you are to have found me out."

The news of Lady Wilde's arrival in London spread like wildfire. She was surprised anyone should bother to take notice, but take notice they did. Invitations flooded the Park Lane mansion. Olivia secretly hoped to use the myriad social requests to finagle time alone in her husband's company, but such was not the case.

Shortly after lunch, she found him secluded in the library, slumped in a leather chair, his booted feet stretched on the ottoman before him. Dressed in a white linen shirt that hung open at the neck and black trousers, he did not look at all the thing. She suspected his green complexion was the result of imbibing far too heavily the night before. Resolving to make her interview as brief as possible, she folded her hands at her waist and cleared her throat.

He glanced over his shoulder. Startled by her arrival in what was his daytime retreat, he blinked at her.

"I beg your pardon, my lord, but I wished a word."

His gaze drifted over her, taking in her appearance with unnerving slowness. The hunger in his eyes was the one thing that bolstered her confidence. There could be no denying it. He found her looks pleasing, and she could build on that if she was wise.

Frowning, he dragged his eyes away from her and sat back. "Yes, what is it?" he snapped.

"We have received several invitations. Not knowing your preference for such matters, I thought it best to inquire."

"I do not wish to attend," he practically barked at her.

"Very well," she countered, her voice quiet but steel edged. "You have no objection to my going without you, I trust?"

He whipped his head around to stare at her.

"After all, I have my own interests to consider. You can hardly be so selfish as to deny me the opportunity to further my introductions."

His lips thinned. "No, of course not," he said. "Do as you like. It is of little consequence to me."

She offered him a chilling smile and inclined her blond head in agreement. "Just so." She turned to take her leave, but hesitated at the threshold. "Shall I tell Carrington to fetch you another drink?" she inquired flippantly. "You look as though you need one."

The glare he gave her would have made a lesser woman weep. "No," he bit out. "I will see to my own needs."

"As you wish," she replied, and quit the room.

Undaunted by his attitude, she marched up the

front stairs muttering under her breath about her desire to give him a lesson in manners, took her seat at the escritoire in her bedroom, and summarily penned her acceptance to every summons she had received.

Who knew? By attending every ball in town, she might unearth some amorous prospects of her own. Brandon had the hateful Lady Chesney. Olivia could just as easily procure a Lord Someone. Verily, it would serve her callous husband right. He obviously held no respect for their marriage vows. Why shouldn't she bend them a tad?

Stage one of her scheme to entice her wayward spouse was under way. He would not ignore her now, not when she had men clamoring at her heels—at least she hoped he wouldn't. Her brow puckered slightly. Oh dear. She hoped she would have men clamoring after her, else she would be very embarrassed indeed.

One week later, the first of Olivia's many boring social events drew uneventfully to a close. Given the lateness of the hour, she chose to take pity on her maid and decided against summoning Jenny.

"Be a dear and help me with my buttons and stays, will you Aunt?"

"Of course, my dear," Edwina readily agreed.

Minutes later, Olivia bid her aunt good night and moved down the darkened hallway, lamp in hand, toward her bedroom. Easing open the door, she noted that the fire was blazing cheerfully in the grate, but the gaslight had been turned down. Expelling a tired sigh, she set the lamp on her dressing table.

Her deft fingers made short work of the last of the

tiny buttons trailing down the back of her pink satin gown. Letting the garment slide over her arms to the floor, she untied her crinoline and stepped free. Sinking into the chair before the mirror, she tugged at the pins holding her hair and shrugged her blond mane loose until it fell loosely down her back.

Sleepily rising from the chair, she unlaced her restrictive corset and with a relieved sigh cast it aside. Arching her spine, she pressed her palms to the middle of her back stretched like a cat. She was just about to untie her shift when something crystal clinked behind her. She gasped in surprise and whirled about to face the shadowy figure of a man lounging in the chair beside the fire. It was Brandon. Even in the dimly lit room, she could feel the weight of his stare.

She made a vain effort to shield herself from his probing gaze. "What are you doing here?"

"Watching you," came his velvety retort. "Go on with your performance. I was enjoying it."

Her performance, as he put it, must have appeared unintentionally erotic. Color scalded her cheeks at the thought of his watching her innocently undress.

"You should have made your presence known," she said, trying to salvage her pride—difficult, given that she was standing in a sheer cotton chemise before the firelight.

"I just did." He got deftly to his feet. Brandy glass in hand, he slowly closed the distance between them. She could almost feel the heat of him. "But don't let me stop you." The smile he gave her was purely sinful. "Go on with what you were doing."

She quelled the childish urge to scamper away from him and forced herself to stand her ground. She had passed a miserable evening fending off one wolf after the next, all of which would have been worthwhile in her campaign to provoke him had he deigned to give her escort.

"Was there something you wanted?" she asked pointedly, disappointment making her bold. "You are not in the habit of visiting my bedchamber in the middle of the night."

He chuckled softly and took a swallow of liquor. "You ask rather provocative questions," he murmured over the rim of his glass.

Her eyes flickered with inner fire. "To which you offer nothing but vague replies."

He shrugged. "Perhaps I was wondering about your evening among polite society. It is nearly three o'clock. What kept you?"

"Given your wicked tendencies," she countered, "I find it difficult to believe you are concerned about my whereabouts after midnight."

"Was it a man?" he asked pointedly. "Is that what detained you?"

She stared at him for a moment, assessing his inquiry. "Naturally. What else?" she remarked sassily.

The pulse in his jaw leaped. "Who?"

"Does there have to be just one?" she taunted.

His eyes narrowed into slits. "What were their names?" he asked through clenched teeth.

"Let me see," she drawled, tapping her chin with her forefinger. "Lord Driscoll indicated a penchant for me."

"Indeed. And in what manner, pray," he bit out, "was his fondness expressed?"

She gave him a flirtatious giggle. "The usual way."

Brandon slammed his glass on the mantel and came to her. He caught her by the shoulders and whirled her about to face him. "Did he touch you?"

Her chin came up a notch. "Why shouldn't he?" came her silk reply.

He swore under his breath and yanked her to him. "He kissed you," he accused, his fingers digging into her upper arms like talons.

"What if he did? What could possibly be wrong in that?" She raised one golden brow. "Surely you can have no objections?"

His breath was hot and moist against her cheek. It smelled of brandy mixed with a faint aroma of tobacco. "You're my wife," he said angrily.

"So I am," she agreed, forcing herself to remain calm. "Are you saying you want to renegotiate the terms of our agreement? Do you want a wife after all, my lord?"

"No, damn you," he growled, covering her mouth with his own. His arms closed around her like bands of steel, crushing her to him in a kiss that was a purely elemental display of ownership.

But it shook her right down to her toes. Her world reeled. Her hands clutched his shoulders. His kiss was born of jealous anger and not deep-seated feelings, but she could not seem to break the erotic spell.

His open mouth slanted over hers with bruising intensity, his tongue stroking hers with savage need. His hands spread across her back, scalding her with his heat, branding her with his passion. Palming her breasts, he caressed her nipples until they peaked against him. He uttered a throaty groan of desire. His hot, wet, open mouth slid down her neck, and then his fingers slipped the flimsy chemise off her shoulder and his mouth covered her bare skin.

"You taste so damned good," he rasped against her neck. His hand smoothed over the column of her neck and he raised his head to capture her mouth once more.

Coming to her senses, she shoved away from him. "You're drunk," she spat.

"You think so?"

Breathless and weak from his passionate onslaught, she clasped the bedpost at her back for support. Whether he was or he wasn't, she could not risk spending the night with him. Not again.

"If you want a woman in your bed, I suggest you look elsewhere. I am sure Lady Chesney will be only too happy to oblige."

"I thought you wanted to learn how to please a man."

"I've had enough pawing for one night."

His heated gaze took in the rapid rise and fall of her chest. He reached out and traced the hard contours of her nipple straining against the thin fabric of her shift. "You're not as unaffected as you claim."

She swatted his hand away. "And you're more foxed than you think."

He laughed at that. Catching her around the waist, he drew her close. She gasped her surprise. "On the contrary, my sweet, there isn't enough brandy in all London to make me stop wanting you," he murmured against her lips.

Startled, her wide eyes searched his hooded gaze, trying to fathom his intentions. He pressed a hard kiss to her lips and let her go.

Before she had time to recover, he was gone. He disappeared into the adjoining room like a sensual phantom of the night, leaving her bereft and confused and quivering all over.

* * *

The next morning, following a meager breakfast, Olivia's thoughts were engrossed as to how she and Brandon might come to reconcile their differences when Carrington presented her with a silver tray. A twinge of apprehension crept up her spine. She slipped the note from the tray.

Thankfully, she noticed it looked like an invitation, not another blackmail threat. Running her finger over the expensive ivory parchment, she examined the missive. It was from Lord and Lady Pratt, whoever they were.

"The footman requested his lordship's immediate reply," the aged butler explained, "but as he is presently indisposed, I thought you might be able to issue a response, my lady."

"Yes, of course." Wrenching herself from her preoccupation with her husband's motivations last night, she tore open the wax seal. Her eyes drifted over the embossed invitation. It was to an intimate dinner party next week. She was about to issue her refusal when a thought occurred to her.

If she held the slightest hope that she might countermand Brandon's wicked liaisons, she must force him to appear with her socially. Of course, she sincerely doubted Lady Chesney was the sort to be put off by a clinging young bride, but it was worth a try. She could not sit idly by whilst that horrid trollop paraded around London with *her* husband.

Besides, if last night's torrid encounter was any indication, he was inclined to be jealous. What better way to show the world—and her saturnine husband— she was a woman of substance and independence than to arrive at a dinner party with him and bestow her attention on all the other men in the room?

She must evoke some emotion from him. If memory served, however, emotion was not his defect. Indeed, he had displayed passion well beyond her maidenly expectations at every turn. The memory of their past sensual liaisons gave her hope for a possible future. After all, could a man respond to a woman with such fire and lack feelings?

"Thank you, Carrington. We shall be pleased to accept. Shall I pen my acceptance while you wait?" Floundering, she glanced about her for some embossed writing paper. She had no idea where Brandon kept the family seal.

Apparently sensing her quandary, Carrington said, "Lord Pratt is an old friend of his lordship's. I sincerely doubt he would require such formalities. I shall merely instruct his footman to expect two for dinner. Would that be satisfactory, my lady?"

Olivia smiled sweetly, warming to her scheme. She had never been capable of artifice before. It was a heady feeling to realize that *she,* a woman who only recently was of very little consequence, could be powerful. She was beginning to like it. "Yes. Thank you, Carrington."

"Shall I inform his lordship you have accepted the invitation?"

Olivia hesitated for a moment. "Er, no. I shall speak to him directly."

"Very good, my lady," Carrington replied, bowing dutifully.

So pleased was she with her machinations that she practically flew up the stairs. Rapping her knuckles against the heavy mahogany door, she awaited his reply.

"Come," his deep, authoritative voice commanded.

Her hand clasped the brass door handle. A tingle of excitement ran down her spine. She opened the door.

Garbed only in a navy paisley silk robe that hung open at the chest, her virile husband stood before her, toweling his thick wet hair dry. She had not anticipated confronting his potent masculinity quite so soon. Vivid recollections of his hard, sinewed chest assailed her. She hesitated in the doorway.

Brandon caught sight of her, and his lips turned down. "That will be all, Saunders."

At Brandon's curt dismissal, the aged valet shuffled his way into the adjoining room and closed the door.

Brandon tossed his towel aside. "Was there something you wanted?" he asked curtly. "Or have you suddenly developed a penchant for watching men dress, along with your latest quirk to garner a lover?"

His sarcasm irked her. "Not at all," she countered coolly. "I merely wished a word. But it can wait." She turned to take her leave.

"Nonsense." He caught her arm. "After all, we are man and wife. Certainly after last night you can have no objections to seeing me in the buff. After all, this will shortly become a common occurrence for you. Acting the part of a blushing innocent will not do," he mocked. "If you plan to acquire a lover worth his salt, you must learn to accept being familiar with a man."

"It is not that," she hastened to explain, despising herself for blushing.

"Then what?"

"I had supposed," she said stiffly, "you desired your privacy. I did not wish to intrude."

A low chuckle rumbled in his well-muscled chest.

"It pleases me to know you consider my desires," he murmured, his voice husky.

She knew he was toying with her, but she could not halt the rapid swell of her chest. His hands slipped over her arms, inching her closer to his provocative masculinity. She could not bring herself to move. The smile he offered her was purely wicked. But, she admitted without an ounce of shame, she liked playing with fire.

"If I were striving to win your affections," he said softly, his tone positively sinful, "I would be deeply gratified by your appearance."

"Would you?"

"Indeed, I would. Perhaps even moved to possess you," he assured her, his hands gently caressing her arms, lulling her into erotic compliance.

His gentle massage sent ripples of pleasure through her.

"How, pray, would such a circumstance come about?" she asked, breathless from the heat of his gaze and the heady sensation of being near him.

Placing his large hands around her waist, he eased her against him and gazed deeply into her jade eyes. "To begin with," he instructed, bending his mouth perilously close to hers, "I might steal a kiss from your sweet lips and press you near to my heart." His voice was deep and husky and warm against her lips.

She quivered. "Might you?"

"Mmm," he purred low in his throat. "If I thought the overture would be well received."

Lifting her eager, parted lips, she asked, "How would I assure you of my eagerness to comply?"

"You might look at me as you are doing now."

She raised her lashes and gazed into his deep blue eyes. "And how is that?"

His hand cupped the side of her face. "Like temptation in the flesh," he whispered in a velvety voice. The pad of his thumb stroked her softly parted lips. "Would you be warm and willing in my arms, my alluring little beauty?"

Her limpid gaze met his smoldering blue. "I would be all those things and more," she told him in a bare whisper, "provided you expressed the need to make me yours."

A slow, seductive smile crept over his sardonic features. He cocked one ebony brow mischievously. "And if I were to make such an overture? How would you reciprocate?" he asked, pressing featherlight kisses at the side of her mouth, her cheek, the tip of her nose, and her eyelids.

Her eyelashes fluttered shut, and she drew a deep, steadying breath. "I . . . would give myself freely to you, bestowing only the warmest of kisses in return for your generous passion."

"Show me how willing you would be," he urged breathlessly against her lips. "I want to feel your lips on mine—soft, warm, and open. Kiss me, Olivia. I cannot wait to taste you."

At the sound of his voice, deep and rough with desire, currents of longing washed over her. Standing on tiptoe, she touched her lips to his. Her kiss was tentative, soft, achingly gentle at first. But when his arms encircled her and brought her hard against him, she whimpered her surrender.

His open mouth slanted over hers with unbridled hunger. She sighed and met the erotic thrusts of his tongue with her own. His lips moved over hers, tasting her fully, lavishing her honeyed mouth with the heat of his own. He groaned, devouring her sweetness like a starving man.

She should have been shocked by her eagerness to revel in his wickedly intimate kisses. The feel of his large masterful hands claiming her body, even as he claimed her lips, thrilled her like nothing she'd ever known. All she could feel, all she could think of was him, and all she wanted was more—more of his burning kisses, more of his tantalizing caresses—regardless of the consequences.

His arm slipped beneath her knees. He lifted her into his arms and carried her to the large canopied bed. Winding her arms around his neck, she issued no objection to being swept off her feet. She felt the velvet coverlet beneath her. The weight of his sinewed body bore down on her, and she reveled in the heady moment. His hands slid over her aching breasts to caress the soft mounds concealed by silken fabric. Her nipples peaked beneath his roving touch.

He raised his mouth from hers, and she released a blissful sigh. Floating on a sensual cloud of joy, she touched her fingertips to his cheek and ran her fingers lightly over his full sensual mouth, wet from the heat of her kiss. His smoldering gaze held her captive. She'd never seen his beautiful eyes look bluer. And, she acknowledged with a modicum of fear, she'd never wanted him to love her more.

But that was not to be—at least not yet. She could not go through with this without some emotional assurances from him that were clearly not forthcoming.

Swallowing aloud, she whispered, her breathing ragged, "I thank you for my lesson, my lord. It was quite . . . riveting."

He stiffened, and the hard lines around his mouth tensed. A flicker of anger swept over his face. "If not enormously diverting," he said cruelly, pulling away from her.

She flinched.

Sitting up, she smoothed her shaky hands over her mussed hair and swallowed back the painful lump in her throat.

"Faith, my lord, you are a wonder," she cried, adopting a playful, flirtatious manner to conceal the depth of her emotions. "After spending the night with your mistress, you are interested in *my* meager concerns. I should count myself fortunate indeed."

His jaw flexed. "I was not with my mistress last night, as you well know," he reminded her, his manner gruff.

The realization that he had not gone into Lady Chesney's arms made Olivia nearly giddy. All was not lost. She still had a chance to win his affections, provided she could arouse his interest. At the moment, he seemed more inclined to fits of rage and mindless desire than undying love. But perhaps passion was a start.

Stripping off his robe, he snatched his gray trousers off the nearby velvet chair. She had to squelch a cry of shock. Averting her gaze from the fetching sight of his bare backside, she slipped from the bed and wandered to the casement window.

"We received an invitation to dine with Lord and Lady Pratt next week," she said. "I took the liberty of accepting."

He let out a long, audible breath. "You did *what*?"

Donning her most innocent expression, she whirled about to face her irate husband. "I thought it the appropriate thing to do. I hope I haven't disappointed you."

His face darkened. He shoved his white linen shirt-tail inside his trousers. "It is not in the least appropriate," he countered sharply.

"If I have made a mistake," she said, "I apologize most sincerely. Have you perchance made other arrangements?"

"Perchance."

She offered him a look of mock concern. "How very awkward for you. Well, it should not be too difficult to send your regrets. I am sure the lady in question will be understanding when she learns you are fulfilling your tedious husbandly duties. After all, Lord Pratt's dinner party will be the perfect venue for me to pursue a suitable collection of eligible males, would you not agree?"

He looked ready to commit murder. "I sincerely doubt Jeremy or his wife would understand your need for, shall we say, male diversions."

"Anymore than your need for frivolous females and excessive drink?" she asked him archly.

The glare he gave her would have made most women cringe. "Jeremy is a gentleman." Brandon looked away from her. "He would never agree to such an arrangement with his wife."

"Whereas you are a rogue," she countered saucily.

He sent her a ferocious look over his shoulder. "And you are a coquette."

She shrugged. "What an unusual friendship you two must share." She adeptly changed the subject. "I simply cannot wait to make his acquaintance. And I am persuaded his wife must be charm itself."

"Christine is a kind, loving woman," Brandon remarked. "Jeremy has no cause for complaint."

She gasped. "Can you possibly be suggesting *I* am not everything your wife should be?"

He expelled a tired sigh. "I expect we both are disappointments to one another."

His words cut her to the quick. Bowing her head, she fought back the prick of tears. "I daresay," she said softly, making her way to the door, "you are correct."

She slipped silently from the room and closed the door.

"Wicked seductress," Brandon spat under his breath when she'd gone. Uncorking the brandy decanter, he helped himself to a stiff drink and downed it in one gulp. It bothered him no end that he found the enticing little vixen infinitely more appealing than any other woman. The gorgeous hussy was bloody difficult to resist.

His hand fisted around the crystal glass. The simple, unalterable fact was the chit was luscious to look at and even more delectable to bed. Pushing that tempting thought from his mind, he sloshed some more brandy in his glass. As he drank, the muscle in his cheek pulsed. She was too damned desirable by half. He polished off the remainder of his brandy and slammed the glass down on the table.

Driving his hands deep into his trouser pockets, he wore a path in the carpet beneath his feet. Had he actually given in to the insane notion of taking her in his arms and letting his mouth linger over hers? His teeth clenched. He dragged his hand through his raven hair. Confound it, yes.

The moment he'd laid eyes on her standing there all soft and vulnerable and incredibly desirable, hot, potent passion roared in his chest like a beast unleashed. He had to touch her.

His jaw tightened. He had fallen prey to her charms like a smitten fool. He had fully enjoyed the lurid prospect of sampling her lovely wares with a slow thoroughness that would have had her panting and begging for more—that is until the full ramifications of his desire and her fervent intention to attract a man, any man, gave him pause.

He swore under his breath. Life in the Queen's service had taught him that self-restraint was always in good regulation. Why was it he had none where his fetching wife was concerned?

Olivia passed a miserable week. Brandon was cold and indifferent. He did his best to avoid her, and she, in turn, not knowing what ploy to try next, was forced to respect the stilted distance he enforced between them. To her utter disappointment, he made no more amorous overtures. The night of the Pratts' dinner party arrived sooner than she would have liked.

The china clock on the mantel in the drawing room chimed the hour of seven. Olivia flexed her gloved hands nervously. She caught sight of herself in the large mirror above the fireplace and fidgeted with her pearl and aquamarine choker. Examining her reflection critically, she twisted her lips. Would she do? The pale blue taffeta gown with the lacy off-the-shoulder neckline seemed too informal. Carrington had suggested they were old friends, which probably meant they were aristocrats. Biting her lower lip, she sighed. Everyone knew she was a commoner.

Aunt Edwina was happily gabbing about the latest titillating developments in the society papers.

"Will I do, do you suppose?" Olivia asked, meeting her aunt's eye in the mirror.

The older woman's gray head bobbed up and down

in agreement. "Oh, yes. I declare, you shall be the toast of the party!"

The door swung open, and Brandon strode in. Olivia looked up. Their eyes met, and her breath caught in her throat. It was the first time they had encountered one another since the incident in his bedroom. She had been on pins and needles most of the evening, worried he might refuse to escort her tonight. She breathed a little easier at the sight of him. Garbed in black evening attire, white silk waistcoat, and crisp white linen shirt, he looked starkly handsome. His smoldering gaze drifted over her with appreciation. A faint flush crept into her cheeks.

"Does she not look lovely, my lord?" Edwina inquired from where she sat on the brown velvet sofa.

His sultry gaze drank Olivia in, lingering on the daring neckline of her gown. "Ravishing," he murmured huskily and closed the door behind him. He crossed the room to the drinks table and lifted the crystal decanter of sherry.

Edwina darted a glance at his broad back and then back to her niece. *"Excellent for your purposes, my dear,"* she mouthed conspiratorially. Her large eyes danced with excitement behind her spectacles. *"At this rate, you will be able to garner several introductions without his objection."*

Olivia paled slightly. She was not particularly interested in garnering attention from anyone but him. It bothered her that he would be too foxed to care what she did. How could she elicit an appropriately jealous response? A wave of disappointment assailed her.

"Aunt, I would like a word alone with my—his lordship," she said, a meaningful gleam in her hazel eyes.

Aunt Edwina burst into nervous laughter. "Oh, yes. You two have a nice little chat," she replied and hastily clambered to her feet. "Enjoy yourselves, my dears," she called out as she sailed over the threshold.

Watching her husband down a second glass of sherry, Olivia heaved a frustrated sigh. "Must you?" she snapped irritably.

He glanced over his shoulder at her. A cynical smile touched his lips. "Yes, as a matter of fact, I must."

Her lips thinned and she looked away. "I wish you wouldn't."

"Why not?" he inquired nonchalantly, helping himself to another.

"I do not like it. I cannot abide you when you do."

He held up his sherry glass in a mock toast. "In that case, I'm afraid we are at an impasse, my dear. You see, I can't abide myself when I don't." He downed the contents of the glass in one gulp.

She toyed with her ivory lace undersleeve and walked to the window to gaze out at the ebony sky. If he planned to get foxed, this evening would be a complete disaster.

"I can't think why you need it."

"Can't you?" he snapped.

She glanced coolly over her shoulder at him. "Only a coward needs a drink to bolster his confidence."

He shrugged. "Well then," he said, his tone biting, "perhaps I am a coward. Does it disappoint you, *dear* wife? Ah, that is right. I forgot. You want nothing to do with your husband."

She turned around to face him, her hands fisted in angry resentment. "Nor you your wife," she flung at him.

He chuckled. "Quite true, my sweet, quite true."

A tap on the door brought their argument to an abrupt end. "Come," Brandon snapped.

Carrington appeared. "I beg your pardon, my lord," he said with a dutiful bow. "It was not my intent to intrude, but this note just arrived for her ladyship. The messenger indicated some urgency in the matter."

Olivia's heart leaped into her throat.

Frowning, Brandon snatched the note from the tray and examined it.

She rushed forward to intercept him. "No, I—"

Brandon's head came up. His penetrating gaze narrowed on her face, noting the pale, tense lines. He glanced down at the unmarked letter. He tapped it against his palm, and a deep pucker marred his forehead.

She flexed her fingers nervously. *God. Oh, God. Please do not let him open it.*

Smirking slightly, he held out his hand. "Your note, my lady," he said, his tone clipped.

Swallowing back her anxiety, she slipped the missive from his fingers and murmured her thanks.

"Open it," he prodded, an acerbic edge to his voice. "You must be eager for the news."

She stared down at the missive and shook her head. She knew the malicious nature of the letter and who had sent it. She stashed the threatening note in her reticule.

Drawing a deep breath, she managed to regain her aplomb. "The hour grows late, my lord. Should we not depart?"

"By all means." He eyed her with cold censure. "I know how *eager* you are to commence further introductions."

Chapter 9

Olivia accepted the footman's assistance in alighting from the carriage and then climbed the brick steps to greet Lord and Lady Pratt.

Dressed in a pale green velvet off-the-shoulder gown, Lady Pratt looked beautiful and elegant. Her auburn hair and large brown eyes gave her an exotic allure. Olivia felt certain she lacked anything as fascinating. Immediately self-conscious, she lowered her gaze to her own gown and wished she had the support of her husband. Smiling warmly, Lady Pratt extended her gloved hands in greeting.

"I am so very pleased to met the woman who stole Brandon's heart." She studied Olivia with open appreciation. "I see now why he abandoned his bachelor ways."

Lord Pratt stood at his wife's side. Suavely garbed in the customary black evening attire, he inclined his head charmingly in agreement.

"We both are eager to make your acquaintance, Lady Wilde," he said.

Tall and slender, he had brown hair, a bushy mustache, and long muttonchop whiskers. His appearance took her back to all those months ago when she'd first laid eyes on Brandon. How utterly foolish she had been to imagine fanciful romantic notions about her dashing young officer.

A pang of sadness struck her heart. She had been gravely mistaken to endow him with anything resembling gallantry.

Bending at the waist, Lord Pratt pressed a polite kiss to Olivia's outstretched hand. "You are a regal beauty, my lady."

Embarrassed, she said softly, "And you are too kind, my lord."

She felt Brandon's brooding gaze upon her. Stealing a glance in his direction, she recognized the smoldering expression in his eyes. *Oh, Brandon, if only you wanted me,* she thought, *I'd be a wife to make you proud.*

Standing rigidly at her side, he dragged his gaze to his host and said with stiff politeness, "It was good of you to invite us."

The butler took Brandon's black hat, walking stick, and cape.

Brandon's lips thinned, and he eyed his good friend with irritation.

Jeremy merely smiled. "We were anxious to meet your lovely bride."

Brandon glared at Jeremy, then looked away. This evening smacked of conspiracy. It was an obvious ploy to ease the wayward Lord Wilde into respectable married life—dull, domesticated bliss with Olivia, till death do them part.

He had to admit, though, allowing himself to steal a covert glance at his scrumptious wife, she was a tantalizing little treat. In truth, marriage to a woman of her lovely attributes would scarcely be a hardship for any man.

He tore his gaze from the luscious sight. No. He had weakened more than once. He refused to be ruled by his nether regions again. He despised the notion of Parker's diabolic machinations. His hand had been forced, and he would never willingly agree to a real marriage.

Regardless of how tempting her body might be, he had no intention of altering his firm convictions. He would not allow her father to control him like a prize bull.

Jeremy graciously extended his arm to Olivia. Smiling her sweetest, she accepted his escort and entered the parlor on her gallant host's arm.

As several gentlemen approached to make her acquaintance, Brandon's lips tightened into a grim line. Jeremy was only too happy to provide the necessary introductions. Not that she needed any, Brandon thought, watching Olivia. The brazen hussy was already receiving love letters from some whelp. Of that much, he was sure. His jaw clenched. Tonight the bees were swarming around the honey. She looked well-pleased with the attention, damn her.

She had been in London less than a fortnight and had managed at least one amorous conquest. His lips twisted. Lessons, indeed—as if she needed advice about how to lure a man. Hell, he himself wanted her more by the minute. It rankled no small degree to realize she'd found someone new to occupy her time.

* * *

This will be far easier than I imagined, Olivia realized with a measure of relief. She glanced about her, a placid smile pinned to her face, as Lord Pratt graciously introduced her to the dozens of dinner guests. Amidst the charming gentlemen eager to regale her with fascinating war stories, one blond man stood out among the crowd. Elegantly clad in a navy frock coat and gray brocade waistcoat, he was the epitome of fashion. A dandified popinjay, she thought, concealing a smile. Perfect for her purposes. Lord Pratt introduced him as Lord Hughes.

"Good evening, Lady Wilde," the man remarked, offering her a flawless bow despite his paunchy middle.

She smiled shyly and dipped her lashes in a demure fashion. "Good evening, my lord." She extended her hand to receive his very forward—albeit sloppy and wet—kiss.

He bestowed his affections with the greatest of ease. Better and better, she thought, retrieving her hand from his clammy grasp.

Straightening to his full height, which by her estimation could be no more than five-feet-eight, he flashed a smile designed to make all the ladies swoon. "I am persuaded I have never gazed upon such beauty as yours."

"Lady Wilde is indeed a diamond beyond price," Jeremy remarked. "Lord Wilde is a king among paupers, to be sure."

"Indeed," Lord Hughes murmured, ogling her as he might a delicious confection.

Bowing over her hand, Jeremy issued a polite excuse to rejoin his wife.

Smiling at her odious admirer, she warmly invited

his attention. Murmuring her agreement to some inane remark he made, her large dark eyes flickered around the room in search of Brandon. She found him.

Standing across the room, his elbow casually propped on the mantel before the fire, he was observing her every movement.

She recognized that hungry, brooding expression. She had seen it once before—at their wedding, when they'd been forced to suffer through that dreadful celebration. Her gaze slid away.

"A lady such as yourself must enjoy receiving male attention," Lord Hughes was saying.

She forced herself to smile at his obvious compliment. Arousing Brandon's covetous, possessive nature was her goal, not becoming Lord Hughes's mistress.

Disinterested in the tiresome man's twaddle, she gushed insipidly, "What a flatterer you are with the ladies, Lord Hughes."

A smile spread across his pudgy, sweat-beaded face. "You must call me, Alfred, my dear," he practically drooled.

The sight of Hughes charming his wife senseless vexed Brandon no small degree. She was flirting with that short stout imbecile! Of course, Brandon had no one to blame but himself. He should have insisted on his conjugal rights from the start and never agreed to this damned arrangement.

His mood vexed him. For some inexplicable reason, the mere idea of another man touching her made his blood boil. Under the circumstances, he had no right to feel resentment. She had stated her desire plain enough, and he had given his tacit consent. Anything else would have been emotional suicide.

And yet, he acknowledged, watching the flirtation

unfolding across the room, he could not abide the way Hughes was salivating over her. Nor could he explain the bizarre reaction he had whenever she was near.

What had happened to his cool, reserved, detached manner? He had worked damned hard at becoming totally immune, first to the hardships of his brutal childhood and then to the rigorous demands of a soldier's life. He absolutely refused to let himself become emotionally invested. Maria Chesney moved him not in the slightest, and yet, his innocent wife made his blood pulse hot.

It was highly doubtful that paunchy old Hughes would be capable of lavishing her with the proper sensual reverence. Perhaps that was it. *Was* he thinking of her best interests? His lips pursed. Hell, no. What supple treasures lay beyond that snug taffeta gown he remembered and liked a little too well. And his memory was working wonders.

As Hughes inched closer to whisper something in her ear, Brandon's fist clenched. Devil take it. It was not to be borne. By George, she was *his* wife. Hadn't she pledged her discretion? He was certain she had, else he never would have consented. What the deuce did she think she was doing, doting in public on a man who was clearly not her husband?

"Wicked siren," he groused under his breath.

Catching sight of Brandon's ferocious glower, Jeremy glanced at Lord Hughes and Lady Wilde.

She looked immensely enthralled by Hughes's far too obvious brand of charm. Her giggles and flirtatious smiles seemed a tad forced, to Jeremy's way of thinking.

He was aware of the occasional glance she darted

in her husband's direction just to make sure he was still engrossed with her performance.

He smiled and shook his head. "If I did not know better, I'd say your wife was trying to make you jealous."

Incredulity jolted Brandon. He could not conceal his reaction. *Jealous?* So that was what the little tart was doing. And he'd fallen for it like a deck of used cards.

Jeremy merely smiled in the face of Brandon's astonishment. "Don't look so surprised. It has been done before."

Brandon's spine straightened. Masking his features behind a stony facade once more, he managed to say, with characteristic nonchalance, "So it has."

"Tell me," Jeremy remarked, forgetting the melodrama for the moment, "why the sudden change of heart?"

"Change of heart?" Brandon echoed, his gaze riveted to his comely bride. *Was* she trying to make him jealous?

"Not that I object to your delightful bride's sudden appearance. On the contrary, I think it was a smashing idea to bring her to London. But I was under the impression you were not entirely sold on the idea of marriage. What persuaded you to see reason?"

Brandon coughed into his hand. He clasped his hands behind his back and rocked back on his heels. "She arrived unannounced," he explained awkwardly.

Jeremy's brows hiked. "I see. Did she indeed? Well then"—he glanced at the young novice charming Lord Hughes like a seasoned professional—"perhaps there is cause for alarm."

Dragging his gaze from the fetching little vixen, Brandon looked at his friend in disbelief.

"Don't underestimate her. There may be more to her frivolous flirtation this evening than I thought."

Brandon shrugged. "Let her have her little diversion. Where is the harm in it?"

"Your lovely bride is young and, I daresay, impressionable. If you do not rein her in"—Jeremy clapped his friend on the shoulder—"and occupy her time more wisely, someone else will."

Brandon gave Jeremy an irritated look. His gaze settled once more on his coquettish wife. A hint of smile touched her full, inviting lips. He remembered the taste of her, like sweet honey. His jaw clenched. The urge to haul her away from that cad and smother her lips with his own threatened to overpower him. He cursed himself for a fool.

The impudent little minx would not draw him in so easily. This ridiculous ploy to make him jealous— if that was what she was doing—was entirely lost on him. After all, he had Maria Chesney waiting in the wings. He did not give a damn what his bride did, he told himself.

The footman rang the dinner bell, and the chattering couples paired to promenade from the drawing room across the marbled front hall to the heavily paneled, dimly lit dining room.

Lord Pratt appeared at Olivia's elbow, blessedly rescuing her from Hughes's trite conversation. "May I take our guest of honor in to dinner?"

Olivia was about to consent when she heard her husband's deep authoritative voice. "I'll show her to the table, Jeremy. If it is all the same to you."

Jeremy politely stepped back and inclined his head. "Of course, Brandon." His gaze settled on Olivia's surprised countenance. "I cannot say as I blame you, not wanting a moment away from your lovely bride, completely understandable."

"Enjoying yourself?" Brandon muttered against her ear when they were alone.

She smiled ever so slightly, inwardly relishing his surly mood. He *was* jealous. Lord, she was glad. Her taxing conversation with the loathsome Hughes had been worth the time. She was not sure how much more of the obnoxious man's pointed innuendos she could innocently ignore.

"No cause for temper, surely," she replied, bestowing a sunny smile at Lord Hughes, who hovered nearby like an eager basset hound. "I am merely commencing my new life as a mature woman of the world. Such a move can come as little surprise to you."

Brandon's fingers dug into her arm. "You are not seriously contemplating coming to an arrangement with that—that fop?" he growled against her ear.

She dismissed his umbrage. "To be truthful, my lord, he has not asked me. I do believe, however, it is merely a matter of time before he does. Of course," she said, on a bored sigh, "as you probably are aware, these arrangements occasionally go awry. We shall just have to wait and see."

"Forget it," he bit out as the two walked a good distance behind the other guests.

Her head jerked up. She stared at him in amazement. "Never say you object?"

His face was a stony mask, but she sensed the mounting fury behind his facade. "I forbid you to speak to him ever again," he ordered. "Is that perfectly clear?"

Her large doe eyes searched his arctic blue ones. "But," she said, the picture of calmness in the face of her husband's simmering temper, "we came to an agreement, you and I. You cannot be so cruel as to alter the terms."

"I alter nothing," came his gruff rejoinder. "I merely reserve the right to be selective."

"May I inquire why?"

"Hughes is a bounder through and through," he growled. "An affair with the likes of him would be a brutal waste of time."

Her brows hiked. "I see. In that case, who *would* you suggest?"

His eyes jerked to her face, his icy gaze sharpening. *"Suggest?"*

"Indeed. Since you do not seem to like my choices, I assume you have someone more suitable in mind."

His jaw clenched and he turned away from her. "No, by God, I do not."

"I must say you have placed me in a rather difficult situation. You deny me Lord Hughes's charming company and object to Lord Driscoll, but offer no substitution. What am I to do?"

The muscle in his cheek throbbed with a vengeance. Pulling out the richly carved walnut chair at the dinner table, he waited, in a gentlemanly fashion, for her to take her seat. Despite his outward appearance of calm, she sensed his seething temper.

Brandon's hand closed over her bare shoulder and stroked her porcelain skin possessively. She stiffened beneath his display of ownership. As his hand slid over her neck and caressed the ivory column, her cheeks flamed red. He deliberately sought to humiliate her. No gentleman would manhandle his wife in public.

Enjoying her discomfort, Brandon's penetrating gaze slid over the elegant blue taffeta dress. His hungry eyes lingering on the daring, tight neckline, he watched the gentle rise and fall of her creamy white globes. A familiar surge of blinding attraction coursed hot and thick through his veins. He had to squash the urge to caress her inviting skin. How he longed to stroke her soft, enticing breasts until she peaked against his open mouth and begged for more.

He leaned his cheek close to hers. To the outside world, it appeared to be a gesture of affection between husband and wife. But Olivia knew better.

"To be candid, madam"—his murmur lashed like a whip—"I do not give a tinker's damn what you do." In sharp contrast to his demeanor, his breath was warm and soft against her skin. A shiver of pleasure crept down her spine.

"Then," she said flippantly, casting him a sidelong glance, "I am free to see whomever I choose."

His face hardened. "Your freedom depends on how lenient I am prepared to be. You seem eager to ingratiate yourself with everyone but your husband."

Her eyes widened.

"That's right, my sweet," he said in a low tone, "you are still *my* wife. And I shall decide your fate. It may be that I want you in my bed after all."

Telltale color streaked across her cheeks. His crude insinuation sparked her anger. She refused to suffer his insolence. She opened her mouth to issue a scathing retort, but the footman had appeared at her elbow with a silver tray. "Your wine, my lady."

Fuming, she had no choice but to quell her retort.

Brandon withdrew and took his seat across from her, his features hard with burning resentment. The liquor he'd poured down his throat had done nothing to alter his attraction to her. The woman possessed an inescapable sensual draw.

* * *

Dinner was a lavish display of pea soup, trout, venison, ham, spring chickens, and lamb. Mercifully, the conversation flowed with ease around Brandon and Olivia. The last course consisted of mouthwatering tarts, creams, and custards. Then it was time for the ladies to withdraw to the drawing room for tea while the men enjoyed their port.

The footman attempted to fill Brandon's glass, but he shook his head in refusal. Surprise flickered across Olivia's face. Taking a leisurely sip of coffee, Brandon's eyes met hers over the rim of his cup. His sensual gaze made her warm. She lowered her lashes and tried to conceal her blush.

Turning away, she slipped from the dining room on the heels of the other ladies and retired to the drawing room. She could not fathom why he had abstained from drinking. Her brow knitted slightly. Dared she hope it was due to her? Was it possible her rakehell husband was actually reforming his ways to please her?

No. She shook her head. It was far too much to hope. A pensive frown played at her lips. What other reason could there be?

Lady Pratt sought Olivia out, interrupting her troubled thoughts.

"Let us take a turn about the room," she said, locking arms with Olivia. "I am eager for us to become better acquainted."

Olivia forced a polite smile. "As am I, Lady Pratt," she said.

"You must call me Christine."

Olivia smiled in reply.

"I am so pleased that Brandon has taken a wife,"

Christine said. "Jeremy feels it is the best thing for him, and I am certain upon meeting you that I agree."

Olivia could think of no reason to be pleased. Thus far, her marriage was a complete sham.

"I wonder," Christine began, searching for the right words, "are you entirely happy?"

Olivia shot her a startled look. Was it that obvious? Had her attempt to appear enthralled with her status as Lady Wilde fallen flat?

Christine smiled in the face of Olivia's obvious dismay. "Men can be moody and a tad difficult at times," she went on, "but you mustn't take it to heart. I suspect it's the war. You must know Brandon's childhood was not a happy one. Poor Jeremy frets over him excessively. He fears Brandon is teetering on the very brink of moral disaster. And I thought perhaps I might be able to help in some way. It cannot be easy for you," she said kindly. "Marriage can be a challenge in the beginning. If there is anything I can do, any advice you may need, pray do not hesitate to take me into your confidence."

Thoroughly depressed, Olivia disengaged her arm and sank down on the gold velvet settee. Christine's openhearted honesty had her on the verge of tears. Everything she had surmised was horribly true.

"You are correct when you say he is . . . difficult," she admitted, her head bowed. "I feel ashamed to confess it to you." She struggled against the painful lump in her throat. "But I fear we do not suit. I do not believe he will ever come to have any sort of regard for me."

Christine sank down beside her. "Oh, but you are wrong. Both Jeremy and I believe he needs you, more than he may know. You must not give up hope."

Olivia laughed, but without humor. "With Lady

Chesney chafing at the bit, what possible hope is there for me?"

"That horrid woman can be no more than a passing fancy."

Olivia expelled a dejected sigh and shrugged her shoulders. "He can just as easily find another, if he is so inclined."

"Is he so inclined?" Christine inquired archly. "He did not appear to be this evening."

Getting to her feet, Olivia wound her lacy handkerchief around her fingers. "I daresay there is little hope for me."

"Don't say that. If you follow the dictates of your heart, in the end you will come together. You'll see."

Olivia was not comforted.

Christine sighed and rose to her feet. "Lord Hughes is not the answer," she counseled sternly. "If you take a lover, you will be making a terrible mistake, one for which your husband may never forgive you."

Olivia had no intention of any involvement with that insufferable man, but she could scarcely admit her plot to win her husband's attention to Lady Pratt.

"Try to work things out with Brandon," Christine urged. "If not for your own sake, then for his."

Olivia drew a deep, frustrated breath. "It is hard to work at something by yourself. Your husband loves you. You cannot imagine how it feels to realize you are not wanted."

"And how do you know that? I declare the man never took his eyes off you all evening. Is that a portrait of a disinterested husband? I think not."

With that provocative remark, Lady Pratt joined the other ladies, who were espousing the excellent character of Florence Nightingale. She had proved how truly useful a woman could be, they all concurred. Her introduction of hygienic standards in military hospitals was revolutionary. It was rumored she might actually be allowed to speak before parliament on the subject.

Olivia turned away and stared into the fire. Was Brandon interested in her? she wondered. Not as a wife, but perhaps . . . as a lover?

As the hour fast approached midnight, the dinner party slowly drew to a close, and Olivia dreaded what she knew was to follow. She would suffer the silence of her moody husband all the way home. Then he would issue a curt good night and find his comfort in Lady Chesney's arms, as she suspected he did every night.

Sensing her husband's presence behind her, she stiffened. The feel of his warm hands on her bare shoulders made her shiver. She had no choice but to accept the navy velvet pelisse he draped around her arms. Was it her imagination, or did his hands linger longer than necessary on her shoulders?

As the two descended the stone steps to the conveyance waiting below, she stole a glance in his direction. Even in the shadows of night, she detected the forbidding expression on his face. She turned away as her heart plummeted.

So much for arousing his interest, she thought with frustration as the footman helped her into the carriage. Bowing her head, she took her seat across from Brandon and toyed with her gloves.

What else was left for her to do? Nothing. Quite plainly, she had played her hand and lost.

Expelling a tired sigh, she turned her attention out the window and felt heartily sorry for herself.

"I have instructed the servants to prepare a bed in the small study adjoining the master suite." His velvety voice cut through the darkness.

Startled, she shot him a wide-eyed look. Did he plan to spend his nights at home, then? "That . . . was good of you," she managed awkwardly. "Thank you."

He dismissed her gratitude with a shrug. "It was originally designed for such a purpose. But my mother was disinclined to visit town."

"I shall, of course, have my maid move my things in the morning."

"No," he countered firmly.

She glanced up at him, taken aback by his sharp tone.

A wicked grin curled his lips. "Do you think me such a rogue that I would allow my wife to be inconvenienced in such a manner?"

Her tongue darted between her lips. "That is extremely gracious of you, my lord. But I have no wish to disturb you."

"I shall take the spare." The note of finality in his voice silenced any further objections. His hooded gaze slid over her. "Believe me, madam," he imparted, his voice rough with desire, "you disturb me without half trying."

Olivia was glad of the darkened carriage. It concealed her confused, flustered response.

Some time later, Olivia awoke from a sound sleep with a start. Sitting up in the enormous canopied bed, she listened to the silence in confusion. Something had undeniably awakened her. But what?

"Stop! No! I won't! I won't . . . do it!" Brandon was shouting. "We haven't enough supplies!"

Pushing back the covers, Olivia slipped from the bed. She scurried across the icy floor to the adjoining room, where her husband slept fitfully.

Easing open the door, she called to him. "Brandon? Brandon, wake up!"

But he did not rouse from his haunted slumber. Thrashing about in the small bed, he kept yelling out nonsensical things. He was dreaming, of course, and obviously about the war. Seeing his fellow veterans at tonight's dinner party must have conjured up painful memories.

Soft moonlight lit the small room. Creeping to the side of the bed, she gazed down at him. The covers were torn apart. He was lying naked in the narrow bed. The thick white scar that she remembered from their wedding night cut across his chest and torso, testimony to the atrocities he had suffered. She placed her arm on his shoulder and shook him.

"Brandon, wake up. It's a dream. You're having a nightmare."

His eyes flew open. Gasping for air, he stared blankly up at her. Recognizing her at last, he tried to sit up. But she sank down on the side of the bed and pressed her palms against his sweat-glistened shoulders, easing him down against the feather mattress.

"It's all right," she said softly. "You were having a bad dream, that's all."

He swallowed hard, but his breathing was still labored.

Her heart went out to him.

Dragging his hands through his hair, he closed his eyes and drew a deep calming breath.

She sensed he was trying to banish the images of his nightmare. "Was it the war?" she asked quietly.

Not particularly interested in divulging the details of the images that visited him nightly, he nodded his head.

"I'm sorry. It must be terrible for you."

"I wish I could ... forget," he admitted quietly, squeezing his eyes shut.

"In time, the horror of it will fade."

"How much time?"

"I don't know." Her voice was whisper soft. "But all pain fades with the passage of time."

He looked at her then, startled by the sight of her sitting on his bed. In the pale moonlight that spilled through the windows, her gossamer thin gown revealed her naked form in a highly erotic light.

Bloody hell. This was the last thing he needed. Her sheer white nightrail billowed around her luscious little body like a cloud of sensual mist. Her long, thick hair flowed loosely down her back and over her shoulders, brushing against the soft swell of her breasts. He dragged his eyes from the tempting sight. "You should be in bed," he said hoarsely.

She laid her hand on his arm. His eyes darted back to her hand lying warm and soft against his skin. "The way you cried out ... I was worried."

Frowning, he turned away from her. "I am sorry I woke you, but I am fine now. Go back to bed," he said harshly.

She did not flee, and she chose to ignore the warning note in his voice—perhaps because tonight, not for the first time, she had glimpsed her husband's true character, and she felt drawn to the sensitive, vulnerable man, compelled to comfort him.

Almost with a will of its own, her hand reached out

to touch the bumpy scar revealed by the rumpled sheets, which barely covered his narrow hips.

"What a terrible hurt this must have been," she whispered softly. She spread her cool palm over his burning skin. His breath hissed between his teeth. "How did it happen?"

He stared at her, hunger burning in his eyes. "A saber ran me through."

Her eyes jerked to his. "Were you frightened?"

He shook his head. "Relieved." His eyes never left hers.

"Relieved? Why?"

Brandon looked away. "I welcomed an end to everything," he admitted on a deep breath.

"But you didn't die."

"Oh, no," he said, a rueful smile titling his lips. "I lived to fight another day and return to England the conquering hero. To my sorrow and yours, no doubt."

Her brow wrinkled slightly. "Why should I have reason to regret you?" she asked, gazing into his eyes.

"I can think of several reasons," he muttered.

She glanced down at the ugly scar. "Was this what your dream was about?" she asked, caressing the mark that marred his otherwise perfectly muscled physique.

"No." His voice was rough and raspy.

"What then?" she urged. "Tell me what upset you. Sharing your pain might ease your plight."

He turned away from her. "After the obscenities I've seen, is it any wonder my sleep is restless?" he snapped.

"No. I only thought . . . *please,* Brandon," she said, floundering to forge some connection with him, "don't keep shutting me out. We are man and wife. Let us help one another."

"What I need you cannot possibly give me," he told her bitterly.

She'd made an emotional inroad with him tonight. She would not give up so easily. "How do you know?" she pressed.

He refused to look at her. "Can't you understand? Have I not made it plain enough? I don't need your help," he said, his tone clipped, "and I don't want it."

"So you claim." Reaching out, she turned his face back to hers. "But I see the demons clawing at you. Almost from the first, you've been angry . . . tormented. Why? What have I done?" she asked, her enormous eyes searching his deep blue ones.

His eyes fluttered shut. Massaging his forehead with his hand, he expelled a ragged sigh. "It is not you. *God,*" he marveled on a husky breath, "if you only knew." He caressed her soft cheek with the back of his hand. "You are so goddamned beautiful. I . . ." He dropped his hand and turned away from her. "Go back to bed, Olivia," he commanded gruffly.

"No," she whispered, slipping her hand into his. She rubbed her cheek against the back of his hand. Her eyes fluttered shut. "Let me help you. *Please,*" she beseeched so softly he had to strain to hear her.

Slowly, inexorably yet haltingly, he drew her near.

He stared deeply into her eyes. "Are you truly certain you want this?" he asked her, his voice low and rough.

She nodded her head. But when she was cradled against his bare chest, a twinge of apprehension assailed her. What if nothing changed between them? What if tomorrow he retreated behind his cold, hard shell and returned to Lady Chesney's arms? Could her heart survive another rejection? She knew she could not bear to be used and deserted. Not again.

She pressed her palms against his chest and felt the thundering of his heart. "Brandon—" she said, panicking.

As if sensing her trepidation, his strong arms gathered her close, and he lips brushed a kiss to her temple.

"Hush," he whispered against her lips, his fingers lightly feathering through her hair. "No more words . . . not tonight. Just let me love you."

His husky voice was her undoing, and his gentle, reassuring manner tugged at her heart. She could not refuse him, even if it meant losing her heart. She wanted what intimacy their lovemaking would bring. She needed it.

"Yes, *please,*" she pleaded softly, raising her parted lips to receive the heat of his kiss. "I want to be with you so much. So very much."

"No more than I want to be with you." His mouth claimed hers in a torrid kiss.

Chapter 10

Eager to feel his body against hers, Olivia arched against Brandon, clinging to him. His mouth slanted over hers, lavishing her lips, her tongue, and the soft recesses of her mouth with tender strokes. His hands feathered lightly over her face, her neck, and slid lower to fondle her aching breasts. Covering his hand with hers, she sighed, craving the rippling flood of pleasure emanating from the heat of his touch.

Trailing hot, wet kisses down her neck, he slipped her nightgown off her shoulder and breathed a kiss against her soft satiny skin. She lay unabashed in all her naked beauty before his smoldering gaze. Her need matched the passionate embers of his desire. He uttered a guttural groan and bent his head once more, his open mouth branding her with his kisses. Taking her taut nipple in his mouth, he stroked the hard pebble with his tongue, and then his hungry mouth closed over her rosy peak and sucked.

She mewed with pleasure. Driving her fingers through his thick raven hair, she arched against him, deliciously pliant in his arms.

Trailing kisses over her stomach, down her abdomen, and across her hip, he eased her legs apart and pressed a kiss to the soft inside of her thigh. His fingers parted her soft, dewy folds and stroked her, making her ache with the need to have him deep within her. Swept away by tiny currents of desire, she moaned and twisted her head on the soft downy pillow. As the exquisite torment burgeoned deep inside her, she caught her lower lip between her teeth and tried to stifle her cry of ecstasy.

And then, to her shock, his mouth was there, kissing, stroking her soft slick petals. She was about to issue a stunned refusal, but his teasing tongue had her writhing on the edge of blissful insanity.

Somewhere in the recesses of her mind, she knew he was no gentleman. To touch his wife in such a shocking way was unheard of. But, she reasoned, as currents of excruciating fulfillment rushed over her and she gave in to the burgeoning flame, she was no lady. She cried out from the aching crescendo deep inside her.

When at last the sweet torture came to an end, he lowered himself against her. His large, probing manhood pressed against her feminine core. Wrapping her silky arms around his velvety back, she drew him against her. Bending his head to her neck, he kissed the pulsing hollow of her throat. She sighed and angled her neck to better receive his kiss. He pressed a kiss behind her ear and nibbled at her earlobe. The harsh sound of his warm breath made her shiver.

Resting his weight on his elbows, he looked down

at her, his arresting blue gaze holding her captive. The fervent tenderness in his eyes made her heart kick against her ribs. This was more than passion, she realized. Her heart sang with joy, for this was what she wanted, what she'd waited for—deep, abiding emotion.

His hips moved against hers, seeking the treasure they both knew lay just beyond this sweet paradise. She lifted her hips to receive him. He watched her reaction as he eased inside her satin sheath. Whimpering at the exquisite feeling of his hard length inside her soft, snug channel, she welcomed his slow penetration. He pressed a gentle kiss to her lips, teasing her with the lazy rhythm of his lovemaking. Unable to bear the sweet agony a moment longer, her hands clutched at his back, urging him to quit his playful toying. He obeyed her frantic command and drove deep, filling her completely. His mouth covered hers, urgently moving over her lips, hungrily devouring her sweet cry of ecstasy.

He was deep within her, almost touching her womb. A sigh of pleasure erupted in her throat. She wrapped her thighs around his hips. Slowly, he withdrew almost completely from her and then sank deeply into her welcoming warmth once more. She moaned and wrapped her arms around his neck, tugging him near. Her lips parted and sought his, craving the heat of his kiss, the warmth of his love.

Wrapping his arms around her, he sealed their passion with a fiery kiss. His mouth slanted over hers, tasting her, loving her, probing her honeyed depths with his tongue. The tempo of their lovemaking changed. His hips slammed against hers, and she met his passionate thrusts, undulating wildly beneath him. Her hungry mouth twisted against his, coveting his savage kisses. She could never get enough of him, this wild, brooding man for whom she cared more deeply than she'd ever imagined possible.

Her hand slid up his back to caress his shoulders, and she reveled in the well-toned muscles flexing beneath her fingers as he drove into her, loving her with strokes that fueled her pleasure and took her to new heights of ecstasy. The rasp of his labored breathing mingled with her own breathless pants. He groaned with the force of his need and drove deep, quickening his powerful thrusts. Eager to reach the glorious pinnacle she knew they would find in each other's arms, she strained against him.

Gasping at the waves of pleasure spiraling deep inside her, she was nearly frantic to reach the other side of this sweet heaven. His mouth found hers once more for a feverish kiss. Whimpering, she convulsed around him, finding that point of blissful abandonment at last.

He shuddered and drove into her one last time, joining her in nirvana. Trembling from the potency of the emotionally charged moment, she hugged him to her. He filled her with his seed.

"Oh God, *Olivia,*" he panted urgently against her cheek, "don't ever leave me. I need you so much, so damned much," he rasped, burying his face in her silky hair.

When the world ceased to career out of control, he rolled onto his back and drew her close. Having found the special rapture they could only find wrapped in each other's arms, they lay quietly together in the afterglow of their lovemaking.

Her cheek was pressed against his chest, her arms wrapped around his broad, strong shoulders. She heaved a dreamy sigh. "Is that the way it is with all lovers?"

He tilted her face up to his. "I wouldn't know," he murmured huskily against her lips. "But I am glad that is the way it is between us." Then he claimed her mouth in a slow, drugging kiss.

Pulling away at last, she sighed and laid her cheek against his heart. Gladdened by the strong, sure beat beneath her ear, a smile touched her lips. "Brandon," she said softly, "tell me about my husband."

A low chuckle rumbled in his chest as his palm lazily caressed the curve of her back. "What do you want to know?" his voice cut through the darkness, swirling around her like velvet.

"What was your childhood like?"

His hand stilled. "I don't remember."

"Everyone remembers their childhood," she persisted gently.

"I don't," he said, a curt finality in his voice.

A prolonged silence spread between them. "Chalmers told me," she whispered into the darkness.

"Told you what?" His voice was flat and tightly controlled, but she sensed his inner turmoil.

"About your mother . . . how she died."

Easing her off his chest, he sat up and presented her with his back. He expelled a deep tortured sigh and hung his head.

She got to her knees and wrapped her arms around his back. Her breasts pressed against his warm skin. Kissing his shoulder, she nestled her face into his neck. "What a terrible time that must have been for you."

He turned his head slightly toward her cheek. "It doesn't matter now," he claimed, but the roughness of his voice indicated the contrary. "It was a long time ago and best forgotten."

"So much pain," she murmured. "I hate to think of you as a vulnerable little boy left alone with that heartless brute of a father. How awful that must have been for you. And now the war has brought you so much more suffering."

He turned around and pressed her back against the pillows. "We have each other tonight," he rasped urgently against her lips as his body came down on top of hers. His coarse chest hair rubbed against her soft breasts, making her ache with desire. "Let's make the most of it."

Before she could utter another word, his mouth captured hers, kissing her with an urgent, blazing need that banished all thought of conversation. His hips rocked against her, teasing her with slow erotic thrusts. His hard shaft pressed against her soft feminine core until she throbbed with longing. Whimpering with need, she arched her hips, eager to feel him deep within her. His lips slanted against hers with increasing ardor.

Clutching her hips, he sank inside her, filling her completely. He moved within her, loving her with long, tormenting strokes until she thought she'd go mad with pleasure. Murmuring her name on a husky whisper of desire, he rubbed his rough cheek against her silky hair.

She wrapped her legs around his waist. Running her hands across his back, she hugged him to her. She tasted the salty skin of his shoulder, then nibbled at his hard muscles. And then her mouth moved hungrily over his face in search of his mouth once more.

"*I love you,*" she rasped against his mouth, lavishing

fierce kisses on his lips. "I love you ... I love you," she whispered over and over again.

He drank in her words, smothering her lips with the heat of his own.

Whether her ardent declaration or her soft moans of pleasure drove him toward climax, he knew not, only that the pinnacle came on him with a force so potent, so intense he could not stem the rushing tide. Clasping her hips, he withdrew almost completely from her. Determined that she find sweet rapture with him, he drove deep inside her satin sheath once more. When she convulsed around him, his body jerked with the force of his own release.

As the heat of passion slowly fizzled out, their lips clung in soft, slow, tender kisses. Not wanting to dispel the tender moment, neither one spoke. Exchanging soft caresses, they explored the wonder of one another until sleep overtook them.

Rolling onto his back, Brandon opened his eyes. The bed was empty. Darting a glance around the room, he found his comely wife standing by the window. Her long corn silk hair was tousled from their vigorous lovemaking. Wild and tangled, it draped down her back like an open invitation to passion.

His greedy eyes drifted over her. His black velvet dressing gown fell haphazardly off her lovely shoulder. She looked lusciously wanton.

A slow smile touched his lips and a tired limpness settled in his bones. It was little wonder. They'd made love all through the night. The first time, they'd been ruled by mindless passion. On the second occasion, he made sure he took his time with her, tenderly coaxing her to the peak of ecstasy again and again.

And the last time, they'd found each other in the night. It was a slow, sleepy, affectionate joining. There was a warm, tender familiarity to their lovemaking, as if they'd been married for a lifetime and were content to lazily cherish one another in the darkness.

His blood ran hot through his veins. He wanted her again this morning. The enticing curve of her dainty neck beckoned his fiery kiss. Admiring her untamed beauty, he watched her with hungry eyes. He'd never known such a feeling. He could not seem to get enough of her, this beguiling little wife of his.

Her adorable turned-up nose and enormous hazel eyes appealed to him like no other he'd ever known. But he did not fail to recognize the perplexed look that crossed her face, nor her pinched mouth.

His smile faded. Something was terribly wrong. Her deeply furrowed brow gave him pause. Puzzled by her strained expression, he lay quietly observing her movements. Was she regretting last night? No. That could not be. He'd felt her passion and seen the depth of her emotions shining in her exotic cat eyes.

His chest tightened at the memory of her fervent cry. *I love you.* Did she love *him*, or what they did together? he wondered. Perhaps it was simply her reaction to the intoxicating pleasure found in the throes of passion.

She darted a glance in his direction. He lowered his lashes, giving her the illusion that he still slept peacefully. But he continued to regard her from beneath heavy lids.

Looking nervously over her shoulder to make sure he was not awake, she slipped from the room. Frowning, he leaned up on one elbow and peered through the open doorway. He watched in some confusion as she lifted the top to her jewelry case and retrieved a folded piece of paper.

He recognized the yellowed parchment immediately. The crease in his brow deepened. What the deuce was she doing? As she unfolded the letter with great care, a sense of dread settled heavily on his heart. It could not be a lover's note, not after the night they'd shared. Could it?

He watched her as she tiptoed across the room and retrieved a piece of paper from the small escritoire. What the blazes was she scribbling so fast and furiously? Not words of love for another man, surely? Could the warm, loving woman he'd held in his arms last night be so deceitful by day?

Despite his reluctance to think ill of her, his eyes could not deceive him. Jealousy sparked his anger. He was sickened by the sight of her haste. Had he actually imagined he was developing feelings for her? What a bloody fool he was. So much for her fervent declaration of love. In the early hours of the morning that followed, she'd slipped from his bed to relish a philandering cad's love letter.

Easing back the covers, he slipped silently from the bed. Stealthy as a ferocious predator, he crossed the master bedroom threshold and approached her from behind.

When he was close enough to touch her, he asked in an acid tone, "Penning your beloved fidelity to me already?"

A surprised cry escaped her lips. She stashed her reply in the desk drawer and swiveled around to face him. Her hand splayed over her chest. *"Brandon,"* she gasped, breathless from nerves, "you frightened me."

His accusing gaze drilled into her. "Who else were you expecting?"

"No one," she said, shoving her admirer's note deep into the pocket of his robe. "I was . . . I was . . . unable to sleep. So I decided . . . to write my father."

"Your father?" he echoed in disbelief. His temper blazed hot at her obvious lie. He arched an eyebrow. "At this hour of the morning?" he queried, his tone sharp.

"I—I thought you were sleeping," she stammered, her cheeks coloring at her paper-thin deception.

"I'm awake now," he commented, drawing her into his arms. The need to possess her, to remove all thoughts of her secret lover from her mind, nearly overwhelmed him.

Sliding his hand behind her neck, he brought her roughly against him. She drew in her breath. Wide-eyed, she searched his cold, unfeeling eyes.

"Come back to bed," he said crudely. "I haven't had my fill of you yet."

If she was dismayed by his rude manner, she did not show it. Like a dutiful wife, she gave a slow nod of her head and allowed him to lead her to his bed.

When he tugged at the tie around her waist and stripped his robe from her, baring her body to his searing gaze, she uttered no objection. He clasped her bare breast in his hand and fondled her, watching her nipples peak in response to his touch. A soft gasp of pleasure escaped her lips.

Bending his head, he covered her nipple with his open mouth and sucked. Hard. Arching her back, she sighed and angled her body closer to his, wanting his warmth. He pushed her down on the cold bed linens. Jealous anger was driving him. Determined to purge her secret lover from her heart, he covered her body with his. His mouth claimed her lips as his own. It was a hard, punishing, brutal kiss. She moaned against his assaulting lips.

But he would not be deterred. Demons were clawing at him. Images of her giving herself to another man, kissing him, loving him as freely and openly as she had Brandon with her beautiful body, fueled his fire. Had she spent a similar night of lovemaking with her secret admirer?

Thrusting his hands into her hair, he held her head captive and ravaged her mouth with his tongue. He wanted to brand her as his own, to absorb her into him completely, to banish all thoughts of another man from her deceiving mind.

Nudging her legs apart, he spread her wide. With one powerful thrust he entered her, driving deep. She gasped against his mouth, but made no move to resist his possession. Quite the contrary. She was dripping with honeyed desire.

Withdrawing from her, he thrust deep once more. Her slick folds tightened around his hard length. Her silky arms held him captive, soothing his ire. Each satiny caress of her loving hands, every fervent, hungry kiss, stole his reason. The tantalizing stroke of her tongue and the ardent caress of her lips melted his icy resolve.

He wanted to treat her cruelly, to ruthlessly use her in return for her wretched duplicity. But her warm, open, loving response melted his anger. All he could think of, all he could feel was her. Moaning against her mouth, he was swept up by the wondrous beauty of the woman lying in his arms. His chest tightened with emotion. He loved her with deep quick strokes, his heartbeat quickening to a fevered pitch.

Her beautiful body writhed beneath him, finding

fulfillment in his fierce, passionate lovemaking. Nearing the point of deep spasms of release, he uttered a hoarse, guttural sound and crushed her mouth beneath his. Capturing her cry of sweet rapture, he poured himself into her, convulsing again and again in the warm comfort of her silken embrace.

No matter what treachery she was capable of, he would never get enough of this woman. She'd found her way around his heart, and there was no going back now.

Hours later, Olivia awoke. Slowly coming out of a deep slumber, she moaned softly, limp from exhaustion. It was little wonder. She'd spent the balance of the night and most of the early hours of dawn making love. Her body rustled the sheets, and her eyes opened.

She tried to push up, but could not. A heavy weight bore down around her midriff. She was naked, she realized, and the large bronzed arm draped across her torso belonged to her husband. The room held a morning chill, but she was toasty warm from the heat of Brandon's body snuggled against hers.

A smile softened her lips. She reached out to touch his cheek, then checked the urge. He looked so young, like a carefree boy, in sleep's gentle repose. She was loath to wake him. His ebony hair curled haphazardly across his brow. The deep crevices that normally marred his forehead were erased; the hard lines that edged his soft full lips were miraculously absent.

Recalling the tenderness of his kisses and his deeply passionate, all-consuming lovemaking, she sighed softly. If only they could share that perfect connection during their waking hours, what a splendid life they could have.

Anxiety clawed at her. What would today bring? Would he retreat behind the painfully familiar cold stone wall, or welcome her with open arms as his wife?

She cringed inwardly, remembering her ardent expression of love. Why had she spoken aloud? It was too soon. And she felt sure it was not at all what he wanted to hear. Thus far, theirs was purely a physical relationship, but she wanted more than that from him. Despite her desire to forge a deeper union, he had made it patently clear that his heart was not now, nor would it ever be, involved.

She cursed herself for a fool. She should have proven herself capable of meeting his physical needs without emotional assurances. By stupidly admitting her feelings, she'd made herself vulnerable. What would a man like him want with a clinging wife? He wanted a lover.

Besides, she was not entirely certain that she did love him—exactly. She glanced at his sleeping figure and sighed. Was love like this? A whirlwind of confusion? Hurt feelings mingled with intense passion? She wasn't sure. She felt drawn to him, of that there could be no doubt. But was that love? She heaved a sigh. No other word seemed appropriate to describe the intensity of her feelings.

Trepidation invaded her heart. Now that he knew her true feelings, would he use her declaration against her? That humiliation would be more than she could bear.

Craven fear took hold. Suddenly, she could not bring herself to face him in the light of day. Being careful not to wake him, she eased from beneath his

arm and slipped from the bed where they'd collapsed
their energy spent in the throes of bittersweet passion

He stirred in his sleep. Murmuring her name, he
rolled onto his stomach. The side of his face rested
against the soft feather mattress. She scurried to the
adjoining room and softly clicked the door shut.

A short while later, Saunders shuffled into the small
room where his master slept. Arching a bushy brow,
he eyed the ransacked bed and discarded billowy
white nightgown with some astonishment.

Brandon opened his eyes. He squinted against the
bright sunshine pouring in through the casement
windows.

"Olivia?" he murmured groggily, reaching for her.

"Not Olivia," came Saunders's voice as he shuffled
into the master bedroom, "but your ever faithful
valet."

Startled, Brandon sat up. The bed was empty.
Frowning, he drove his fingers through his rumpled
hair.

Saunders cocked a brow. "I trust your lordship
passed a satisfactory night?" he inquired, casting a
dubious glance at the hopelessly tangled bedding.

Kicking the sheets free from his legs, Brandon fixed
his aged valet with a chilling glare and leaned back
against the headboard, folding his arms over his chest.

"Does my lord require a drink this morning? A
glass of port, perhaps?"

"No," Brandon bit out, "his lordship does not. I'll
take coffee, hot and black. And plenty of it."

Saunders managed to conceal his look of surprise.
"Very good, my lord."

"What the deuce time is it, anyway?" Brandon demanded after a lusty yawn.

"Nearly eleven, my lord."

"I see," Brandon murmured, a pensive scowl playing at his lips. Remembering his wife's deception, he snatched his velvet robe from the end of the bed and quickly dug through the pockets.

Empty.

His lips thinned. He threw the garment aside and jumped from the bed. Scouring her escritoire, he tore open the drawers. Her hastily written reply was nowhere to be found.

Observing his lordship's bizarre behavior, Saunders's brows furrowed. "My lord, is something amiss?"

"No, nothing," Brandon muttered, rubbing his rough, stubbled chin with his palm.

Eyeing her jewelry case with curiosity, he threw open the lid and dug through her glimmering pile of jewels. Swearing under his breath, he shoved the top closed and expelled an infuriated sigh.

Her disappearance this morning left a gnawing doubt in his belly. Had she scampered off, fresh from his bed, to meet her secret lover? Was that why she was in such a hurry to pen her reply?

Turning his gaze out the window, he clenched his jaw. Who the devil was the bastard anyway? Driscoll? Hughes? No. She'd have better taste than to dally with them. He crossed the room to the china basin to splash some cold water on his face. Resting his palms on the sides of the basin, he swore under his breath. Bloody hell. He needed to release some of his tension, or he'd explode. Dabbing his face dry, he commanded over his shoulder, "Fetch my riding clothes, Saunders."

"A brisk ride is just the thing after an exhausting night, I always say."

Brandon glared at his manservant and tossed the towel aside.

A light tap sounded at the drawing room door.

Olivia was ill prepared to come face to face with Brandon after their torrid night of passion, and her stomach jangled with nervous energy. If he pressed her for an explanation of her ridiculous claim to love him, she would simply say it was her reaction to passion.

Furthermore, she had no clear recollection of saying those words specifically. Satisfied she could face him without flushing to her roots, she squared her shoulders and said, "Come in." Smoothing her hands hastily over her hair, she cleared her throat and braced herself for the encounter.

To her relief and disappointment, Carrington appeared, bearing a note on a silver tray.

As she unfolded the note, a shiver of dread crept over her. She knew before reading the contents it was another threat from that disgusting Winterbottom.

Sinking onto the brown velvet sofa, she scanned the page with horror.

"My lady," Carrington inquired, "is something the matter?"

"What?" she asked, distracted by the scrawled missive.

"You seem distraught. It is not bad news, I hope. Should I fetch his lordship?"

"No," she said too quickly. "That won't be necessary. I—it is nothing." She folded the letter to conceal its ugly contents. "Just something I wasn't expecting, that is all."

"Very good, my lady." So saying, the butler took his leave.

Olivia gazed down at her lap. Slowly, she unfolded the disgusting note. She could scarcely bring herself to read it. Her hands shook as she gazed down at the shocking contents.

> *You didn't keep our appointment. That wasn't very nice. I waited for you like a right nice gentleman. I don't fancy having my patience tried.*
>
> *Unless you agree to pay me one thousand pounds, I shall inform his lordship of the truth and show him the letter penned by your dearly departed slut of a mother. We shall see if your good name or your lily white marriage can survive the scandal.*
>
> *If you're thinking of double-crossing me, don't. I am smarter than you think. Don't disappoint me, either, or I'll make you sorry you were ever born, even if it was on the wrong side of the blanket.*

She swallowed back her apprehension. Getting swiftly to her feet, she turned the letter over and over in her hands and paced the small confines of the parlor.

She must *do* something.

But what? She could not possibly pay Winterbottom without arousing Brandon's suspicions. Their dawn encounter had been far too close for comfort. She was enormously glad he had believed her ruse.

Coming to a halt, she stared down at the vile letter and rapped it against her knuckles. She had to discover the truth for herself. The Duke of Kent would know if her blackmailer's insinuations were true. Provided he consented to meet with her, she might be able to formulate a plan to thwart Winterbottom. But first, she must discover if such a letter actually existed. One way or the other, she would rid herself of the hateful pest.

She jumped at the sound of a knock at the parlor door. Talons of dread closed around her heart. She could not face Brandon—not now, not in this pathetic state.

"I—just a minute," she called out in a shaky voice. Concealing the note in her bodice, she swallowed hard and braced herself for what was to come.

Carrington stepped into the room once again. Relief flooded through her, and she expelled the breath she'd been holding.

"Lord Hughes is here, my lady. He requests an interview."

Taken aback, she asked, "Where is his lordship?"

"His lordship is not at home."

"Oh," she replied, dejected. Had he gone to Lady Chesney? Had last night meant no more to him than the fleeting passion of their wedding night? He could not be so heartless, could he? Hadn't he said he needed her last night?

Needing is not loving, an insidious voice whispered in her head.

"My lady?" Carrington pressed at seeing her dismay. "Shall I show Lord Hughes in?"

"No. Kindly send Lord Hughes away."

"As you wish, my lady." Carrington bowed and departed, bearing her terse reply.

She wandered to the fireplace. Placing her hand on the mantel, she bowed her head in misery and closed her eyes.

"Oh, Brandon, if only you loved me," she whispered aloud. "Just a little."

She desperately wanted to take him into her confidence, to rely on his steely strength of purpose as she had once been able to trust in her father. How she longed for a confidant!

But she dared not speak of Winterbottom's threats, nor his foul lies, to another living soul. She could not risk it.

All the same, her heart ached for a trusted ally. If only that person could be her husband. How wonderful it would be to share her woes with Brandon with the sure and certain knowledge he would not abandon her.

But she could never involve him in Winterbottom's scheme. She would have to deal with her malevolent blackmailer on her own. Somehow.

Reining in his feisty mount to a brisk walk, Brandon wiped the back of his arm across his sweaty brow. He patted the hunter's neck and murmured words of appreciation for a fine gallop. Despite the hour, the park was unusually crowded, but he'd enjoyed the ride. The crisp air had helped clear his head.

"I say," Maria Chesney remarked, "you look vaguely familiar. Though I must say I am hard put to recall your name." Steering her chestnut mare toward him, she offered him a purely sexual smile.

Slowing his horse to fall in step with hers, he flashed her a cool smile. Her pointed barb was not unexpected. He had not seen her since the debacle at Lady Bloomsberry's ball.

"Lovely day for a ride," he remarked noncommittally.

She glanced at him askance. "If I did not know better," she said, her lips twisting with amusement, "I'd be inclined to believe the horrid little rumor whizzing about town."

"And what rumor might that be?"

"They say you have fallen for that ridiculous little wife of yours and have chosen to abandon me altogether. Say it isn't so," she purred seductively. "I shall never survive the ignominy of it."

Brandon's mouth set in a sarcastic smile. "You should know better than to listen to idle chatter, Maria."

"I knew it," she cried with ugly conceit. "I could never lose you, not to a pristine child. What can a green girl like her possibly offer a real man like you?"

Brandon weighed her question for a long moment. "If you cannot guess," he drawled, "then you are more limited than I ever imagined."

Her smile slid from her face. Pulling her mount up short, she glared at him. "Can you honestly tell me that little twit has aroused your interest?"

One corner of Brandon's mouth lifted slightly. He brought his horse to an abrupt halt. Leaning forward, he rested his forearms against the pommel of his saddle. "I don't recall *honesty* being something you ever valued. But since you've asked, she has aroused far more than merely my interest."

Maria recoiled as if he'd struck her. "Well, I never," she huffed, insulted. She kicked her mount to a brisk trot and disappeared into the thickening crowd.

Shaking his head, Brandon turned his horse toward the park exit and headed for home. He was about to dismount when he caught sight of a round, balding gentleman descending the stone steps.

Incensed, Brandon leaped from his horse and

tossed the reins at Ned, who quickly tethered the beast to a nearby hitching post.

Barreling down on his unsuspecting prey, Brandon did not so much as pause to remove his riding gloves. Lord Hughes caught sight of him. "Good day, my lord," he blurted and hurried on his stout legs toward the safety of his carriage.

But Brandon caught him up short. Leaning into the conveyance, he demanded, "What the hell are *you* doing here?"

Hughes gawked at him as if he were a candidate for bedlam. Opening his snuff box, he took a pinch. "I should think it would be obvious," he remarked haughtily. "I came to visit your lovely bride, whom you so grossly neglect."

A look of blazing fury crossed Brandon's face. "If I ever catch you near her again," he bit out, "I'll wring your fat neck. Is that perfectly clear?"

Hughes's Adam's apple bobbed up and down. Terrified, he hastily nodded his agreement. Turning away from the odious caller, Brandon marched up the stone steps.

"Where is my wife?" he growled at Carrington.

"In the parlor, my lord," Carrington replied, accepting his master's leather gloves and riding crop.

Storming across the opulent front hall, he threw open the parlor door. It banged against the wall.

Startled, Olivia gasped in surprise and turned around to find her husband's tall, broad frame nearly filling the doorway.

Arms akimbo, he stood glaring at her. His nostrils flared with rage. "Lord Hughes was just here."

"Yes," she replied, swiftly concealing Winterbottom's note behind her back, "he was. I wondered where you were," she ventured to say, her nervousness appallingly evident.

"Did you?" He kicked the door shut with his booted foot.

Her large eyes locked with his furious glare. "Yes," she said quietly. Her gaze swept over his riding breeches and linen shirt. It clung to his chest with enviable closeness. "I presume you went out for a ride. Did you enjoy it?" she asked, striving for civil conversation. "It is a lovely day."

He fixed her a look of burning contempt. "Is it? I hadn't noticed."

By God! How could he have been so bloody gullible as to believe in her adoring kisses? He was gone not forty-five minutes, and the little witch was entertaining another man behind his back. What an idiot he was to imagine last night meant a thing to her. She'd deceived him with the likes of Lord Hughes, no less.

Inching back toward the fireplace, she tried to conceal the note she slipped into the flames. But Brandon was wise to her deception.

His lips thinned. "Did you enjoy your morning, my sweet?" he asked her nastily.

"It was passable," she murmured. Her attempts to kick the remnants of the letter into the fire were less than subtle.

"Only passable? Well, we must do something about that," he mocked, his tone vicious. "Mustn't we?"

Her large hazel eyes searched his enraged face. "Brandon, what has happened? You are angry with me. Why? What have I done to displease you?"

He came to stand over her, a furious snarl twisting his lips. "Perhaps I don't like it when my wife crawls out of my bed like a common doxy to meet another man behind my back."

Her eyes rounded in disbelief. Before she could contain her reaction, her hand connected in a loud smack against his cheek. His head jerked back from the force of her unexpected blow. With an angry growl, he grabbed her by the arms and yanked her roughly against him.

He glared down at her with burning, accusing eyes. Passion pulsed hot through his veins. He was about to give in to the overwhelming urge to smother her lips with his and crush her devotion to that vile miscreant when he saw tears in her eyes.

His desire wilted. *"Olivia,"* he said, his tone gentling.

But she wrenched free of him. Gathering her skirts, she brushed past him and fled from the room.

Swearing under his breath, Brandon marched to the drinks table. He was about to pour himself a stiff brandy, but hesitated. Staring at the crystal decanter, he scowled. Slamming the stopper back into the decanter, he turned away, disgusted with himself.

"Damn her!" he spat angrily.

She was in every way as her calculating father had described, a rose on the verge of bloom. She was also a wicked vixen who coveted clandestine love letters and connived to meet men behind his back while he could not stop thinking about her—the way her skin was like polished ivory, how her long, luxurious tresses of gold caressed her shoulders, beckoning him to enter the sensual fray, her softly enticing round hips that were scarcely wide enough to bear the children which she had promised him on their wedding day.

Remembering how incredible making love to her had been last night, desire coursed like molten lava through his veins. She'd fit him like a second skin and made him forget the consequences of their marriage and what taking her to his bed could mean, something he'd sworn he would never do.

Incensed beyond measure by his weakness, he braced his hands against the mantel and gazed down at the flickering flames. A small corner of the note she'd tossed into the grate remained untouched by the fire. Grabbing the poker, he dragged the slip of parchment from the grate and crouched down on his haunches to read it. What he saw written there gave him pause.

You didn't keep our appointment. That wasn't very nice.

A deep frown marred his forehead. What the devil did that mean? And more important, why hadn't she kept the secret rendezvous with her lover?

Chapter 11

That night Olivia descended the stairs for dinner only to find another hideous letter awaiting her. She stared at the note, anxiety tightening her stomach into a sickening knot.

With a shaky hand, she accepted the missive from Carrington. "Thank you," she managed to say.

"From your latest paramour?" Brandon purred over her shoulder. "Or am I not permitted to know?"

Surprised by his presence, for it was not his habit to dine at home, she glanced up sharply. *"Latest paramour?"* She slipped the sealed threat up her sleeve. "I am sure I do not know what you mean, my lord." She turned away from him.

But his hand slipped around her upper arm, halting her intended retreat. He flashed her a smile, but his eyes were cold and accusing. "You cannot imagine what a relief that is to me."

Lowering her lashes, Olivia stiffened. In taut

silence, the two walked into the dining room. Gathering her skirts, she sank into the scarlet-velvet-cushioned chair one of the footmen had pulled out for her. Her husband took his seat at the head of the table in a large, heavily carved walnut chair.

She darted a nervous glance around the table. "Where is Aunt Edwina?" she inquired, noting the table was set for two.

"In her room."

Olivia cast him an agitated look.

He merely smiled with chilling civility. "I thought perhaps we might dine alone together this evening."

Trepidation flared in her breast. "Oh," she said with some discomfort, lowering her gaze to her plate. "I see."

Waving away the offer of claret, he draped his linen napkin across his lap and looked at her. "Come, my dear, do not look so crestfallen. Surely you can survive an evening with your husband and suffer no ill effects?"

His words hit their mark with painful accuracy. She lowered her lashes to conceal her hurt. "Yes, of course."

He sampled cook's pea soup with relish. "Tell me," he goaded, "does that bounder Driscoll still strike your fancy? Or have you settled on Hughes in your quest for male diversion?"

She did not miss the biting edge in his voice. Shaking her head, she fought back her revulsion at the mere thought of Lord Hughes in her bed. "Certainly not, my lord," she murmured quietly, toying with her pea soup. She was in awe that he could bring himself to eat. Her stomach was tighter than a drum.

"Then why do you covet their love letters?" he asked her pointedly.

Her head snapped up. His dark penetrating gaze drilled into her.

"*Love letters?*" she echoed, a sense of dread engulfing her. "What . . . do you mean?"

He dabbed the edges of his mouth with his napkin and threw it on the table in anger. "The one you received the night of Jeremy's dinner," he said with icy succinctness. "The one you read this morning, thinking your movements unobserved, and the one you threw in the fire, hoping I would not notice. *Those* love letters."

She dropped her spoon with a loud clatter. "I don't know what you are talking about," she told him, struggling for calm. "I have received no love letters."

He sat back and weighed her inept response. For a long, hard moment, he accessed her pale face. "Why didn't you keep your appointment with him, this lover of yours?" he demanded.

She gaped at him, fear tugging at her heart. "*You read it.*"

He shrugged his shoulder. "Enough to know you were to enjoy a clandestine meeting with the whelp." His features hardened. "Why the hell didn't you?"

She despised the idea that he thought her unfaithful, but she could not risk discovery. The real intent of those letters would destroy her tenuous marriage.

Bowing her head, she twisted the napkin between her fingers. "I cannot credit your reaction, my lord. I am persuaded Lady Chesney will ease whatever discomfort you may feel at the loss of my companionship. Faith, all London knows you prefer her company to mine."

"*Prefer her?*" he breathed in disbelief. Catching her chin in his palm, he turned her face to his. "You little idiot,'' he said vehemently. "Don't you know it's you I want?''

She blinked at him. *"Me?"* she breathed, incredulity mingling with hope. "But I thought—''

"How could you be so bloody stupid as to think I would dally with a woman like her when I had someone as wonderful as you in my bed?'' His voice was silky soft and yet harsh with need.

Staring at him in disbelief, she wet her lips. "But,'' she sputtered, "everyone says . . . the papers . . . I saw you with her, and you are so rarely at home.''

"You should know better than to believe idle gossip,'' he coaxed in a velvety voice. "It is rarely ever true.''

Her lashes fluttered shut. "Brandon, please don't trifle with me,'' she begged, on the verge of tears. "Not now. I could not bear it. Not with everything that's happened.''

"Who is trifling?'' he murmured huskily against her lips. "It can hardly come as a surprise to learn I want you.''

"Oh, Brandon," she sighed, weakening. She leaned in to him and his mouth captured hers. She gave herself up to the heated splendor of his kiss.

His mouth slanted over hers, warm and tender, and his hands moved to caress her, sliding greedily over her arms. Before she knew what he was about, he tugged the note from beneath her sleeve.

Olivia cried out in shock. Stunned by his hateful deception, she recoiled from him.

"Now, madam, we shall know the truth of it,'' he announced, a cold, calculating gleam in his eye.

Appalled by his heartless manipulation, she pleaded, almost in tears, *"Brandon, please.* Do not.''

His gaze swept over her. "What's the trouble, my

impudent little hussy?'' he asked. ''Afraid I might call the bounder out and end your sordid love affair?''

She shook her head and closed her eyes in abject misery. ''It is not what you think.''

But he would not be deterred. With a triumphant flourish, he tore open the letter. As his eyes traveled the page riddled with threats and demands for money, his mouth fell open.

Olivia covered her face with her hands.

Swallowing hard, he placed the letter on the table and stared down at its vile contents. By George, he had been a fool. This was no love letter. His wife was being blackmailed. Stunned and deeply regretful, he asked her quietly, ''What is it he knows about you that is worth a thousand pounds?''

Brushing at the corner of her eyes with her fingertips, she tried to stem the tide of tears. ''What does it matter?'' she snapped.

''Is it a lover?'' he asked her roughly. ''Is that what he hopes to blackmail you with?''

But she was too distraught to answer.

''Are you in love with someone else? Does he love you?'' When she offered no reply, he spat at her, ''Answer me, damn you!''

''No,'' she choked out. ''I've never known any man but you.'' She raised her watery eyes to his. ''In your heart, you know it is true.''

His eyes swerved away from her, for she had hit upon the truth. Drawing a deep breath, he stared down at the note for a long moment.

''I have been unbearably cruel,'' he stated with contrition, meticulously refolding the letter. ''I have no excuse.'' The lines about his mouth tensed. ''I simply could not bear the thought of you wanting someone else.''

His confession elicited a loud sob from her, swiftly followed by a wellspring of tears. He raised his hand to caress her hair, but hesitated. She would scarcely want his comfort after the devious manner in which he'd tricked her.

"Olivia," he urged gently, "you must confide in me. Who is this man? What possible reason could he have for blackmailing you?"

She shook her head. "I cannot tell you," she sniffled.

Brandon tipped her chin upward, and his intense blue gaze searched her tear-stained face. "For God's sake, why not? If you have no lover to hide, what are you keeping from me?"

Squeezing her eyes shut, she turned away from him. "You don't understand."

"I am trying to understand," he countered with mounting frustration, "but I need your help."

"I dare not confide in you," she whispered, shaking her head.

"Good Lord, Olivia. What secret is so terrible that you would be willing to pay one thousand pounds to keep it quiet?"

She raised her teary eyes to his. "Please," she implored him, "I beg of you, do not press me. I . . . cannot explain. But you must believe me, you are the only man who has ever touched me. Yours"—she caressed his cheek lovingly with her quivering fingertips—"are the only lips I've ever kissed."

He buried his face in her palm and breathed a kiss there. "Olivia. What can he possibly know about you that is so damning?" he asked gently, covering her hand with the warmth of his own.

Retrieving her hand from his grasp, she turned

away from him and tried to rise from the table. But he caught her arm, holding her fast.

"At least tell me his identity," he beseeched her. "You must allow me that much."

"He once worked for my father," she mumbled softly. "More than that I do not know."

Brandon's brows snapped together. *"Your father? What has he to do with this?"*

"Nothing. Brandon, please," she cried in desperate supplication, "if you have any regard for me at all, you will trust me and respect my wish not to divulge the true meaning behind these threats. I beg of you, give me time to sort this out on my own."

Drawing her near, he caressed her cheek with his palm. "I do care for you," he told her, his voice low and husky. "But I cannot agree to your terms. I must know why he hopes to gain a thousand pounds in return for his silence. You *must* tell me."

"I cannot risk losing you," she whimpered, her voice raw.

"Then tell me," he urged, his eyes compelling. "The truth cannot possibly be as bad as all that."

Shaking her head, she said, "What you ask is impossible," and withdrew from him.

He vaulted to his feet. His arm snaked out, grabbing her around the waist. "Olivia," he appealed to her, "tell me now and end this folly. Once and for all, let us have truth between us."

She shook her head. "I cannot."

His dark blue eyes held a cold, purposeful sheen. "In that case, you leave me no choice but to pursue the matter on my own."

"Pursue it then," she lashed out at him angrily. "It will be to your own detriment."

With that cryptic warning, she pulled free of him and hurried from the room.

Alone with his troubled thoughts, Brandon sank into his chair. "Damn and blast."

Despite his wife's fervent pleas, he was intent on ferreting out the truth. Gazing down at the sinister note, a pensive frown crossed his face. As much as he loathed the idea, he needed to pay a call on his father-in-law.

It lacked ten o'clock when Brandon arrived at Belgrave Square. He was relieved to be admitted. After his hostile refusal to see his father-in-law or, for that matter, heed his warnings to reform his wicked ways, he was concerned Parker might hold a grudge and treat Brandon with the disrespect he deserved.

The butler showed him into the now familiar study. He glanced at the gauche desk complete with savage dragons. A smile softened his features.

With a stroke of a pen, he'd sealed his fate in this very room. Little did he know that the beautiful, fragile woman offered in the marital bargain would alter his life so completely. Had he really balked at the arrangement? he wondered wryly. What a pigheaded idiot he'd been.

The door opened behind him. He swung around to face Parker.

"I trust you have not run through your entire allowance," the elder gentleman said curtly, "and come begging for more."

Brandon's lips twisted, but he reckoned he deserved the rebuke.

"May I offer you a drink? Some brandy, perhaps? As I recall, you are rather partial to spirits."

Brandon stiffened at the jibe. "None for me, thanks."

His father-in-law arched a surprised brow. With a nonchalant shrug, he splashed a small amount of brandy in a glass and palmed the snifter.

Reaching into his breast pocket, Brandon retrieved the blackmail note. He thrust it at his father-in-law. "Read it."

Gilbert gave Brandon a queer look. Setting his glass on the table, he accepted the parchment. Reclining in the wing chair beside the roaring fire, he glanced down at the hastily scrawled missive. A frown touched his forehead.

I've been more than patient, little miss, but your time is running out. If you don't pay me one thousand pounds by week's end, I'll tell the whole world your dirty little secret. I doubt your husband would take kindly to that. I'm warning you for the last time. Give me what's mine.

Gilbert glanced up sharply at Brandon. "What the devil is the meaning of this?"

Brandon shrugged and dropped into the chair across from his perplexed father-in-law. "I don't know. I thought perhaps you might be able to shed some light on the matter."

"Why me?" Parker asked in confusion.

"Olivia refuses to speak of it."

Gilbert's faced clouded over. "You mean to say *Olivia* is the recipient of this—this disgusting threat?"

Brandon nodded. "She is—this and others like it, I have reason to suspect."

Gilbert vaulted to his feet. "You are her husband. For God's sake," he thundered, rubbing his forehead, "it is your responsibility to see to her protection. Can you not perform the simplest of duties?"

Brandon's jaw clenched. "Believe me," he said brusquely, "I have tried everything I know to force a confession from her. She is determined to keep the unseemly truth from me at all costs. It might be easier if you would consent to aid me."

Gilbert stared at Brandon, a look of utter disbelief etched on his face.

Brandon expelled a sigh. "Let us put our dislike for one another aside for the time being. It is Olivia who must concern us now."

Gilbert's lips pinched. "Very well. I shall try to set aside my bias toward you. Because of Olivia, and only because of her, I will aid you. What is it you want of me?"

"I care not for your reasons," Brandon countered coolly, "only that you agree. I have not been able to pry from her the man's identity. Apparently, you know him."

Gilbert whirled about in surprise. "*I* know him?"

"He was in your employ. I am assuming it must have been some time ago."

"In *my* employ?" Gilbert echoed with a dark scowl. "This is too fantastic!"

"Perhaps, but is nonetheless true. Can you not think of someone who held a vendetta against you or who might wish to become wealthy by harassing your daughter? Try to remember, if you can," Brandon pressed with urgency. "Was there anyone who was dismissed without cause? Or perhaps someone who held a grudge?"

"Do you honestly expect me to recall every man I ever hired?" came Gilbert's irritated reply. "It would be a waste of time. I have given many men the opportunity to earn their keep. Not all of them are grateful to me." He paused to gaze down at the fire. His hand curled into a fist on the mantel. "I shall deal with him," he groused under his breath. "He'll be sorry he ever opened his wretched mouth."

Brandon's eyebrows furrowed. He felt certain Parker knew more than he was saying. "If you know this man's identity, it would be better to say so now, rather than risk Olivia's well-being to protect your own interests."

Parker whirled about to face Brandon. "How dare you infer such a thing!" Parker fumed. "My daughter is more precious to me than life itself."

"Based on my dealings with you, I am persuaded there is nothing you would not do. I am asking you for the last time," he ground out, sensing Parker's duplicity, "what do you know about this man?"

"No more than you," Parker replied evasively.

Brandon gave him a murderous glare.

"You have come to me for help. I have consented to aid you. Do not give me cause to regret my decision."

"If you risk Olivia's safety," Brandon warned, his tone lethal, "I'll kill you."

"Do you truly believe I would ever harm a hair on her head?" He cast a disparaging glance at his son-in-law. "Olivia means more to me than a wastrel like you can ever imagine."

"She is *my* wife. And I give you fair warning," Brandon charged, an ominous gleam in his eye, "if you are hiding something that may be damaging to her, you will wish you were never born."

"We are wasting valuable time. This can have nothing whatsoever to do with me," Gilbert muttered harshly. "If it did, the miscreant would have come directly to me and not plagued my daughter."

"Possibly," Brandon allowed, still distrustful of his cunning father-in-law.

"For God's sake, man, can you not see my one wish is to free my daughter from this waking nightmare?"

"Then we are in agreement," Brandon said, nodding slowly. "Considering the gravity of his threat, I think we should contact Scotland Yard."

Parker took a dim view of involving the authorities. "Think, man. Do you fancy a scandal? Go to the Yard," he blustered, waving his hand in the air for emphasis, "and all London will hear of it."

Brandon's eyes narrowed. "Hear what, precisely? That a man who once worked for you is tormenting my wife? What possible scandal can there be in that? Unless, of course," he said, a dubious look in his eye, "you know something I do not."

Gilbert frowned. "Of course not," he snapped irritably. "The best course of action is to hire an investigator. For Olivia's sake, we do not want news of this perfidy to circulate. I have just the sort of man for the job. I've used him countless times before." His eyes glazed with a vindictive light. "He'll catch the bastard and give him what for," he vowed.

Brandon could well imagine the sort of man to which Parker referred and how many times he'd contracted for similar services. Rubbing the tension from his neck, he wrestled with the unsettling prejudice he had about hiring someone of that ilk. The idea of Olivia's being subjected to blackmail, however, distressed him far too greatly to hesitate. He, too, was eager for a quick resolution.

"If you are convinced your man is the most expedient method," Brandon uttered stiffly, "I'll agree to it." He fixed Gilbert with a pointed glare. "But be sure Olivia's well-being is your one true aim, or you'll have to reckon with me.''

Gilbert shrugged Brandon's caution aside. "Now," he muttered, casting a disparaging glance at his son-in-law, "if you will allow me to go about my business, we may have a resolution to our problem by day-break.''

Bright morning sun crept over the city, but Olivia awoke feeling morose. She glanced at the door leading to Brandon's room. Pain stabbed at her heart. He had undoubtedly resumed his wild ways with Lady Chesney and would not be up for hours yet.

Very late last night, she had heard him come in. Despite her misgivings, she'd foolishly longed for him to come to her. His footsteps had approached the connecting door, and she'd prayed he would open it, but after an agonizing moment, he had moved away.

Tears had pricked her eyes. She'd rolled onto her side and wept until exhaustion overtook her and she finally fell asleep.

One thought sustained her. She must uncover the truth about her birth for herself and thereby foil Winterbottom's vile blackmail attempts. The duke would know the truth.

Pushing back the coverlet, she slipped from the warm refuge of bed and quietly summoned her maid to help her dress. Easing her bedroom door open, she tiptoed down the front stairs and hurried out the street door, escaping the sleepy Park Lane mansion without notice.

She had it on good authority that the Duke of Kent resided in Grosvenor Square whilst in town, and she

made haste there. Her only hope was that he had
come up from the country by now. Otherwise, she
would have no way of contacting him save for the
written word, and she could not risk committing her
suspicions to paper.

In very little time, she arrived at the enormous stone
mansion which belonged to the duke. Olivia quivered
with trepidation. What if he refused to see her? Worse
yet, what if he was incensed by her questions? She
heaved a sigh. No help for it. She must get to the
bottom of this, one way or the other.

One thing troubled her, however. How would it
feel to come face to face with her real father—if,
indeed, the duke *was* her natural father? Odd,
undoubtedly so. But she must persevere. Her future
depended on it, not to mention the future of her
precarious marriage. Besides, it couldn't really be
true.

She gazed up at the stone facade and knew a
moment of anxiety. Drawing a deep breath, she bolstered her nerve and, lifting her crinoline skirts,
mounted the steps. She rapped the bronze boar's
head knocker against the black lacquered door and
waited.

An officious looking butler greeted her.

Despite the churning in her stomach, she managed
to say, "I wish an audience with the duke, if you
please."

With a dour look on his face, the manservant
gawked at her. "At this hour?"

"Oh, yes, please. It is most important. I must speak
to him on an urgent matter."

"Go away," he muttered, attempting to shut the
street door in her face.

"No, please! I beg of you. Let me see him, it will

only be for a moment. I shan't go away until I do," she added with staunch determination that seemed to sway him.

Heaving an irritated sigh, the aged butler inquired, "Whom shall I say is calling?"

"Lady Wilde."

"One moment, my lady." He admitted her into the opulent front hall. It dazzled her senses. The life-size marble statues surrounded by large leafy plants astounded her. She waited on pins and needles in the enormous foyer for the manservant to return.

"If you would be so good as to follow me?" the butler announced.

"Yes, certainly," Olivia replied, unable to contain her anxiety.

Traversing the lavish front hall, she trailed behind the servant toward large white-paneled doors. Upon entering what was obviously the drawing room, Olivia was struck almost immediately by the youthful appearance of the duke.

Dark blond hair graced a strong countenance that revealed two large questioning brown eyes. As her startled gaze traveled the length of him, she allowed that he cut a dashing figure, dressed as he was in a gray frock coat and trousers. But the gentleman in question clearly could not be her father.

A smile graced his good-looking features and he laughed. "I take it from your expression you are somewhat surprised to make my acquaintance. I must confess, I am equally at a loss. I do not normally receive callers before breakfast. Nor do I believe I have had the pleasure of making your acquaintance, Lady Wilde."

His inquiry was rewarded with an owlish stare. "You

cannot be the duke," she sputtered. "The man I am looking for would be much older."

An easy smile played around his lips. "Ah," he said. "You have mistaken me for my grandfather. A common mistake. My father passed away several years ago."

"I suppose I must have," she mumbled, despondent at the discovery.

"I am sorry to disappoint you, but my grandfather is rather ill and is in no fit condition to receive visitors."

She glanced up at him, greatly distressed. "You mean he won't see me?" she whispered, paling at the thought that her trip was wasted. Now she would never learn the truth and thwart her blackmailer. Sinking down onto the red velvet sofa, she mumbled aloud, "But he must see me. He must."

"I am afraid that is quite impossible."

Seeing her anguish, the gentleman's forehead puckered. Coming to her side, he sat beside her and gazed pensively at her downhearted face. "Pray do not look so put out. You mustn't make yourself ill over it. Perhaps I may be of assistance in some way?"

She shook her head. "No. It is the duke I need to see." She lifted her eyes to his in earnest petition. "Please, would it not be possible, just for a moment, to see him? It is most urgent that I speak with him."

His grandson shook his head. "What you ask is quite impossible. His mind is not what it once was. One never knows what might set him off. Your appearance might well do him harm."

"I see," she murmured. "If you will not grant me a few moments with him, then I must be going." She got abruptly to her feet. "I apologize for intruding on your privacy. I would not have done so were my need not great."

"One moment," he stalled, catching her by the arm. "I cannot very well send you on your way without knowing what you wished to see my grandfather about. Whatever it is, clearly it is a source of great torment for you." He offered her a sunny smile. "Come, tell me what is grieving you so. I may be of some help."

She glanced at the gallant stranger who might, in fact, be a blood relation. A shiver assailed her. How would he feel to learn there was a chance they were related? It was too preposterous. She could neither prove nor deny her suspicions without speaking to the duke, and until such time, she could not afford to bandy gossip. Besides, she had the distinct impression, gazing about her at the lavish home, that he would take a dim view of slandering his grandfather's good name, and rightly so.

"I do not believe that would be wise. I apologize for intruding on your morning. If I am forbidden an audience with the duke, then I must bid you good day."

Heaving a dejected sigh, he said, "Very well. I will permit you to see him, Lady Wilde. But only for a moment."

Startled by his change of heart, she looked at him, her mouth parted in surprise, her eager countenance beaming her thanks.

"If you disturb him," he cautioned, his eyes locked with hers, "I will insist you leave immediately."

"Yes, of course. I have no wish to disturb him. I cannot thank you enough. You cannot know how important this is to me."

"I suspect I shortly shall," he remarked wryly.

As they moved up the plush gold staircase and down the wide hall, her heart thudded in her chest. Pausing at the threshold, he advised in a low tone, "Remember, he is not himself."

Nodding her head, she entered the dimly lit room. A large canopied bed occupied the far wall. Propped against a heap of pillows was a frail, aged man. At his side sat a nursemaid. She glanced up at Olivia's intrusion.

"It is all right, Daisy," the marquis explained. "Lady Wilde wishes a word."

Daisy nodded and resumed her reading.

Olivia crept forward to the side of the bed and peered down at the duke. His breathing was heavy and labored, as if his lungs were wizened with passage of time. His eyes were shut, but she was not certain he slept.

From the foot of the bed, his son spoke to him. "Grandfather," he practically shouted to be heard by the old man, "Lady Wilde is here to see you."

The duke's eyes fluttered opened, and he focused on Olivia. *"Amelia?"* he whispered, his wrinkled hand reaching for her face.

Stunned by his words, Olivia quelled the urge to pull away. Instead, she leaned closer. The man was a stranger to her, and yet, she realized with a sinking sensation in her stomach, he had been far more important than she ever knew.

"It is you," he rejoiced, touching her hair and her cheek with his shaky palm.

"His mind slips back in time," his grandson explained to her.

Nodding her head, Olivia said, "I am Amelia's daughter. Do you remember me? My name is Olivia."

He frowned at that. "No. I never saw our baby."

Our baby? Despite the feeling of uneasiness that invaded her chest, Olivia seized on his remark.

"Then . . . you are quite certain Amelia carried your child?" she asked, dreading his reply, and yet desperate to learn the truth.

"He cannot know what he is saying," his grandson scoffed from the foot of the bed.

Olivia ignored him and gazed down at the duke. His brow furrowed deeply as if his mind was muddled. "My child? You are my daughter?" he asked her with some confusion.

Tears pricked Olivia's eyes. She nodded. "I believe so . . . yes, your grace. I was hoping you might be able to remember, to tell me what happened. Please try."

"Oh," he gasped, exhausted from the effort. He laid back against the pillows once more. "It was a long time ago. You were so pretty. So very lovely. My Amelia. My beautiful Amelia. How I adored you."

"Yes, but what happened?" Olivia prodded.

"The country is beautiful this time of year. But we mustn't tell a soul."

Frustrated that his mind was obviously wandering, she pressed, "What happened in the country?"

"Nothing happened," his grandson snapped. "It is obvious he does not know what you are talking about."

Tears welled in the duke's eyes. "You kept our secret so well. My one regret was that I never saw the child. And then . . . you left me all alone. I was heartbroken. Oh, Amelia, why did you have to go away?" he sobbed. "I miss you, my love. I miss you so."

Observing his grandfather's distress, the marquis stepped in. "That is enough for today, Grandfather. Rest, and think no more of it."

"Please," Olivia pleaded with the marquis, "I must know. Just a few minutes more."

The marquis glared at her. "What more can you possibly wish to know? Can you not see he is not in his right mind? What he says today, he will disavow tomorrow. I am sorry, Lady Wilde, but this has been a waste of time. I must ask you to leave."

Olivia glanced down one last time at the man who, despite his son's adamant claim, she now believed in her heart was her real father. She squeezed his blue-veined hand. "Good-bye," she whispered and pressed a kiss to his weathered cheek.

He smiled at her and touched one crooked finger to the pearl lavaliere that lay against her neck. "You still have it. I hoped you would cherish it, as I cherished you. We will be together again, Amelia," he vowed, patting her cheek with his hand. "And I shall spoil you with the Queen's jewels, my love, as I was never able to do before."

"Yes," Olivia replied softly, "I would like that."

The marquis took her by the arm and dragged her none too gently down the hall. She almost lost her footing twice.

They were halfway down the front stairs before he paused to address her. "I took pity on you, Lady Wilde, and permitted you to see my grandfather," he said, "something I now regret. If you wish to profess that gibberish outside this house, I shall deny it. My *grand*mother, the Duchess of Kent, is still in possession of her faculties. *She* can attest to the nature of my *grand*father's character and any vile details you should choose to dredge up."

"Pray, be at ease," Olivia replied, laying her hand on his arm. "I have lived these eighteen years under a very different impression. Believe me, I am as appalled and disturbed by his admission as you. I have no wish to repeat what was heard here today."

"Excellent. Then I see no need to continue what has been for me a thoroughly disagreeable acquaintance."

Thrusting her toward the door like a common harlot, he gave curt instructions to the butler to have her shown out. Before she could utter a word, the marquis turned his back on her and strode across the front hall to the parlor.

Olivia was hastily removed from the town house and emerged into the square in confusion. Dazed by the startling revelation that the duke apparently was, in fact, her father—that there was a strong possibility her mother had taken a lover—she practically stumbled down the stone steps. Preoccupied by the shocking turn of events, she had no clear sense of where she was walking, only that she needed to clear her head and digest the full impact of her disturbing interview with the man who might well be her father.

Chapter 12

The streets were not crowded. In fact, the only person about was a milkmaid. It occurred to Olivia that the maid seemed strangely out of place in Grosvenor Square. She was indeed far from St. James's Park where most of the maids sold milk from the cow. Having other much more pressing matters on her mind, Olivia turned away and paid the woman's offer of warm milk no heed.

A shadow appeared in her path. She glanced up and frowned at the large figure blocking her way.

Then her eyes flew wide, for the man was horribly familiar. He offered her a broad, wicked grin.

Olivia gasped and backed away. But before she could turn and run, his arm snaked out. Grabbing her around the neck, he darted a quick glance around to make sure no one had noticed and hauled her toward a nearby wagon.

The shiny gleam of the blade was all she saw, but

she felt the cold edge against her neck. Swallowing, she closed her eyes and fought nearly overwhelming, nauseating fear.

"P-p-please," she stammered, forcing back the tears that stung her eyes. "I'll pay you whatever you ask."

"Oh, aye." His noxious breath was hot and oppressive against her face. "That you will, sweetheart, that and more. Much more."

Whimpering to be free, she struggled against him. But he tightened his grip. A cry of pain escaped her. Her heart beat frantically, almost painfully. "You must release me," she told him, the blood rushing in her ears with a deafening roar, "so I may make the proper arrangements for payment."

He sniggered aloud. "Not on your life. I've had enough of your double-crossing. I ain't gonna wait no more."

She gulped back her panic. "You must understand," she coaxed desperately, "these things take time. I cannot very well ask my husband for such a sum without arousing his suspicion."

"You've 'ad all the time yer going' t' get," he said against her ear.

Overwrought by his brutality, she cried, *"Please,* you must listen to reason. A-at first, I wasn't sure. Without seeing the letter, how could I know for certain?"

"I gots proof. I told y' that, didn'a I?" he railed.

She winced at his vise-like grip around her neck. "Y-y-yes," she stammered, wetting her lips, "b-but I needed to confirm your story for myself. You must understand."

"Oh, aye, I understand. You ain't goin' t' pay me," he charged, arching her back hard against him.

She groaned in pain. He was breaking her spine. "I—I will. I promise."

"We'll, see, me lovely." Glancing up and down the street, he maneuvered her into the back of the rickety old wagon. His knife was an ever present threat pressed against Olivia's back. The milkmaid darted a glance around to see who was watching. When she was satisfied no one took notice, she opened the back doors.

Boosting her up, Winterbottom shoved Olivia inside. Her knee hit the hard wooden floor. She grimaced in pain and tried to get to her feet, but the throb in her leg was almost crippling. Her cumbersome crinoline added to her paralysis. He gave her a shove. Thrown off balance, she landed on all fours. Struggling to gain her equilibrium, she scrambled about and tried to jump from the cart, but the hefty milkmaid blocked her way.

Backing away, Olivia curled into a miserable ball on the straw-strewn floor. "Why are you doing this?"

Winterbottom shrugged and stashed the blade in his belt. "It's a living, ain't it?"

"Kidnapping me won't get you your money," she spat.

"Who said anythin' 'bout kidnapping?" he asked, leering.

Terror struck at her heart. She stared at him in mute horror.

Throwing back his head, he roared with laughter and closed the doors to the wobbly conveyance.

"Watch her, Bess," he advised, closing the two women in.

Trembling with apprehension, Olivia rubbed her sore knee. Her hair had been pulled loose and had fallen in disarray. Her hands shaking, she fumbled with the stray pieces in an insane effort to repair the damage.

"I wouldn't bother with that, ducky," Bess advised with an evil smirk. "Where yer going', won't matter much what y' look like."

Struggling to calm her shattered nerves, Olivia wet her lips. "Where are we going?"

"You'll see, me lovely. All in good time. My Clive's got a plan."

Olivia eyed the portly woman with trepidation. "What sort of plan?"

"To get what he deserves," Bess snapped, "that's what."

"And how does he propose to do that? It does him no good to abduct me. The money will never be his. If any harm should come to me—"

"Just shut it, Miss high and mighty. My Clive knows what 'e's 'bout." Bess let her disparaging gaze rake over Olivia. "Canna say I care much for the likes o' you. The less y'know, the better. Now come 'ere."

When Olivia made no move to comply, Bess crawled forward and yanked her by the arm. She hauled Olivia about and tugged her arms behind her back. Olivia uttered a cry of pain. "You're hurting me."

But Bess tugged even harder, winding coarse rope around Olivia's wrists until it seemed the blood had ceased to flow.

"Please, you're breaking my arm!"

Bess snickered. "Oh, aye?" she asked maliciously. "I'm right sorry, *my lady*."

Swinging Olivia around like a sack of flour, Bess grabbed her ankles. Olivia kicked at her hateful captor, but it was no use. The beefy woman was far too strong. Olivia was helpless to fend her off.

Her task completed, Bess sat back and drew a deep breath. Exhausted from the fray, she dragged the back of her hand across her sweaty brow.

"Why are you doing this to me?" Olivia demanded, near the point of hysterical tears.

Drawing a filthy rag from her pocket, Bess came for her. Wide-eyed, Olivia shook her head and squirmed in a vain effort to escape being gagged. Bess grabbed a clump of Olivia's hair and yanked her head back. Olivia's moan of pain was silenced by a dirty rag stuffed in her mouth and bound at the back of her head.

Bess sat back and crossed her sausage-like arms over her sagging breasts. "That'll fix you," she muttered with a satisfied nod of her head.

Leaning her back against the wall, Olivia gave in to her maelstrom of emotion. Tears streamed down her cheeks.

No one knew where she was. She'd sneaked out of the house this morning quite deliberately. How could she have been so stupid? Why had she not realized Winterbottom's evil intent?

After his appearance in Green Park, she should have suspected he would lie in wait for her.

She was doomed. Even if he chose to spare her life, what possible future could she and Brandon share? No amount of money could change the possibility she'd been born on the wrong side of the blanket.

Brandon awoke that morning with every intention of telling his wife about his meeting with her father. He rapped against the door which led to her bedroom. Hearing no reply, he frowned and turned the handle. To his astonishment, the room was empty. The upstairs maid and charwoman were seeing to their daily duties.

"Where is her ladyship?" Brandon asked.

Bobbing a polite curtsy, the maid clasped her feather duster nervously. "I am sure I do not know, my lord. She rose early and left without so much as touching her breakfast this morn."

Frowning, Brandon left the room and descended the stairs in search of what breakfast could be had. He found Edwina happily installed in the breakfast room. She was finishing a large portion of porridge.

Excellent. Whatever else she might be, the old woman was a veritable fountain of information.

"Where is Olivia?" he asked, taking his seat at the head of the large mahogany table.

Pausing over her breakfast, Edwina blinked at him. "I was given to understand she was still abed, my lord." Her cheeks pinkened at the scandalous insinuation.

Dismissing her embarrassment, Brandon frowned. "She isn't."

As he swallowed the strong black coffee, his mind wandered to the meeting last night with Parker. Brandon could not shake the unsettling feeling that Parker was being less than honest.

"Perhaps," the old woman ventured to guess, after a momentary silence, "she has gone for a ride before breakfast. She does love a brisk trot around the track." With that, she hastily dabbed at her lips and got laboriously to her feet.

Unjustifiably annoyed, Brandon muttered his thanks and took another sip of the aromatic brew. Where the devil *had* Olivia gone?

Apprehension crept over him. She would not be so foolish as to try to handle this man on her own, would she? No. He shook his head. Olivia had more sense than that.

Confident that his wife's judgment was sound, he

was about to consume his morning meal of eggs and sausage when Carrington interrupted his lordship's solitary breakfast.

"A letter arrived for you, my lord."

Eager for news from Parker, Brandon snapped up the missive and tore it open. "Very good, Carrington. That will be all."

He was expecting an update on the investigation. Instead, he found himself the recipient of a threat.

> *I've got something I think you want. If you ever hope to see your pretty little wife again, meet me at Charing Cross pier at midnight. Five thousand pounds ensures her safe return.*

He smashed his fist down on the table. The china jumped and clattered.

"Bloody devil," he gritted under his breath.

Brandon shoved his chair back, scraping it against the floor, then strode from the breakfast room and into the library. Hastily retrieving parchment and pen, he scribbled a quick note to Parker. So much for his man. The investigator had proven utterly useless. Guilt consumed Brandon. If any harm came to Olivia due to his lack of foresight, he could never forgive himself.

"Have this delivered to Belgrave Square immediately," he instructed, brushing past Carrington on his way into the front hall. "It is imperative my father-in-law receives it posthaste."

Before the aged manservant could inquire what was amiss, Brandon threw open the street door and shouted to Ned, "Fetch my horse!"

Frowning, Carrington followed him. "Should her ladyship ask for you, where shall I say you have gone?"

"Her ladyship will not ask," Brandon replied grimly over his shoulder. He let the street door bang shut on his heels.

Carrington and downstairs maid, Prudence, exchanged confused glances. They hurried to the drawing room, where Carrington pulled back the drapes and the two peered through the window. With some confusion, they watched the master bellowing orders.

"Quick as y' like, my lord," Ned replied, jumping to do his master's bidding.

Ned brought the mount around and held the bit while Brandon got a leg up. "Lovely morning fer a ride, my lord."

Snapping up the reins, Brandon said gravely, "I haven't the time to admire the weather, Ned. I'm off to pay a call on my banker."

With that, he kicked the enormous hunter into a canter and headed toward King William Street.

What felt like hours later, Olivia lay limp and cold in the dark wagon, awaiting the horrible fate Winterbottom had in store for her. Stiff and achy all over, she heard the rattling of the wagon doors and tried to wriggle into a sitting position. The ropes dug painfully into her flesh. She winced and abandoned her attempt.

Winterbottom jumped inside. Coming to stand over her, he reached down and hauled her roughly to her feet. Eyes wild, she moaned her objection, but he merely dragged her from the wagon and shoved her off the edge. She fell. When she recovered her breath and the pain lessened, she glanced around her.

Night had fallen, and she was at the docks. Terrified, she darted a look at her captor.

He smirked. "No, I ain't gonna drown ya."

"Not yet, least ways," Bess chimed in, her laugh wicked.

Olivia felt ill. Talons of fear clutched at her heart, but one thought consoled her. Without her, he would gain nothing. Brandon would scarcely pay for Winterbottom's silence if the illegitimate Lady Wilde suffered an unfortunate accident.

Taking her roughly by the arm, Winterbottom dragged her toward the water's edge. Twisting against him, she groaned her objection and tried to fight him.

But it was no use. Uttering an irritated curse under his breath, he tossed her over his shoulder like a sack of potatoes. His shoulder dug into her ribs, and she cringed from the pain. Setting her abruptly on her feet, he shoved her toward the wooden ladder that led to the black abyss. She darted a terrified glance at the frigid water and back at Winterbottom.

Smirking at her, he grabbed her bound wrists and threaded a piece of rope through the knot. Violently shaking her head, she whimpered a plea for him to spare her, but he took no notice of her petition.

"No worries, me lovely," he advised in a horrible voice. "Yer husband has only t' bring the blunt and all will be well."

With that, he shoved her off the pier. She hit the glassy water with a hard smack. The weight of her crinoline dragged her down, deep beneath the murky surface. As she plunged into the icy river, she thought for one panicked moment he planned to let her drown. But then she felt a hard tug on the rope. She was being lifted from her watery grave. Choking and sputtering, she emerged from the dark, icy Thames.

He secured the rope around the top of the weathered ladder. She hung waist deep in her cold onyx prison.

Crouching down, he called down to her. " 'Is lordship should be arrivin' right 'bout now. If he done like he was told, you've got no worries. Just hang on. We'll see if 'e's a man o' 'is word."

Groaning in distress, she struggled against the pressure on her wrists. The ropes cut into her flesh like a knife.

Dangling in the watery trap, she felt as if her hands would be severed from her wrists. In desperation, she kicked at the wooden ladder. But it was no use. The rungs were covered with slippery slime.

Armed with the designated sum and a loaded pistol, Brandon waited for his blackmailer to appear. The eerie sound of water lapping against the wooden pier permeated the night stillness. The occasional roar of a foghorn cut the thick mist. Hoisting his collar, Brandon shrugged off the damp, chill air.

Checking his pocket watch, he frowned. Where the devil was Parker? It was nearly midnight. He and his worthless investigator were due to arrive by now.

He should have gone to the authorities and had the matter handled professionally. Because of his foolhardy decision to trust Parker, his wife had been abducted. Brandon's mouth thinned with anger. Her life might well be in danger.

It was too late for recriminations. Scotland Yard's involvement would mean inquiries, and time was not something Brandon had. If he tried to delay the meeting in order for the Yard to begin their investigation, the blackguard who'd abducted Olivia would doubtless become desperate.

Footsteps approached through the dense fog. Brandon tensed. Prepared to encounter his wife's malignant kidnapper, Brandon slipped his hand over the pistol stashed inside his coat.

His father-in-law emerged from the heavy mist. Brandon's lips thinned, but the tension eased out of his shoulders. "You took your time," he muttered.

"It is just twelve o'clock," Parker replied tersely. Waving his gloved hand, he muttered, "My man, O'Reilly."

Brandon glanced at the stout man lurking in the shadows. He gave a curt nod of his head.

O'Reilly tipped his hat. "My lord."

Parker shivered in the night's chill. "What now?" he demanded with impatience.

"We wait," Brandon explained, his tone clipped.

Parker gave O'Reilly a nod. With that, the investigator slipped behind a large wooden crate to conceal his presence.

Brandon watched the man retrieve a pistol from his coat and slink into position. He frowned and dragged his gaze to Parker. "What are you about?" he growled angrily.

Yawning lustily, Parker remarked, "Merely taking precautions."

Brandon snorted with derision. He could well imagine what precautions O'Reilly had in mind—shoot first, ask questions later. "I'll handle this as I see fit," Brandon cautioned in a lethal tone. "She is my wife."

"And *my* daughter," Parker reminded him coolly.

Brandon looked away. He would never forgive himself, if, due to his damnable jealousy, she was lost to him forever.

"If you think I intend to wait here all night—"

"Hush!" Brandon snapped, raising his hand to silence his overbearing father-in-law.

Footfalls sounded through the thick fog. The culprit was approaching.

"Well now, it is about time." Parker rubbed his hands together, whether to ward off the cold or out of relish, Brandon could not be certain. It made him uneasy nonetheless. He could not quite shake the feeling that Parker was up to his old devices.

"Let me do the talking," Brandon advised sharply.

Parker glanced at Brandon with disdain.

Brandon glared at him. Distrust lingered in his heated gaze. But he did not have time to probe into Parker's intentions, for the villain appeared. Garbed in tattered, dirt-smudged clothing, he looked the part of a grubby thief to perfection.

"Here now," he groused, pointing at Parker. "What y' bring him for? I got nothin' t' say to 'im."

"I should think not, Winterbottom," Parker said, his hostility barely concealed.

Brandon's head turned sharply. His eyes narrowed into arctic blue slits. "You know him?"

"He was in my employ for a short period of time, yes," the older man admitted. "Under the circumstances, he'd be well advised to keep his filthy mouth shut. The prompt return of my daughter is all that interests me."

"Aye," Winterbottom muttered, scratching his scruffy chin, "I 'spect so. But yer not the one payin'." He turned his greedy attention to Brandon. "All I want is me money and she's yers, milord."

Brandon sent Parker an aggravated glare. "Before

I pay you a farthing," he told Winterbottom, "I want assurances my wife is alive and well."

"You cannot expect him to tell you the truth," Parker interjected gruffly. "The man is a vagrant. The moment you pay him, you sign Olivia's death warrant."

"I've no reason to believe that," Brandon said, a meaningful glare in his eye. His one aim was to retrieve Olivia from Winterbottom's grimy clutches. Quite frankly, he did not give a tinker's damn what transpired between Parker and the unsavory criminal. "Whatever business you two have may be sorted out *after* Olivia is returned to me safe and sound."

"I know this man's character," Parker protested. "He is the lowest sort of vermin."

Before Brandon could issue a curt rebuttal, a shot exploded. Winterbottom clutched his chest and fell to the ground. O'Reilly emerged, pistol in hand.

"Good work," Parker commended, staring down at Winterbottom's bloodied body.

Enraged, Brandon turned on his father-in-law. Uttering a furious growl, he grabbed him by the collar. "Damn you," he spat with venom. "You planned this. You knew his identity all along."

"I had reason to suspect he might be involved. More than that I did not know. Believe me, if I had allowed his vile tongue to wag a moment longer, you would have regretted it."

Brandon glowered at him. Disgusted, he shoved him away. "If Olivia comes to harm because of your rash conduct," he vowed ferociously, "I'll make you regret the day you were born."

"You'll need to find her first. I suggest you direct your anger to the situation at hand. I may have just done you the biggest favor of your life."

"By shooting him?" Brandon accused with blistering contempt.

"Silencing is a better word."

Whistles shrieked out, signaling the arrival of the bobbies. The shot had aroused their suspicion. O'Reilly stashed his pistol inside his coat and slunk into the misty darkness.

Crouching down on one knee, Brandon yanked the wounded culprit from the ground. "Where is my wife?" he gritted.

"I'll not say now," Winterbottom gasped.

Brandon sent a frigid glance over his shoulder in Parker's direction. "Shall I let him finish the job then? Or are you at least interested in staying alive?"

"She's . . . she's on the pier. In the water," Winterbottom choked out. "If th' tide comes in, she'll drown."

Brandon shoved him to the ground and ran toward the pier. Darting a frantic gaze about him, he squinted through the soupy mist. Cupping his hands to his mouth, he shouted, "Olivia! Where are you?"

He thought he heard someone moaning and the splash of water near the end of the pier. Tearing off his black overcoat and cutaway, he dived into the icy depths and emerged beside her. She was hanging neck deep in the water, straining to keep her mouth above the rising tide.

"It's all right. I'm here now."

Grabbing hold of the flimsy ladder, Brandon got a leg up. He wrapped his arm around her waist and hoisted her out of her watery prison. Gasping and coughing, she leaned against him.

"I've got you. Just a little further now," he assured her, breathless from the effort to lift her waterlogged body and his own weight from the frigid depths, "and you'll be safe."

By the time they reached the pier, bobbies were swarming the docks. Brandon yanked the gag from around Olivia's mouth. Before she could utter a sound, he caught her face between his hands and kissed her on the mouth.

"Thank God I got you back," he whispered urgently against her bruised lips.

He hugged her fiercely to him. Sobbing her relief, she clung to him. He tugged at the ropes around her wrists, and she winced in pain. Crouching down, he unraveled the ropes binding her ankles. She could do no more than cry.

Winterbottom's irate wife, Bess, was strenuously resisting a young bobbie. "I ain't going' nowhere. I done nothin' wrong."

"That's for the magistrate to decide."

Olivia shuddered and buried her face in Brandon's shoulder. He wrapped his overcoat around her shoulders and held her close.

"Don't think of it," he murmured, brushing her wet, muddy hair back from her face. "They cannot hurt you anymore. I've got you now."

One of the bobbies approached them. Tipping his tall, stiff hat, he asked, "Are you all right, my lord?"

"No," Brandon replied with harsh candor. "But we will be."

"What can you tell us about the wounded bloke?" he asked, glancing over his shoulder at the wounded man lying on the ground a few yards away.

"Brandon," Olivia whimpered, clinging to him, "Take me home. Please take me home."

Brandon cast a glance over Olivia's head. Parker was busy issuing a lengthy statement. Brandon's lips twisted. No doubt the story he related was generously one-sided. O'Reilly was conspicuously absent.

Frowning, he muttered, "I can tell you nothing. I've never seen him before in my life." With that, he swept Olivia into his arms and cradled her against his chest. She was shaking from the cold and the shock of being abducted and nearly meeting her death. "My wife needs a doctor."

"Right, my lord. We can see you both safely home."

Brandon shook his head. "That won't be necessary. My carriage is waiting for us."

The young bobbie tipped his hat. "As you like, my lord."

Brandon walked from the cold, foggy docks to the warmth of his carriage. At seeing Lord Wilde soaked to the bone and carrying the equally drenched Lady Wilde in his arms, Ned jumped down to help.

"Get us home as fast as you can," Brandon instructed over his shoulder. Setting Olivia gently on the squab seat, he jumped in beside her and wrapped the woolen throw around her shivering body. Holding her close, he tried to stem the tide of her convulsive shivers.

Olivia sighed. She turned her head on the soft downy pillow, and her eyes fluttered open. Momentarily disoriented, she gazed unknowingly about her. Brandon was sitting in a chair beside the bed. At seeing her awake, he sat forward. For a moment, she stared at him in blank confusion. Then her eyes lit with recognition.

"Oh, it is you," she said, her voice heavy with sleep.

He covered her hands with his own. "Who else?" He smiled at her.

"I am glad you're here," she murmured sleepily.

"How are you feeling?"

Her throat was terribly parched, and she ached from head to toe. "I'm . . . sore," she murmured, shifting against the pillows to push herself up into a sitting position.

His strong hands made quick work of her failed attempts. When she was propped against the lacy pillows, he pulled the blankets around her like a doting husband and sat on the edge of the bed grinning at her.

"Hungry?" He brushed a stray lock of blond hair behind her ear.

"Ravenous." She tried to smile and moaned at the effort. Her fingertips traced the raw bruises in the corners of her mouth.

He took her hand and pressed a kiss to her raw, red wrist. "The doctor says you'll be tender for the next few days, but after that you'll be good as new."

Her brow knitted. "Doctor?" she echoed with some confusion. "I can't seem to recall . . ."

He offered her a crooked smile, and her heart melted.

"I shouldn't imagine you would. When I finally got you home, you were suffering from exposure and, I suspect, a good deal of shock."

Vivid images of her traumatic ordeal came rushing to the forefront of her mind. "It was unbearable . . ." She faltered as the horror of her experience assailed her. A painful lump formed in her throat, nearly gagging her. "To be tied up and treated like that . . . and when he threw me into the water, I thought . . ." She swallowed convulsively. "I thought I might die," she admitted, her eyes welling with tears. "And I would never see you again."

His arms went around her, and he hugged her to him. "Hush," he urged, brushing his lips against her temple. "Try not to think of it."

For a long time, he held her, both of them basking in the warm nearness of the other, their need for one another silently shown.

"Olivia," he said at length, "there's something I need to say. Something that must be made clear between us."

Dread threatened to consume her. She did not want to hear this, but she knew she could not stop him from speaking his mind. Whatever the consequences to their shaky marriage, she would have to face them. She was only glad of this quiet time together before he imparted the cruel, unvarnished truth: He did not love her, nor did he want her as his wife. The sooner she accepted the harsh reality, the better. She would survive. Somehow.

Tilting her chin up to his, he gazed down at her face. His thumb brushed her cheek with loving reverence. "When I received that blasted ransom note from Winterbottom and was faced with the very real prospect of losing you, I couldn't think straight for want of seeing you again, safe and sound."

She blinked at him, her jade eyes large with surprise. "I don't understand. What are you saying?"

"Isn't it obvious to you?"

"What?" she asked in confusion.

Sighing, he drew her close once more and brushed a kiss to the top of her head. "Olivia, I've been such a bloody fool. The way I feel about you . . . it's— I—care for you more deeply than I ever thought possible," he admitted. "I could not bear the thought of being vulnerable, laying my heart open to another person. I realize now how wrong I was to shut you out. But I'd been doing it for so long, I wasn't sure what else to do. I was afraid," he admitted with a roguish grin that had her heart fluttering in her chest. "Afraid of loving you too much. I was bent on self-protection. But I was wrong, terribly wrong to have hurt you. I never meant to cause you pain, you must believe that. You are everything a man longs for in a wife. I am damned fortunate to have you. Like a selfish fool, I allowed my pride to eclipse my love for you."

He tipped her face up toward his. "Can you find it in your heart to forgive me for being such a pigheaded idiot?" he asked, searching her eyes for a glimmer of hope.

She reached up to gently cup his cheek. "I think that can be arranged," she whispered, blinking back her tears. "Oh, Brandon," she sighed, wrapping her arms around him. She pressed her cheek against his chest and her eyes fluttered shut. "If you only knew. I've wanted to tell you for so long—"

"May I interrupt this moving interlude?" her father inquired with mild sarcasm from where he stood in the doorway.

Brandon's head came around. At the sight of his overbearing relative, he frowned. Releasing Olivia, he set her gently from him and slipped off the bed. "I don't suppose there is any way I can stop you," he said crisply.

Ignoring his son-in-law's attitude, Parker approached his daughter's bedside. Smiling, he took her hands in his and squeezed them. "Thank heaven you are safe."

Olivia lowered her gaze. "Yes. I am extremely fortunate to be alive."

Parker frowned at her cool reception and straightened from her bedside. "So," he snapped, casting a frigid gaze over his shoulder toward Brandon, "you have succeeded in turning her against me."

Brandon crossed his arms over his chest. "I doubt that would be possible," he replied evenly. "Olivia has a kind, giving nature. She would not turn from you on my say so, nor have I given it."

"I believe you know the basis for my reticence, Father," Olivia murmured softly. "It has precious little to do with my husband."

Parker frowned at her. "Never say you believe that mongrel Winterbottom! He would have said anything to garner a hefty sum."

Olivia's features tensed, and she turned away. "I have reason to believe what he said."

He stared at her for a long moment, and a frown creased his forehead. "What has gotten into you, Olivia?" he asked, assessing her. "You are not at all yourself, my dear."

"On the contrary, Father," she said, lifting her eyes to his, "I am more myself than ever before."

His gaze sharpened. "No, my dear,' he countered, "you are not. The woman I see before me is a mere shadow of her former self. I raised you to be gentle and refined, not belligerent and demanding."

She squared her jaw. "I merely wish to know the truth surrounding Winterbottom's claims. Is that such a crime?"

"No, of course not," he said with maddening calm. "It is really quite simple. The man was a bounder through and through. He lied in the hope of successfully blackmailing you. That is all there is to it. Now," he said, his voice strict, "you are overwrought and need your rest. We will speak of this when you are more yourself."

"As soon as I am well," she countered, a defiant

gleam in her eye, "I plan to discover the whole truth behind his accusations for myself."

"Very well," he said stiffly, "if that is what you wish, but you will be wasting your time. Winterbottom is nothing more than a scoundrel."

"That may be," she allowed, boldly arching her chin in defiance. "But I am determined, nonetheless."

Her father nodded his head. "Very well. If there is no way I can convince you of the futility of your effort, I shall take my leave." He turned on his heel and strode haughtily from the bedroom.

Brandon sighed. Unfolding his arms from across his chest, he shoved away from the wall and approached the bed. Planting his hand on either side of her slender hips, he leaned down. "I think it's about time you told me everything," he advised, gazing deeply into her eyes.

Gulping, she turned whiter and lowered her gaze to the coverlet. "I—I don't know where to start," she stalled.

Catching her chin, he turned her face back to his. "Let's try the beginning, shall we?" he murmured, a determined look in his eye.

Chapter 13

Olivia finished her explanation of the events that had led to her kidnapping. She darted a glance at Brandon. He was frowning.

"Why the devil didn't you confide in me earlier?" he asked, his manner gruff with frustration.

Disappointed by his anger, she pleaded with him. "How could I? With things the way they were between us," she mumbled, bowing her head, "can you honestly tell me you would have aided me without prejudice?"

He grunted a reply. Dash it all, he did not like being reminded of his unfeeling conduct toward his wife. The notion he'd been such an ogre that she was afraid to divulge the reason behind her blackmail threats did not sit well with him. Dragging his hand through his hair, he prowled the room, reflecting on what his comportment should have been.

"Does it . . . disappoint you?" she asked softly, every fiber of her being dreading his reply.

Halting in his tracks, he swiveled around. His brows drew together. "Does what disappoint me?" he repeated, not following her line of thought.

Her gaze swerved away. "To learn that I am"—she gulped back the words—"that I may have been born . . . well, illegitimate."

Shaking his head, he replied, "That my dearly departed father brought his own death about through drink and debauchery there can be no question," he drawled. "And you are asking *me*"—he drilled his finger against his chest for emphasis—"if I object to your questionable birth?" He shook his head. "I think not, my love. Besides, if it is true," he teased, his smile wry, "I have married above my station in life and should be very thankful, indeed, for your parents' past indiscretions."

"Are you?" she pressed breathlessly, her eyes searching his. "I couldn't blame you if you weren't. After all, you have your title to consider. If the truth was ever revealed—"

He caught her by the shoulders. "I don't give a damn who your father was—or is, do you hear?" The fierce conviction in his voice brought tears to her eyes. He cupped her cheek lovingly with his hand. "All I care about is *you,*" he vowed, gazing deeply into her eyes.

She burst into tears. Covering her face with her hands, she sobbed out, "I've been so worried. I thought you would be angry, disgusted, even shocked, as I myself was, by the news. But worse than that, I feared you would turn from me. I could not bear that."

He pulled her hands away from her face. "That is

one thing I will never do," he rasped, burying his face in her hands.

She stared at him through glistening eyes. "I couldn't bear the thought of losing you. That's why I refused to confide in you."

"I do believe"—he brushed her hair back from her forehead—"the aged vicar said something to the effect of till death do us part. You'll not be rid of me so easily, my love."

"I do not want to be rid of you, Brandon. Not ever. I *do* love you," she whispered. "Truly."

"Show me," he breathed thickly. "Show me how much you love me." Pressing her back against the soft pillows, he blanketed her soft body with the weight of his own. "I need to feel you close to me."

"Oh, Brandon," she sighed. Raising her softly parted lips to his, she wound her arms around his back and drew him near. His mouth covered hers, stealing her breath and warming her heart. He tugged at the lavender ribbon that held her nightgown closed. Slowly, with a sensual deliberateness that made her shiver with desire, he slid the soft fabric from her shoulders.

She fumbled with the buttons on his waistcoat, eager to feel his rough chest hair and velvety skin pressed against her. He laughed at her haste and made short work of the clothing that kept them apart.

Their hungry mouths twisted together even as their roaming hands and open mouths caressed, tasted, loved one another. With every stroke, every tantalizing caress, their fiery need grew stronger until they were swept away by a burning passion.

When at last neither could bear the sweet temptation a moment longer, they came together with a heartrending tenderness that shook them both. And then a feverish intensity of emotion overtook them, altering the complexion of their lovemaking.

Locked in a lover's embrace, they soared toward the sensual peak of ecstasy just beyond the sweet agony. In the exquisite moment of fulfillment, shattering, inexpressible joy swept over them, and they melded together in the blissful harmony of their love.

In the tranquillity that followed, Olivia lay sprawled against Brandon's chest. Happy and replete, she toyed playfully with his thick black chest hair, her fingers teasing the nipple hidden beneath.

"Brandon?" she questioned softly.

His arms tightened around her possessively. "Hmm?" he murmured, sleepily pressing a kiss to the top of her head.

"Why did you marry me?"

He stiffened perceptibly. Taken unawares, he uttered an awkward laugh. He tipped her face to his, his palm splayed possessively against the column of her neck. "It was love at first sight," he murmured against her lips. "What else?"

She gave him a skeptical look.

"Can you doubt it?" he whispered, his mouth nuzzling her neck.

"I am not entirely . . . certain," she admitted tentatively.

He rolled on top of her, covering her body with his own. "Allow me to convince you," he said thickly against her mouth.

His lips were warm and soft. The heat of his kiss quickly dispelled any doubt from her mind. Sighing her sweet surrender, she slid her hand around his neck and pulled him to her, devouring his mouth with her own.

* * *

That afternoon, Inspector Bowles arrived from Scotland Yard. The family was asked to gather in the drawing room to issue statements. When they were all comfortably assembled, the tall slender inspector in the plaid sack coat addressed them. Toying with his mustache, he cleared his throat. "If we are all ready, then, I'd like to begin." He surveyed the occupants for any objections.

"No need for you to be here, Edwina," Gilbert remarked, signaling his sister to take her leave. "You can hardly shed any light on the recent turn of events."

Edwina looked slightly dejected. But, nodding her head obediently, she got to her feet and was about to take her leave when Olivia stopped her.

"On the contrary," Olivia said kindly, openly countermanding her father, "you are part of this family. As such, you have every right to remain. Indeed, it is our express wish," she said, covering Brandon's hand with her own, "that you stay."

Happiness blossomed on her aunt's pudgy face. She glanced at Brandon to ensure his compliance. He smiled at her, giving her ease. "You are entirely welcome to remain, if you so desire."

Irritation darkened Gilbert's countenance. "I cannot think why you would like to," he muttered from where he stood by the mantel, "but if it fulfills your morbid curiosity, then by all means remain as long as you like."

"Thank you, Gilbert." She took her seat in the corner once more.

The inspector adjusted his spectacles. "Very good," he said, rocking back on his heels. "If we are ready?"

"By all means," Brandon remarked from behind his wife's chair, his hand an ever gentle reassurance on her shoulder. "We are all eager to put the unpleasant episode behind us." Smiling up at him, Olivia squeezed his hand. Her father eyed the gesture with contempt.

"It may come as a comfort to you, Lady Wilde," the inspector said, "to learn the culprit has met his end."

Olivia's eyes widened slightly. "You mean he's dead?"

Edwina gasped in dismay, and her brother shot her a quelling look. Her hand flew to her lips, ensuring her reactions would remain silent in future.

"Yes," the inspector replied. "I fear the wounds inflicted during the fray were too much for him to sustain. He'll not bother you further."

"I see," Olivia murmured, digesting the full weight of the situation. "Thank you for telling me."

Dragging his disapproving gaze from his sister, Parker turned to address Inspector Bowles. "It comes as a relief to know my daughter is safe," he remarked, at his most haughty.

Brandon glowered at him. "I am persuaded *all* our hearts are deeply gladdened by Olivia's narrow escape. Proceed, Inspector."

"As to that, the exact nature of the late Mr. Winterbottom's involvement with Lady Wilde is somewhat hazy." Bowles was clearly struggling with the awkward topic.

"No need to dance around it, Inspector," Brandon said, his manner forthright. "My wife was being blackmailed. Winterbottom hoped I would pay him handsomely for her safe return. He was entirely correct." Brandon glanced down at Olivia. "I would have paid him any amount in exchange for her safe return," he murmured softly, his warm gaze caressing her.

The inspector nodded his head and furiously jotted notes in his little black book.

"What was the nature of Winterbottom's blackmailing threats? He must have had good reason to imagine you'd pay such a hefty sum."

Immediately affronted, Gilbert stepped forward. "See here, no reason to delve into all that," he snapped. "I have no wish to see my daughter upset by that man's vile suggestions."

The inspector arched his brow. "I see. Very well. If it is a sensitive topic, we can leave off for today— if it pleases his lordship?" he inquired of Brandon.

Brandon nodded his tacit approval.

"It scarcely matters much now, seeing as he's dead. There won't be a trial. The case is closed."

The color drained from Olivia's face. "If that is all you require of us, Inspector," she said, getting swiftly to her feet, "I am rather tired."

"Yes, of course, Lady Wilde," Bowles replied, offering her a polite smile.

"That was painless enough," Gilbert said, pleased with the brevity of the interview.

Inspector Bowles hesitated for a moment. "Just one thing troubles me, Mr. Parker—a slight matter that bears some mentioning."

Gilbert's eyes narrowed. "And what might that be?" he asked, his tone curt.

"How is it Winterbottom had no weapon when we arrived?"

Gilbert shrugged. "I am sure I don't know."

"But you did shoot the man, did you not," the inspector asked, "in self-defense?"

"In all the confusion, it is difficult to know who

shot at whom. I cooperated fully with your men at
the time of the incident. I am certain my actions are
outlined appropriately in my statement. My conduct
resulted in the safe return of my daughter, which
should be your main concern.''

The pulse in Brandon's cheek throbbed. He glowered at his father-in-law, but for Olivia's sake, he managed to rein in his temper.

''The important thing is,'' Gilbert went on to say,
unruffled by Brandon's glare, ''Lady Wilde is safe
and the villain is no longer a threat.''

''Yes, of course.'' The inspector knew a curt dismissal when he heard one. He snapped his leather-
bound book shut. ''In a high-profile case like this,''
he explained to Brandon, ''we need to be sure of all
our facts. You understand, my lord?''

Brandon's burning, reproachful gaze never left his
father-in-law's smug face. ''We are *all* deeply gratified
by your scrupulous attention to detail, I am sure.''

''Indeed,'' Olivia interjected, folding her hands at
her waist. ''It is reassuring to know Scotland Yard is
so thorough.''

''Only too happy to be of assistance, Lady Wilde.''

''If there is nothing more, I fear my wife is excessively weary,'' Brandon explained.

''Right you are, my lord,'' the inspector replied,
stashing his notepad and pencil in his breast pocket.

Brandon walked to the bellpull. ''Carrington will
show you out. Good day, Inspector.''

''Good afternoon, my lord, ladies, sir.''

As soon as the inspector had taken his leave, Brandon turned on his father-in-law. ''You can add murder
to your list of offenses,'' he accused.

Gilbert merely sniffed his disapproval. ''Winterbottom was the lowest sort of person imaginable. I do

not regret he is no longer on this earth. Can you honestly tell me you feel different?''

Brandon's jaw clenched. ''No,'' he admitted begrudgingly. ''After what he put Olivia through''— he wrapped his arm around her shoulders—''I won't play the hypocrite and claim I am sorry he is gone. But I will never share your cavalier attitude toward killing a man, either.''

''I did what needed to be done,'' Parker remarked, at his most arrogant. ''Nothing more, nothing less.''

A look of consternation crossed Olivia's face. ''You cannot mean to say you went to the docks *intending* to take his life, Father?''

A hard, determined expression crossed his face. ''I would do anything in this world to keep you safe,'' he told her solemnly. ''Anything at all.''

She looked appalled. ''Even commit murder?''

''Yes. Even that, if it meant the preservation of your well-being.''

''Ah yes,'' Brandon retorted, ''the ever noble, loving father. It didn't hurt that taking his life benefited you no small degree, did it?''

Gilbert frowned. ''Don't be absurd,'' he countered harshly. ''I've not had dealings with the man in years. He was a liar and a cheat. The cur would have said anything to get money.''

Disillusioned, Olivia lifted her agonized eyes to his. ''He did not have to resort to lying, did he, Father?''

''I do not know what that blackguard told you, but it was lies. All of it. *That* I guarantee you.''

''Is the duke a liar, as well?'' Olivia charged.

A look of surprise crossed her father's face. *''The duke?''* he breathed.

''Yes. I went to see him. He seemed to confirm the truth.'' She bowed her head. ''He recognized this.''

Lifting the precious pendant from around her neck, she gazed down at the lavaliere. "How is that possible," she asked him pointedly, "unless he was the man who gave it to my mother?"

Her father scoffed at her. "That blithering old fool would have said anything. I am appalled to learn I raised such an imbecile for a daughter."

"And what of mother's letter?" Olivia pressed with vigor. "Is that a fiction, as well?"

His brow creased. "What letter?"

"You *know* what letter." Averting her gaze, she swallowed hard. "About . . . my real father . . . the truth surrounding my birth."

Gilbert's eyes narrowed. "What truth is that, may I ask?"

"Evidence that I am not your daughter."

Her father looked stunned. "You cannot be serious."

"I am afraid so," she murmured.

"I will not tolerate veiled accusations from my own daughter," he roared, slicing his hand through the air.

"Please, Father. I have the right to know," she countered, her voice steely with resolve.

"Very well," he allowed. "We shall pursue this insane line of questioning to the bitter end. Tell me, where is it, this *revealing* letter?" he asked with cool contempt.

She bowed her head. "In Winterbottom's possession," she admitted with some chagrin. "He stumbled across it years ago."

"And only *now* decided to come forward?" he questioned, his tone caustic. Shaking his head at her, he chortled at her stupidity. "Do you honestly believe I would have allowed such a letter to exist, let alone leave my possession?"

Olivia's head snapped up. "But he had it," she said, a faint note of hysteria in her voice. Coming to her side, Brandon put his arm around her waist. She looked up at him, her expression puzzled. "He threatened to show it to you," she cried, distressed by the idea that Winterbottom could have been lying all the time. "He must have had it. He planned to destroy me, my marriage, my life—everything that mattered most in the world to me."

"He was bluffing," her father countered brusquely. "And like a milksop fool, you took him at his word."

Brandon drew Olivia close. "If he was bluffing," he inquired, "why would he go to the trouble of kidnapping Olivia?"

"Money," Parker replied briskly. "It was all he ever was after. When you did not pay promptly, he resorted to more devious tactics."

"But why Olivia? There must be countless other women on whom to prey."

"Few with her particular background. If you will recall, she is a commoner who has recently been elevated to an aristocratic station."

"As I recall, you were more than a little anxious to silence him at the docks. If you have nothing to hide," Brandon asked, his tone razor sharp, "why not let him talk? What harm can idle prattle do?"

"I was thinking of my daughter!" Parker stormed at Brandon. His son-in-law's pointed accusations rattled his icy exterior at last. "Olivia has been through enough. I saw no reason to give his filthy insinuations credence."

"If what Olivia maintains is true, you had good reason for wanting him dead."

"For once, you are entirely correct. My daughter's life was at stake," Parker replied grimly.

"A life you endangered by your rash actions."

"Hardly," the old man scoffed.

"Stop it!" Olivia cried, covering her ears. "Just stop!"

Brandon rubbed her back, trying to ease her upset. "I think it best that we continue this conversation at a more suitable time."

"No need," Parker said grimly. "I have told the truth. She is my daughter, and that is all there is to it."

"Not quite," Edwina asserted from her corner of the room.

Parker whirled about, his face a portrait of blank disbelief. "Hold your tongue, woman," he growled under his breath.

"The child has a right to know the truth, Gilbert."

"The truth?" he spat. "That her mother possessed the morals of an alley cat?"

"You drove her to it," Edwina admonished him, "just as you are driving Olivia away. You do not know how to love people, Gilbert. You stifle them. And they all turn away in the end."

"Be silent!" he thundered.

She shook her head. "I used to be frightened of your temper, Gilbert. Do you know that? I am not proud of how I cowered in the face of your rage. But I have watched Olivia these past few months." She turned her gaze toward her niece. "I admire her so," she said, her eyes brimming with affection. "She has grown into her own woman, and I am proud of her. I envy her the ability to speak her own mind as I longed to do so often, but lacked the courage."

"She is far more outspoken than is seemly," Parker muttered.

"Outspoken?" Olivia sputtered, her eyes welling

with tears. "If it is outspoken to need to know the truth about my own father, then I happily plead guilty to such a fault."

"You know the truth!" he railed. "I have adored you since the day you came into this world. All I have ever done is love you. And this," he said with disgust, *"this* is how you repay me—with hateful accusations and the most vile suspicions!"

"Must you always think of yourself?" Olivia screamed at him, losing her struggle for control. "I believe I am the duke's daughter. If you have an ounce of regard for me, Father, you will forsake your pride and tell me the truth."

"The truth? You ask me for the one thing I do not even know myself!"

Her forehead wrinkled. "What do you mean?" she asked.

Sighing, he massaged his temples between his thumb and forefinger. "Your mother took the duke to her bed," he explained quietly, "but she continued to fulfill her wifely duty to me. How can I possibly know who fathered you?"

Stricken by his words, Olivia gawked at him. "You mean . . . you forced her to be your wife, knowing she loved another?"

"She *was* my wife! I had every right to believe I could persuade her to forget him, to make her love me as I loved her."

Lost in a sea of turmoil, Olivia slumped down on the sofa. "Then," she murmured, "I can never really be sure whose child I am."

Edwina came to her side. "Your mother always claimed you were her love child," she explained, brushing her hair with affection. "And I believe her."

"You would," her brother spat.

Ignoring Gilbert's rancor, Edwina spoke to Olivia. "You asked me many times if I knew the initials FK. I am ashamed to admit that I lied to protect your feelings. Those are the duke's initials, and the pendant you wear around your neck was a token of his esteem for your late mother."

"I knew I would come to rue the day you insisted I let you give her that blasted thing. I should have destroyed it when I had the chance."

Disregarding her father's outburst, Olivia pressed her aunt with urgency, "what about the letter? Was it real? Did it exist?"

"That, I cannot answer," Edwina said on a defeated sigh. She turned to look at her brother.

He expelled an impatient sigh. "Yes," he admitted, "that much is true. Winterbottom stumbled upon it and demanded payment for his silence. I dismissed him immediately and burned the letter."

"Then," Olivia murmured, disheartened, "he never really had any proof at all."

Brandon came to her side. "All that matters is that your mother was in love with the duke, and you are their child."

Parker laughed. "You would like to think that, wouldn't you?"

Brandon fixed his father-in-law with a frosty glare. "I am merely thinking of my wife's happiness. She must have some closure to this."

"*Your wife,*" Parker spat. "A woman you barely recognized for months whilst you dallied in London with every sort of trollop imaginable."

"Please, Father, don't," Olivia interjected, bereft and deeply troubled. Her head was spinning.

"Do you know why he married you," he fumed, "this fortune hunter you love so much?"

Her hand came up. "Fortune hunter?" She repeated dully. "What are you talking about?"

"That's a lie," Brandon snarled.

"Is it?" her father taunted.

Brandon's hands fisted in anger. "Damn you, Parker. We had an agreement," he blazed. "It would be just like you to go back on your word."

Dumbstruck, Olivia looked at Brandon. "Agreement? What agreement?"

"It is rather simple, my dear," her father explained caustically. "Your precious husband inherited a pile of debts. He was in dire need of a hefty sum to bail him out—in a word, a rich heiress. *That's* why he married you."

Olivia stared at Brandon. "Is this true?" she breathed in horrified disbelief. "Is that why you married me?"

"Have you never wondered at his lackluster attitude toward your union?" her father inquired.

"Olivia, don't listen to him," Brandon ground out fiercely.

"Why shouldn't I?"

"He is twisting everything to suit his own ends. You know he despises me. He is bent on making us miserable," Brandon insisted.

Olivia got to her feet. "You cannot twist the truth." She fought the bile that rose in her throat.

"I'm not trying to twist anything. Just . . . let me explain," Brandon said.

"What is there to explain?" she asked. "Either you did or you didn't."

He shook his head. "It is not as simple as that."

"I think it is," she countered firmly.

"Many marriages, particularly among the peerage, are arranged between virtual strangers. There is nothing untoward in that."

She stared at him, suspicion lurking in her eyes. "Why *did* you marry me?" she asked, her voice wavering with pain. "It wasn't for love, was it?"

He looked ill.

Oh God, oh God. Her heart plummeted. Her tormented eyes beseeched him. "Was it truly only . . . for money?" she asked, her searching gaze on his face. "Is that why you married a complete stranger? For *money?*" she gasped, sickened by the prospect.

"Olivia, please understand all men are in want of a generous dowry." He paused for a moment, searching for the right words. "Gentlemen sometimes find themselves in a position where they must marry rich heiresses. It does not mean I do not love you."

Repulsed, she backed away from him. "Gentleman? Our marriage was nothing more than a means to get your hands on my dowry, and you dare refer to yourself as a *gentleman?*"

The pulse in his cheek leaped. "I am not proud of the circumstances preceding our marriage. I won't deny that. But this changes nothing between us. I love you."

She turned her back on him, her breath coming in fits and starts, and fought the nearly overwhelming need to bawl her eyes out. "How could you marry me solely for my dowry?" she asked, hugging her waist, "and then lie about it?"

Grabbing her by the shoulders, he whirled her around to face him. "I never lied to you," he countered fiercely. "I just—I wanted to spare you the unsavory truth."

The private moments they'd shared, the passion, the tenderness—lies. All of it lies. "How could you be so heartless?" she choked out. "Lord, I've been such a fool, such a naive, stupid fool."

"No, you haven't." He swallowed convulsively. "Nothing has changed between us."

She wrenched free of him and stumbled backward. "Everything has changed."

Turning to face her father, she stared at him, hurt and disillusioned. "I never dreamed, never imagined you were capable of such treachery."

"Treachery?" His brow darkened. "What utter rubbish. I secured a place for you among the peerage. You should be grateful to me."

"You used me to secure your own selfish ends. I was sold to the highest bidder like one of your prized paintings, and you expect me to be *grateful*?"

"I handled the situation with the utmost care and saw to it you would have a place among the peerage. I have always taken your best interests into consideration."

"You mean your own interests, don't you, Father? I had no wish for money to be the basis of my marriage," she cried, "and you knew it! You may have been successful at coercing his lordship into marrying me, but I will not have you orchestrate my life as well. There is no undoing the damage you have caused, nor will I forgive you for it."

"What gibberish is this?" he demanded. "Your husband has shamed you, not I."

"You went to great lengths to garner the title of Lady Wilde for your daughter and secure a place among the peerage for your grandchildren. You must have known there'd be a high price," she said bitterly.

Her father looked stunned by her words. "This is too fantastic."

Ignoring her father's outrage, Brandon took Olivia's hands in his. "Please, Olivia, try to understand. My reasons for marrying you have nothing to do with what has blossomed between us. Looking back on it now, I am persuaded your dowry would not have been sufficient incentive had I not felt something for you that first day we met. You must believe that.''

"How magnanimous you are, my lord. Do you imagine, in your infinite conceit, that I could ever regard you in the same light, knowing the truth about you?''

"The truth is,'' he said gravely, "I love you. I always have and I always will. I would do anything to take away the hurt in your eyes. By God, I made a mistake, Olivia. I freely and openly admit it. *Please* try to understand. Is human frailty unforgivable in your eyes? I gave my word.'' He cast a furious glare at her double-crossing father. "I vowed never to tell you the circumstances surrounding our hasty nuptials. And then,'' he explained, his voice tight with emotion, "later, when you asked me why I chose you, I couldn't bring myself to reveal the truth for fear of hurting you.''

"How noble you are,'' she said in a strangled voice. "Forgive me if I don't fall at your feet.''

"If you loved me,'' he countered firmly, "nothing in the world could change that.''

"I don't love you,'' she cried hysterically. "I don't see how I ever could have thought I did.''

Stricken, he stared at her.

She lifted her crinoline skirts and fled the room.

"Olivia!" Her name tore from him an agonized cry.

But she did not stop. She keep running, desperate to escape the torment pounding through her brain. *He married you for your money. Your money. Your money.*

Even when she reached her room and threw herself onto the bed in a heap of misery, she could not stem the rush of pain nor the hot tears that cascaded down her cheeks.

* * *

Brandon fixed his father-in-law with a hateful glare. Enraged, he closed the distance between them in swift, angry strides. Grabbing a fistful of Parker's collar, Brandon shook him hard enough to rattle his teeth. "You bastard!" he growled, nearly strangling him. "You just could not allow us to be happy, could you?"

"If I could not have her," Gilbert gasped in reply, "then why should you? I've spent my life loving her."

Brandon shoved him away. "Get out," he snarled, "before I throw you out."

Brandon yanked open the drawing room door. He tore up the front steps two at a time and tried the handle to the master bedroom. It was locked. He could hear Olivia's tormented sobbing from within. "Let me in," he called to her through the door.

"Go away."

He braced his hands on the door frame and drew a deep breath. "You cannot hide forever."

"I've nothing to say to you," she sobbed.

"Please, Olivia, let me in."

Silence.

"How can we resolve anything if you refuse to speak to me?"

"Go away."

"I can't go away," he moaned, resting his forehead against the door. "Olivia, *please,* I beg of you, speak to me."

Silence.

"I love you. Doesn't that matter?"

Silence.

Pounding his fists on the door, he said sharply, "Open this damned door."

Silence.

"Olivia!" he stormed, banging on the door with renewed vigor.

But she refused to answer him.

"Very well," he told her, his voice resolute, "I will wait for you to come out."

Slumping down on the floor, he bent his knee and rested his forearm across his leg. Leaning his head back, his eyes drifted closed. "I can't lose you," he vowed in a tortured voice. "You mean too much to me. Our love cannot end due to a foolish misunderstanding."

Day drifted into evening, which gave way to night, and still Olivia remained closeted behind locked doors.

Greatly distressed at the sight of his master slumped on the floor outside the mistress's bedroom, his aged valet suggested his lordship relinquish his post.

"Go away," Brandon muttered.

"But, my lord, you cannot intend to stay here all night," Saunders pressed.

Brandon raised his despondent gaze to his valet. "Leave me alone. She must see me," he said with conviction. "She must."

Heaving a defeated sigh, Saunders went in search of his bed for the night.

With a soft click, the door fell open. Scrubbing the sleep from his eyes, Brandon got to his feet. Pushing the door wide, he stood on the threshold, staring blankly at Olivia.

With help of her maid, she was emptying the drawers of all her possessions. His forehead puckered with worry. Stepping into the room, he eased the door shut behind him.

"That will be all, Jenny," she said, dismissing her maid.

"What are you doing?" he asked warily when Jennifer had left the room.

"What does it look like?"

"You're packing."

"How clever you are, my lord," she countered.

He dragged his hand through his hair and took a step closer. "Where are you going?"

"Anywhere, as long as it is far away from here."

"Cloverton Hall?" he croaked.

She shook her head. "That was never my home."

"Then where?" he pressed, with a sense of urgency.

"I shall be leaving for the country directly."

"Where? What part of the country?"

She paused for a moment to look at him. His eyes were bloodshot from lack of sleep and a day's growth of beard darkened his features.

"What I do or whom I fancy," she stated coldly, her once vibrant countenance devoid of all emotion, "can hardly be of significance to you."

He caught her by the arm. "Perhaps I have no wish for my wife to depart for the country. What then?"

She cast a disdainful glance at his hand. "Your wishes do not enter into it," she uttered coolly. "I shall be taking my aunt and my maid with me. Surely you can have no objections. You have never been partial to my relations."

He shook her. "I'll never grant you a divorce," he said with savage intent. "You'll never be free of me. Ever. Do you hear? I won't let you go," he vowed passionately.

"Do you honestly believe you can hold me here

against my will—lock me in a dungeon or a hidden tower room, as you would a mad relative?"

Crestfallen, he released her and sank down on the end of the bed, his head in his hands. "I'm sorry." His voice nearly cracked from the depth of his emotion. "Sorry for everything. Sorry for the way I've treated you, for not being the sort of husband you deserve. And for ever letting your father hurt you."

"Only my father?" she queried, her tone frosty. "Am I to suppose you consider your conduct praiseworthy?"

He glanced up at her sharply. "No," he countered with conviction, shaking his head, "never that."

She offered him a humorless smile. "I am enormously relieved to hear it," she drawled. "How fortunate I am to have such an *honorable* husband."

He gazed at her in disbelief. "Surely," he said, incredulous, "you cannot regard me in the same light as him."

"Can't I?"

"His motivations were far worse than mine. You must grant me that."

She eyed him with cool contempt, but issued no reply.

"My one flaw was in trusting him. I never should have given my word."

"Only one flaw?" she queried. "How nice for you."

He gulped. "Had I been wiser, I never would have let him speak the truth. I shall never forgive myself."

"I wager you are disappointed," she muttered, slamming the top dresser drawer shut. "I expect you thought it better we go on living a lie. But I, for one, would never want that kind of a marriage."

He squeezed his eyes shut. "I know that. You deserve more, much more." He looked at her, his eyes brimming with regret. "Can't you see? Don't you know how much I love you? I need you. Don't turn away from me, please. I can't bear the thought of losing you."

Unmoved, she proceeded with her packing.

"Haven't you heard a word I've said?" he demanded, infuriated by her cruel indifference.

Concentrating on folding her shift, she murmured coolly, "I've heard *all* your words."

He cringed and scrubbed his hand over his face. "What can I say? What can I do? There must be something," he said in desperation. "Tell me. Whatever you want, I'll do it. Just tell me what you want from me."

She walked to the open trunk and placed the neatly folded pile of clothing inside. "Nothing. I want nothing from you," she remarked, her manner totally detached, "save to never see your face again."

"You cannot mean that."

"I do mean it."

"I've said I'm sorry. What more do you want?" He floundered for a solution. "I cannot turn back the hands of time. Lord knows I wish I could, but I cannot. What's done is done. I would give anything to undo it."

She kept methodically stacking her belongings in her trunk.

Exasperated, he vaulted to his feet. Grabbing her by the arm, he whirled her about to face him.

"Please, Olivia," he begged, dragging her against him, "speak to me. *Say* something. Anything."

She raised her eyes to his. "You're hurting me," she said, her glare wintry.

Bewildered, he stared at the cold, distant woman in his arms. "Is that all you have to say to me?"

His eyes searched her face for some semblance of emotion. "After all we have meant to one another, will you not at least listen to reason?"

"Meant to one another?" she echoed. "What precisely was I to you?" she asked bitterly.

"You are my wife," he rasped.

She gave him a frigid glare. "Another woman in your bed, you mean. But what can one lover matter to you"—she mimicked the callous words he'd once used to hurt her—"when you've so many to choose from?"

His eyes drifted shut in abject misery. "God, Olivia," he vowed, "you are the only woman in the world for me. Haven't I made that clear to you?"

"Indeed, you have. A man in your position would do well to espouse a rich heiress."

He stared down at her, the color draining from his face. "You cannot truly believe that."

"How can I not?"

He blanched at the recrimination in her voice. "Then all is lost? There is no hope for us?"

Her wooden posture and steely silence gave him his answer. He dropped his arms to his sides and let her go.

"You're leaving me." It was not a question.

"Yes."

He cast a tormented glance at her. "You won't stay with me and be my wife, my comforter, my world?"

"No."

With an anguished cry, he said, "I won't let you leave me! Do you hear? I will keep you by me always."

"You cannot force me to remain with you," she stated, aloof in the face of his outburst.

"Olivia, please, I beg of you, forgive me. Don't leave me. I cannot bear it. How will I survive without you? My life is nothing without you. If you walk out that door, you condemn me to a life of darkness."

She ignored his pleas.

"What will I do? How can I go on, knowing you are in some distant part of the country without me?"

Presenting her back to him, she silently closed the top to her trunk and locked it.

Clasping her by the shoulders, he turned her around to face him. "You cannot mean to go and never come back to me," he said. "You would not be so cruel as to leave without hearing me out."

"Nothing you can say will alter my opinion," she said, impervious to his petitions.

She slipped her heavy silk mantle from the end of the bed. Donning her Empress hat, she smoothed her hand over her immaculate hair and draped the expensive wrap around her shoulders.

"Olivia, don't go!" he cried. "Stay with me and be my wife."

Unaffected, she marched quietly from the room and descended the stairs in stoic silence.

He ran after her. "How will I contact you?"

She quickened her gait down the stairs, but he caught her up short.

"You are my wife, for God's sake," he insisted. "You cannot think to never speak to me again."

"Very well, if you are inclined to write," she said briskly as she tugged on her buff-colored kid gloves, "Mr. Hendricks has acted as solicitor to my father in the past. You may contact me through him." She raised cool, reproachful eyes to his. "I am sure you are well acquainted with the man. He must stand out in your memory as very useful. He provided you with access to your newly acquired wealth."

He grimaced at her tone. "I don't give a damn

about the blasted money!" he vowed. "It is you I want." His voice grated with emotion. "God, Olivia"— his blue eyes filled with pain and remorse—"please believe that."

She lowered her gaze and waited for him to let her pass.

His shoulders slumped. Defeated, he released her.

She picked up her skirts, hurried down the front stairs, and sailed across the street door threshold. Eager to seek refuge in the carriage waiting below where Aunt Edwina sat ready to depart, she hastened down the stone steps. The footman helped her into the conveyance.

Practically collapsing on the squab seat beside her aunt, she buried her face in her hands.

"Go!" she cried out, desperate to escape Brandon's presence. "Please . . . just go."

The carriage jostled over the cobblestone streets. Her shoulders shook and tears poured down her cheeks.

"There, there child," her aunt said, her gentle tone soothing.

"Oh, Aunt." Olivia wept copiously. "What am I to do? I love him so much. My heart is breaking in two."

Edwina wrapped her arms around her distraught niece and patted her head. "So is his," she murmured quietly. "So is his."

Brandon stormed back inside, slamming the street door in his wake. He pushed open the drawing room doors, crossed the room toward the drinks table, and removed the crystal stopper from the brandy decanter. After sloshing a hefty portion of liquor into his glass and heedless of any spillage, he slammed the decanter down and snatched up the glass. He was about to pour the brandy down his throat and reach for another and another and another still when he stopped.

He stared at the glass.

Uttering a ferocious growl, he threw the glass against the wall, splattering the amber liquid and smashing the crystal into tiny pieces.

Clutching his head between his hands, he stumbled to the brown velvet sofa and sat down. He rested his elbows on his knees and squeezed his skull between his palms. His shoulders shook. For the first time since he was a boy, he gave in to heart-wrenching sobs.

Chapter 14

Six months later

A knock sounded at the library door, where Brandon was quietly ensconced by the fire trying to sort out what would become of his life should Olivia be lost to him forever.

Glancing at the clock, he frowned. It was nearly midnight. "Come," he called out.

Carrington stepped into the dimly lit room. "My lord, I fear we have a problem."

Brandon's head came up and his brow furrowed. "What sort of problem?"

"Me," a hatefully familiar voice called out.

Brandon's jaw clenched at the sight of his father-in-law. Slamming his fists down on the leather chair, he vaulted to his feet.

"I am sorry, my lord. He refused to leave," Carrington explained, flustered.

"Very well, Carrington. That will be all."

"Yes, my lord." The elderly servant bowed.

When the two men were alone, Brandon eyed his father-in-law with icy contempt. "You've got one hell of a lot of nerve showing up here."

Parker shut the door. "I had no choice."

"You are not welcome in this house."

"I understand your feelings toward me perfectly, and I respect your decision. Ordinarily, I would not have intruded on your privacy. But I am at wits' end," he admitted. "I have heard not a single word from Olivia. That damned fool Hendricks is as tight-lipped as ever. I am going out of my mind not knowing how she fares." He tossed his hat and gloves onto the settee. "You must tell me what you know."

Brandon sank down in the chair beside the fire. "Precious little. She has refused all my letters and given strict instructions that I am not to know where she is residing."

"I see," Gilbert muttered, frowning. "It is worse than I feared. I thought perhaps her anger rested solely on me, but I see she has chosen to reject you as well."

"Does it surprise you?" Brandon asked bitterly. "What did you think would happen when she learned the truth? Fall down at my feet and thank me for marrying her?"

Parker scrubbed his forehead with his fist. "I wasn't thinking clearly at the time," he confessed. "What I said, I said in a moment of anger. You see, I love her more than life itself, and you were taking her from me. I don't have much aside from wealth. She is the most precious thing in the world to me. I never dreamed . . . I never thought . . . I would never intentionally hurt her."

Brandon slanted him a derisive look. "It is too late for recriminations. The damage has been done, and there is no way of undoing it."

"Don't you think I know that?" Parker snapped. "Don't you realize I have tortured myself day and night, wishing I had chosen a different path?"

"But you didn't," Brandon reminded him.

Parker heaved an unhappy sigh. "I merely want to know if she is well and happy. That would be enough for me. In time, I hope to make it up to her. The things I've done were not noble, but they were all born out of my love for her. By arranging a marriage to you, I thought to give her something more than I could ever offer her. I so wanted to protect her from the truth of her birth. Can you not understand that?"

Brandon slowly nodded his head. "I think I can, yes. But you went too far."

"I realize that. And I am heartily sorry for my actions. Would that I could take them back."

"You cannot," Brandon said, getting to his feet. "None of us can." He opened the library door, signaling their brief discussion was at an end.

"I expect you are right," Parker concurred, sadly collecting his things and walking slowly toward the door. He paused for a moment on the threshold. "I know you harbor no affection toward me. I cannot say as I blame you. But if you could see your way clear . . . that is to say, if you hear from her, anything at all, I would be much obliged to know, just hear, that she is all right."

It was on the tip of Brandon's tongue to refuse him. But seeing his father-in-law in such dire straits, his heart softened. "I sincerely doubt I shall hear from her," he said stiffly. "But should I learn of her whereabouts, I shall inform you of her well being."

"Thank you. You cannot imagine how much that would mean to me."

Brandon gave a curt nod of his head. "The servants will show you out."

The following morning, fed up with this vexing cat-and-mouse game, Brandon decided to take matters into his own hands, and he paid a call in Chancery Lane. Olivia was his lawfully wedded wife. He had the right to know her whereabouts, and he intended to find out this very morning.

Entering the dimly lit room that smelled of rotting paper and old leather, Brandon's gaze wandered over the tattered volumes bulging from Mr. Hendricks's bookshelves. The dour gentleman depicted in the portrait mounted on the dark green wall looked appropriately stodgy.

Brandon tugged at his silk cravat, which seemed to be suffocating him, and sank down in the leather chair before the cluttered desk.

Blanching, the solicitor affixed his spectacles to his enormous nose and examined the pile of unopened letters before him. Recognizing the bold script and red wax seal, Brandon flexed his sweaty palms over his knees.

"Well, Lord Wilde," the solicitor said, obviously uncomfortable. "I need not tell you that this situation is, er, well, to say the least . . . unusual."

Brandon shifted in the hard chair and tugged at his linen shirtsleeves. "She is my wife," he said curtly. "I have the right to know her whereabouts."

The white-haired gentleman's watery blue eyes narrowed over the rim of his spectacles. "So you do. But she has left express wishes to the contrary, which puts this office in a rather delicate situation."

Perhaps it was the atmosphere of the stuffy office that made Brandon's throat feel constricted, or the fact he was loath to impart the embarrassing details of his wife's estrangement. In any event, he was eager to be done with this business.

"And you are her estranged husband," the solicitor pointed out.

Bitterness and resentment welled up inside Brandon. "Has my wife issued a plea for divorce?" he asked sharply.

The solicitor raised his brows, amazed by Brandon's scandalous inquiry. "Er, no. She has not. A well-respected gentlewoman is hardly likely to do such a thing, my lord."

"Well then," Brandon said, leaning forward, his arctic blue gaze pinning the solicitor, "if my wife has not seen fit to pursue the matter legally, why should my desire to contact her bother you so bloody much?"

The solicitor swallowed audibly and adjusted his wire-rimmed spectacles. "She has requested complete privacy. Not even her father knows her current residence. As I have told him countless times—to my own detriment, I might add—I am not at liberty to divulge her present whereabouts."

Flashing him a predatory smile, Brandon sat back. "You are at liberty to do whatever you want. Perhaps I may be more persuasive than my father-in-law."

The solicitor cleared his throat. "My lord, you do not seem to comprehend me. Your wife has returned every letter you have forwarded through this office—unopened."

"So you delight in reminding me," Brandon remarked.

Hendricks cleared his throat. "In the face of her rejection, I strenuously advise you to let the matter lie."

Brandon's lips thinned. "For how long?"

"Until such time as she deems it appropriate to speak to you."

"No," came Brandon's clipped rejoinder. "I *must* know how she fares. If you will not tell me, I shall employ other methods, but find her I will."

Brandon's tone held a steely note of purpose that gave the aged solicitor pause. Sitting back, Hendricks uttered an exasperated sigh.

"My heart goes out to you, truly it does. But I am powerless to aid you without countermanding the wishes of my client."

Brandon clenched his fists. "How can I possibly hope to make amends if she refuses to accept my letters and you prevent me from seeing her?"

The solicitor looked distressed at that. "I understand your plight, my lord, but there is nothing I can do. I am here to execute your wife's wishes. Nothing more."

Shoving back his chair, Brandon got to his feet. Grabbing Hendricks by the scruff of his neck, he hauled the portly man across the desk. "I must know where she is," he gritted. "Thanks to Her Majesty's excellent training, I learned many useful techniques in the Crimea to wheedle the truth out of a man. Believe me, I can be very persuasive when I want to be. I intend to stop at nothing until I do."

Hendricks recoiled from Brandon's malevolent expression. "I've no doubt you can," he croaked.

"I shall hound you day and night until you divulge

her whereabouts. Your life will not be your own. Every waking moment, you will sense my presence like a wraith haunting your every step. Make it easy on yourself," he coaxed icily. "Tell me where she is."

Hendricks's pudgy face beaded with perspiration. "I say, my lord—he gulped—"no reason for violence, surely?"

Brandon flashed a chilling smile and tightened his grip. "Tell me what I want to know and I'll be on my way."

"She's living in a cottage near Sandringham," Hendricks blurted. "Ask the villagers for directions."

"That wasn't terribly difficult, was it?"

The terrified solicitor shook his head.

Shoving the stout man back down into his chair, Brandon adjusted his shirtsleeves.

"There is another matter I wish you to see to immediately, a certain letter I wish drafted. And I think you are just the man to do it."

Hendricks mopped his damp brow with his lace-edged handkerchief. "Yes, yes, of course. Whatever you wish, my lord."

"Excellent," Brandon remarked, taking his seat once more.

Brandon steered his mount down the narrow lane. He had been given to understand the cottage where Olivia resided with her aunt was at the top of the next hill. As he neared the quaint thatched-roof cottage, he slowed his mount and slipped down to tether the beast at the hitching post. Shifting his saddlebag over his shoulder, he started up the gravel path toward the bright green door.

As he came into view, Aunt Edwina peered up at

him from where she was tending the flower beds. She blinked at him as if she'd seen an aberration of some kind. Then, lumbering quickly to her feet, she made haste for the door, calling to Olivia. Brandon caught up with the old woman and gently silenced her announcement.

"Let me," he whispered, pressing his fingertip to her gaping mouth. "I want it to be a surprise."

Edwina gawked at him. "Oh, my lord"—she gulped—"it will be a surprise, believe you me. In more ways than one."

He merely smiled at her and entered the cottage.

"Stay here," he ordered her. "I want a few moments alone with Olivia."

Edwina nodded her head. "Yes, I very much suspect you will, my lord."

At hearing the dulcet tones of his wife calling to her aunt, he rounded the corner, which led to a cheerful front room flooded with bright sunshine. To his amazement, Olivia was bent before the fire, clearing away the ashes.

He came to an abrupt standstill. His breath caught at the sight of her, and he watched in stunned disbelief as she stood up from her hunched position and straightened, rubbing her lower back.

His heart slammed against his ribs. Lord. Raking his hand through his hair, he stared unblinkingly at the slight round protrusion straining against the soft fabric of her apron. She was with child. *His* child, he realized. He was going to be a father.

"Olivia," he called out, his voice low and rough edged.

Her back stiffened perceptibly. She whirled about in surprise and stared at him for a long moment, as if she could not believe her eyes.

He hovered in the doorway, feeling a million different things all at once, but unable to express any of them.

Drawing a deep, calming breath, she asked quietly, "How did you find me?"

He shook his head. "It doesn't matter now. I *had* to see you. You must have known that, sooner of later, I would find you. Did you think I could go on living without seeing you again?"

She offered no reply, only continued to stare at him.

"God, Olivia," he breathed. "I cannot believe it is really you. After all this time." Dropping his saddlebag, he rushed toward her. Desperate to touch her, he reached out for her.

But she turned her back on him, maintaining the icy distance between them. He dropped his arms to his sides and expelled a defeated sigh.

"You should not have come," she insisted, her voice wavering with emotion.

"How could I stay away?" Taking her by the shoulders, he turned her to face him.

"It would have been better for us both if you hadn't come."

Capturing her gaze with his, he shook his head slowly. "My journey was not in vain," he countered. He glanced down at her abdomen. A smile graced his features, and he spread his palm over the evidence of her pregnancy. "I have learned I am to be a father. Surely," he said, smiling at her, "that was worth the trouble?"

She lowered her lashes to shield her eyes from his probing gaze. "It is of no consequence."

"No consequence?" he echoed in astonishment. "The hell it isn't."

"Please, Brandon, don't do this."

Ignoring her pleas, he asked, "When is the baby due?"

"Two months," she told him unhappily.

"So soon?"

Wordlessly, she nodded her head.

"You must come back to me," he urged her. "If not for yourself, then for the baby."

She shook her head.

"Do you think I intend to allow my child to be born here? To never know our baby? The child we created together out of love?"

She squeezed her eyes shut. "Please . . . don't," she begged in a barely audible whisper.

His finger slipped beneath her chin to tilt her face upward. "Don't what?" he asked, his eyes searching hers. "Tell you that I love you, that I adore you, that I cannot bear another moment on this earth without you? And that I want this baby just as much as you do?"

She swallowed back the tears that threatened to fall and turned away from him. "Words come so easily to you," she murmured, crossing the room to look out the window, "but they are meaningless. If you have any regard for me at all, you will stop this folly and leave me in peace. No gentleman would torture me so."

He turned her around to face him. Brushing the tears from her cheeks with the pad of his thumb, he shook his head at her. "Then I am not a gentleman, because I am not leaving. Not now. Not ever."

She opened her mouth to gainsay him, but he spoke over her.

"After you've heard what I've come to say, if you still wish me to leave, I will go. But first, hear me out.

Please, Olivia, give me one last chance to prove myself to you.''

Sniffling, she nodded her head. ''You leave me little choice in the matter. I will hear you out, but that is all.''

He grinned at her. ''I can ask for nothing more.''

Crossing the room to his saddlebag, he retrieved a parchment letter that bore the seal of Hendricks's firm and handed it to her. She frowned at him.

''Go on,'' he coaxed, ''read it.''

Accepting the heavy ivory parchment, she tore open the seal. As her eyes pored over the contents of the letter, she glanced up at him in surprise. ''Is this true?'' she breathed, taken aback by the legal declaration.

He nodded his head. ''Yes. All of it. I don't want your money, Olivia. There can be no doubt in your mind now.''

''But this means you have no rights to my fortune. No money at all. How will you live?'' she asked, astonishment mingling with happiness.

''We will live on what I make as an officer in the Queen's army. I have taken steps to resume my commission. Will you consent to be a soldier's wife?''

Heaving a deep sigh, she refolded the letter. Slowly, she crossed the room to the fireplace, mentally weighing his offer. ''No,'' she said finally. ''I daresay I'd make a terrible officer's wife.''

He looked flabbergasted. ''But . . .'' he stammered, growing paler, ''I have no other way of supporting you and our baby. I . . . you must agree,'' he insisted, desperate. ''Please, Olivia, I beg of you, reconsider. I know it is not much of a life, but it is all I can offer you.'' Floundering for a way to prove himself, he swallowed audibly. ''How else can I prove my love to you? What more can I do? I have nothing else to offer you.''

She tossed the letter into the fire.

His brows puckered. ''What are you doing?''

She uttered a cheerful sigh and dusted off her hands. Arms akimbo, she turned to look at him. ''What does it look like?'' she asked him saucily.

He gave her a queer look. ''I don't . . . understand. Why did you burn the letter? I meant what I said. I do not want a farthing from you.''

She shook her head at him. ''You might be willing to live like a pauper, but I am not.'' She sashayed her way across the room to where he stood. ''After all,'' she remarked, smoothing her palms over his broad chest, ''I am a duke's daughter, and we have our reputations to keep up.'' She wound her arms around his neck.

''No,'' he told her firmly, taking hold of her arms. ''I won't accept your fortune, Olivia. Our marriage will not be based on money. I love you. I want that clearly understood.''

''Oh, it is understood. Very clearly,'' she breathed, tilting his face to receive her kiss.

He raised his mouth slightly and gazed into her eyes. ''Heed me well,'' he whispered. ''I am determined *not* to live on your money.''

''Very well,'' she sighed. ''We shall live on the very hefty proceeds from my father's fortune.''

A low rumble of laughter erupted from his throat. ''You are very wicked, Lady Wilde,'' he murmured between heated kisses.

''Mmmm, almost as wicked as you, Lord Wilde,'' she concurred, tugging his head close to press a kiss to his parted lips.

His hands moved to caress the swelling of their

child. The baby gave a hard kick, startling them both into laughter.

"See how your son takes after you?" she teased, covering his hand with her own.

Resting his forehead against hers, he said in a husky murmur, "On the contrary. Your daughter shares your stubborn streak, my love."

"Mmm," she whispered, leaning into him, "I do hope so."

A low sound of amusement rumbled in his chest and his arms tightened around her. He kissed her with all the reckless abandon and abounding love in his heart.

Epilogue

Olivia woke in the middle of the night, experiencing the initial pains of labor. A long, hard contraction gripped her. She gasped in pain and reached for Brandon. He sat bolt upright in bed.

"Is it the baby?" he demanded anxiously.

She nodded and managed quite calmly to say, "Could you fetch the doctor? I think it is time."

As a soldier, Brandon had faced armed enemies, but he was totally unprepared for this. He jumped from the bed and tugged on his pants, but did not bother with his shirt or his boots. He dashed across the room and tugged on the bellpull.

"Don't worry darling," he tried to assure her, "everything is going to be fine." She nodded her head. But his anxious shout to the upstairs maid that the baby was coming belied his fears. "Fetch the doctor and be quick about it," he ordered the young girl.

"Yes, my lord." She bobbed a curtsy and darted a startled look at Olivia before she fled the room.

He rushed to Olivia's side. He felt helpless and miserable, unable to stop the pains that gripped her. Holding her hand, he beseeched her, "Olivia, pray, do not have the baby before Dr. Coleburn arrives."

"I'll try not to," Olivia murmured with a nervous, frightened smile.

A man chuckled from the doorway. "No fear of that, my lord," the doctor said, coming to stand beside the bed where Olivia lay. Setting his black leather bag on the nightstand, he smiled down at the young woman about to give birth. "How long?" he asked, shrugging off his coat and rolling up his sleeves.

"Several hours," Olivia gasped just before another contraction took hold, rendering her speechless.

The doctor merely nodded and glanced at the bewildered Brandon. "I will call you when the baby comes," he said with a curt nod. Before the expectant father could object, the upstairs maid closed the door in his concerned face. Digging his hands into his pockets, Brandon trudged down the hall to take refuge in the boudoir.

Late morning turned to early afternoon, and still no word came. Brandon paced anxiously before the fireplace, nearly wearing a hole in the carpet.

"This is her first baby, my lord. It is not uncommon for it to take long," Edwina remarked. Brandon nodded his head and sank down in the chair opposite the kind, concerned old woman. Neither one dared voice their deep-seated worry: Olivia might die trying to bring forth his child.

No. Brandon refused to dwell on that unholy prospect and pushed the thought from his mind. But his fears were not assuaged, for he could hear her moans of pain, followed by Dr. Coleburn's low encouragement.

When he heard Olivia cry out, he could stand it no more. He flung open the door and raced down the hall. Bursting into the room, he stopped short at the sight of Olivia straining to give birth. Dr. Coleburn paid no heed to Brandon's entrance. He was too busy guiding the child into the world. Brandon stared half dazed at his child being born.

There was a lusty wail and the young maid exclaimed jubilantly, "It's a girl!"

"A girl," Olivia whispered. She fell back against the pillows in an exhausted heap.

Brandon rushed to her side. "Olivia," he breathed, clasping her hand in his. Her eyes fluttered open and she smiled at him.

"Brandon," she whispered, touching her fingers to his cheek lightly. "We have a daughter."

He offered her a lopsided grin. "So I saw. Hush, my love," he replied, brushing damp golden tendrils of hair from her face and gently kissing her lips. "We'll talk later. You need your rest."

Her eyes fluttered shut.

"You have a fine, healthy baby girl, my lord," the doctor said as the baby, freshly cleaned and swaddled in linen, was handed to her mother.

Olivia took her baby in her arms and looked upon her small, precious bundle. "Oh," she breathed, tears of joy glistening in her eyes. "Brandon, she is beautiful. She has the tiniest hands, fingers, arms, and legs I've ever seen!"

Brandon smiled down at the child. "And the sweetest face I've ever seen. What shall we name her?"

"I was thinking . . . Amelia. After my mother."

"Then Amelia it is, my love."

Olivia smiled contentedly. Her eyes drifted shut.
The maid took the child from her and handed the
tiny bundle to Brandon. He awkwardly accepted the
babe and gazed down at the child in awe. His heart
was nearly bursting with love—love for the perfect
little creature clasping his finger with her little fist
and love for his beautiful wife, who had nurtured his
seed so lovingly and endured the agonizing hardship
of birth to bring precious little Amelia into the world.

The doctor smiled as he watched Brandon. "My
lord, I should tell you the birth was a trial for your
wife. The child was larger than most. She'll need
plenty of rest if she is to recover fully."

Brandon glanced up in concern. "Is she . . ." He
could not bring himself to say the words.

Dr. Coleburn shook his head. An easy smile played
around his lips as he washed his hands in the porcelain basin. "She is fine and will give you many more,
I wager."

Brandon breathed a sigh of relief. "Thank God for
that," he said, glancing down at his sleeping wife, his
gaze full of love and wonderment. His daughter slept
peacefully in his arms. He reveled in the joyous
moment, his heart swelling with emotion.

Rather than return home immediately, he and
Olivia had decided to remain in the happy cloister
of the countryside cottage, where they might enjoy
the honeymoon they never had. But Brandon had
been insistent that the child be born in the regal
comfort of the restored family estate, where the finest
medical attention was available. Given her long labor,
he was glad of his decision.

"Now that my clever wife has restored Cloverton
Hall to its former glory," Brandon had explained

with a roguish grin, "it is the only fitting place for the next Marlborough heir to be born."

Olivia had raised one golden brow. "Indeed? And shall I labor in the same room as you were born, struggling to bring forth your exalted son for your pleasure, my lord?" she asked him, a teasing gleam in her eye.

Brandon had blanched. "Good God, no. At least," he said, "I hope not."

Olivia had laughed and threaded her arm through her husband's. Basking in the moment of easy closeness that had so quickly blossomed between them, she rested her head against his broad shoulder.

Gazing up at him, all the love in the world shining in her large dark eyes, she had mused happily, "You are hoping for a girl, then?"

"As bonny fair as her mother," he had replied, tilting her face toward his to receive his kiss.

She laughed. "I'll see what can be done, my lord."

She had made all his dreams come true, he thought, gazing at her now through loving eyes. He could not imagine being happier than he was this day.

A few days later, Brandon entered the large chamber where mother and child were happily ensconced in the majestic canopied bed. He still could not believe the tiny new addition cradled in Olivia's arms belonged to him, nor, for that matter, how utterly one woman had changed his life. Smiling at her, he approached the side of the bed and traced his daughter's chubby cheeks, round with milk.

Olivia glanced down at her angelic child suckling hungrily. "She has her father's appetite," she said with an amused smile.

"Mmmm," Brandon mused, a wicked glint in hi gorgeous blue eyes, "and her mother's stamina."

"Lucky girl," Olivia murmured, enjoying the quic kiss he pressed against her lips.

Sighing, Brandon sank down on the side of the be and stretched his arm across the headboard behind her. At seeing his somber expression, Olivia knew a once something was amiss.

"What is it?" she asked, her eyes searching hi dour countenance. "I do believe you look somewha unhappy, my lord. Never say you have grown bore with me already?"

One end of his mouth lifted slightly. "Not in million years."

"Then what, pray, is darkening your brow?" sh pressed with good humor. "God is in His heaven, w have a beautiful baby girl, and all is right with th world."

Lowering his gaze, he clasped Olivia's hand in his "Your father is here," he said bluntly.

A long pause seemed to penetrate the room.

"I see," she murmured, feeling the full ramifica tions of Parker's presence.

"Do you want me to send him away? I wasn't sur how you might feel."

She heaved a deep sigh and laid her head bac against the pillows. "I don't know. I am not certai of my feelings."

"I should not have troubled you with this." Bran don lifted his arm from around her and moved t get up. "I'll send him away, and we'll think no mor of it."

But she stopped him. "No. Wait." She searche his face, her brow deeply furrowed. "Why did yo tell me? You hate him. You must have intended to have him put out. Why didn't you?"

Brandon expelled a sigh and rubbed the tension from the back of his neck. He shrugged. "What you say is true enough," he admitted. "But if you could see him as he is now—I do believe he is sincerely contrite."

Olivia laughed mirthlessly. "Only because he wants something."

"Perhaps," Brandon allowed, "but I remember what it was like when we were separated. I cannot help but feel some sympathy for the man."

"Do you compare your conduct to his?" she asked, startled by his change of heart.

Brandon shook his head. "No. I compare my heart-ache to his loss."

Olivia looked away and worried her lip with her teeth. "What of my heartache? You cannot imagine the agonies I have suffered at seeing his character revealed in such a heinous light."

"I can well imagine it."

She glanced up at him. "And do you think his character substantially altered?"

"In truth, I do not know. That is something for him to express in his own time and manner."

"Yes. But will he?"

"If he is truly sorry for what he has done, in your heart you will know it. His regret will be painfully evident, as was mine."

"Perhaps, in time," she ventured to say, following his train of thought, "I might accept his love and we could be reconciled."

Brandon nodded. "Provided he is able to sustain the changes. You may be able to forge a more honest relationship with him."

Olivia nodded her head. "Yes, I would like that."

"Excellent. I shall tell him there is hope. But for now, my love," he whispered, cupping her cheek with his palm, "I wish to spend every waking hour with you and our new baby."

She said, her voice sultry, "No interruptions, my lord?"

Grinning, he shook his head. "Not a one."

"I think that can be arranged," she whispered, sealing her promise with a kiss. His arm went around her, drawing her near to receive the warmth of his love and the soft satiny caress of his lips. They were happy at last.

Put a Little Romance in Your Life With
Betina Krahn

__**Hidden Fire** 0-8217-5793-8	$5.99US/$7.50CAN
__**Love's Brazen Fire** 0-8217-5691-5	$5.99US/$7.50CAN
__**Midnight Magic** 0-8217-4994-3	$4.99US/$5.99CAN
__**Passion's Ransom** 0-8217-5130-1	$5.99US/$6.99CAN
__**Passion's Treasure** 0-8217-6039-4	$5.99US/$7.50CAN
__**Rebel Passion** 0-8217-5526-9	$5.99US/$7.50CAN

Call toll free **1-888-345-BOOK** to order by phone or use this coupon to order by mail.

Name _____

Address _____

City _____ State _____ Zip _____

Please send me the books I have checked above.

I am enclosing	$_____
Plus postage and handling*	$_____
Sales tax (in New York and Tennessee)	$_____
Total amount enclosed	$_____

*Add $2.50 for the first book and $.50 for each additional book.

Send check or money order (no cash or CODs) to:

Kensington Publishing Corp., 850 Third Avenue, New York, NY 10022

Prices and Numbers subject to change without notice.

All orders subject to availability.

Check out our website at **www.kensingtonbooks.com**

Celebrate Romance With Two of Today's Hottest Authors

Meagan McKinney

__In the Dark	$6.99US/$8.99CAN	0-8217-6341-5
__The Fortune Hunter	$6.50US/$8.00CAN	0-8217-6037-8
__Gentle from the Night	$5.99US/$7.50CAN	0-8217-5803-9
__A Man to Slay Dragons	$5.99US/$6.99CAN	0-8217-5345-2
__My Wicked Enchantress	$5.99US/$7.50CAN	0-8217-5661-3
__No Choice But Surrender	$5.99US/$7.50CAN	0-8217-5859-4

Meryl Sawyer

__Thunder Island	$6.99US/$8.99CAN	0-8217-6378-4
__Half Moon Bay	$6.50US/$8.00CAN	0-8217-6144-7
__The Hideaway	$5.99US/$7.50CAN	0-8217-5780-6
__Tempting Fate	$6.50US/$8.00CAN	0-8217-5858-6
__Unforgettable	$6.50US/$8.00CAN	0-8217-5564-1

Call toll free **1-888-345-BOOK** to order by phone, use this coupon to order by mail, or order online at **www.kensingtonbooks.com**.

Name _____

Address _____

City _____ State _____ Zip _____

Please send me the books I have checked above.

I am enclosing	$_____
Plus postage and handling*	$_____
Sales tax (in New York and Tennessee only)	$_____
Total amount enclosed	$_____

*Add $2.50 for the first book and $.50 for each additional book.

Send check or money order (no cash or CODs) to:

Kensington Publishing Corp., Dept. C.O., 850 Third Avenue, New York, NY 10022

Prices and numbers subject to change without notice.

All orders subject to availability.

Visit our website at **www.kensingtonbooks.com**.